The Dishwater Duchess of Wylder, Wyoming

by

Sharon Shipley

a sequel to
The Wylder Ghost and Blossom Cherry

The Wylder West Series

The Dishwater Duchess of Wylder, Wyoming

COPYRIGHT © 2022 by Sharon Shipley

Cover Art by *Samantha Keating*

The Wild Rose Press, Inc.
PO Box 708
Adams Basin, NY 14410-0708
Visit us at www.thewildrosepress.com

Publishing History
First Edition, 2023
Trade Paperback ISBN 978-1-5092-4830-8
Digital ISBN 978-1-5092-4831-5

The Wylder West Series
Published in the United States of America

"Gentlemen! Gentlemen!" Miss Adelaide chuckled throatily. "Rein in your impatience. Prepare to be delighted and content. I assure you! We all know why we are here, gentlemen. Have your purses ready, prepare your hearts to rejoice, and set your minds open to a rare possibility and opportunity. Raise your hand, nod, or even wave a silk Chinese fan to place your bid.!" Miss Adelaide jested to laughter but impatient laughter, attested by one lone voice.

"Well! Let's get this rodeo started, Miss Addie!"

"The bidding will begin shortly. Until then, avail yourself of our libations and our bounteous buffet for your other appetites." Her husky chuckle came again, promising everything, followed by expectant nervous laughter and an increase of cutlery clatter.

The room quieted.

"Gentlemen all, and a few rogues, without further ado," Miss Adelaide announced, "I present for your pleasure, as your reward, a young miss straight from Ireland. An unspoiled Irish lass fresh from Londonderry County for your bidding…"

Cat then realized few, if any, had ever witnessed her back in the kitchens here or at the Longhorn. She was an unknown to most, and even then, they'd scarce recognize her out of the drab brown dress and the cap that had concealed her conspicuous hair.

Books by Sharon Shipley

SARY'S GOLD: shortlisted for best Western by Chanticleer reviews and a Grand Prize winning script.

SARY'S DIAMONDS: A hot African adventure.

SARY AND THE MAHARAJAH'S EMERALDS: Romance in torrid India.

THE WYLDER GHOST AND BLOSSOM CHERRY: A paranormal romance between a notorious dead gunslinger and a mortal.

BEAST IN THE MOON: Erotic dystopian Sci-Fi.

THE MONSTER FACTORY: Adult, coming-of-age horror.

THE GIRL FROM CONVICT LAKE: Psychological thriller.

DANFORTH THE DRAGON: A children's book.

Dedication

Thank you,
to my brilliant and dedicated editor, Nan Swanson,
and to my husband's undying patience...

Prologue

"Please? Help me?"

The girl, halfway between childhood and young woman, waited shivering by the drab tent nearest her ma and pa's.

"What yer want?" A man's voice gravelly with slumber. "Only chanct ta leave this hellhole is sleep!" The woman next to him grumbled, "What is it, Cat?"

"They're worse. Ma and Pa. They be perishin' sick! Please, can ye be helpin'?"

"I look like a physician?" The sarcasm was thick as the snow fog circling the tent.

"But what should I be doin'?" the child wailed as she shifted foot to foot at the tent flap in the bitterness of early dawn. The girl's voice would break a stone angel's heart, but not theirs.

"Haul yer carcass up, Bessie! Go see to it, so I can get some kip 'fore the feckin' sun come up," the man growled, which hinted he entertained no back-sass.

The woman, shivering beneath her scrap of quilt, grunted a question. "They's so hot, hunh? Blessed way to be, I'd wager." She grumbled as she waddled through snow after the girl.

The child tucked her hands into her armpits. "They can't breathe. Their throats're swelled up, sure."

The woman ducked into the tent, took one look at the two tortured figures, male and female, with sounds scraping from throats in rasping whipsaws. The woman backed. She wouldn't look at the girl, until when she did, she sent evil eyes the child's way.

"Nothin' I can do. Ain't a miracle worker, neither." She softened her voice. "Pack snow around 'em. If they last till mornin', maybe…" She hastened back to her tent beneath the water tower on the tattered outskirts of Wylder, Wyoming.

****

The child's white face was pinched paler now, surrounded by a wilderness of black spring-coiled hair—snared for now under a tatty plaid shawl wrapped tight about shoulders and head and safety-pinned under her chin. She stood quaking beside the two shallow mounds already gathering a blessing of frosty grave covering in the rawness of the earth.

A crude cross made of packing crate pieces and twine leaned between them, upon which Cat scratched names and dates with a miner's pick and sharp rock. No one came near the sole mourner industriously scraping, her tongue stuck between her lips. Only a soul with the maleficence of Satan's minions would have no pity. Whispers and sideways glances slid off like geese on ice when she raised her head to seek guidance, while flames roared behind her as someone tossed a firebrand into her tent. She barely noticed.

Job finished, she swayed as snow feathered like sequins on her tangled raven hair and piled around boots worn to shreds. She might as well have gone barefoot.

She stayed rooted, as if, waiting long enough, this would be a nightmare and Ma and Pa would rise from the mound and boil acorn coffee, or maybe some folk would tell her what to do. But the few brave or piteous souls in distant attendance gave a short grace of mumbled words while drifting back to their huddled tents, and none seemed to take further interest. When her feet seemed two blocks of wood, she finally turned to go.

Where, she wasn't sure, and that lack of knowledge hit her like ice trickling down her neck.

All she owned was in bulky bundles, one made of a discarded saddlebag slung over her shoulder and the other of feedstore burlap. She clutched the bundles to her chest as if they were a lifeline. She could not drag the trunks, with their pathetic remainder of clothing, pots, and bric-a-brac.

Shaking herself as though waking from a long sleep, the child stared down those eyes peering from the shelter of their tents, and tightening her arms about her burdens, headed to the trampled path she only kenned led to the frontier town of Wylder.

Chapter One
Sanctuary

Madame Levi Gruenwald stood in the doorway—or Madame Solange, as she was known in former glory days, and no better than she should be. She blenched, hand to chest, calculating the girl with the plaid shawl and pinched face. Oh, why had she opened the door? In the old days, this vagabond, despite her thin face, would be snatched in before scum collected on cold cocoa.

Memories wended regretfully back over missed opportunities of yore. This scrap would have fetched a pretty price among her old clients, and she the mistress of her business, in place of being the dull wife of Levi Gruenwald, Lord and Master of the Longhorn Saloon. She scarce needed more grunt work, and this bereft child looked more needy than helpful. Nevertheless, dormant Christian charity kicked Madame in the bustle, and she impulsively opened the door a crack to allow the child, satisfyingly grateful, to scuttle in.

After the child had gulped a mug of bitter black tea tasting as if brewed with rusty nails, and had eaten a dry biscuit, Madame Solange learned she was an orphan—orphaned because of the dread scourge of typhoid fever. By that time, it was too late, but not too late for the girl who would become the wild-haired beauty Catriona…

Chapter Two
Wylder Strangers, Airs and Graces

The man, six feet tall, stepped off first, with the grace of a horse bred for racing, all elegant limbs and fluid motion, only just turning stiff with age; silver waves swept from a widow's peak, saving him from baldness. It suited him well, as did his strong aristocratic nose, but his dress spoke more eloquently of his place in the pantheon of titles—The Most Noble Duke Greville of Sandringham Cloisters. He searched the platform, no doubt expecting a porter but seeing only a lout spitting tobacco juice at a stray cat.

Smiling, bemused, he lent a hand to a fine lady, equivalent in all respects. Tall for a woman, almost six feet, slender, high-bosomed, she carried herself like a prow on a ship, nose high as if sniffing the air for something bad. She noted air no different than Wylder always produced—horses, mud, or dust, with the lurking spice of pine and cedar—and conceded the atmosphere was better than London's, thick with the acid yellow devil's-brew of coal and low-lying vapors from the rancid River Thames.

Behind this vision, a slim foot clad in a soft kid shoe the shade of tea roses and tied with ribbons about a lean ankle, completely unsuitable for Wylder thoroughfares, summer or winter, stepped cautiously off the last Pullman step as if into a pigsty, skirts held high rather more to show shapely legs of a fine-boned woman whose flesh was pallid as whey milk under a mass of soft brown hair worn in a fashionable pouf. Soft curls framed a heart-shaped face.

It was only later that Madame, watching as usual from the Longhorn Saloon for possible trade, learned the younger high-born lady's manner was as acid is to iron, and some of the soft curls pinned on. Steely in desires, tart in her demands despite the pretty face—if not for her, Madame often pondered, none of the rest would have happened.

****

Lady Daphne, the elder female, watched His Grace's back as he crossed the rough street, following his lordly figure with an assessing gaze, as all women of her status were prone to do. Striking, with his lion's mane of silvery hair, noble aristocratic nose, and flat paunch, he sidestepped ruts, erratic rattling carts, and the odd horse and rider as he made his way to a gaudy establishment proclaiming itself to be the Longhorn Saloon.

Still, vexingly, he seemed a tad peaky as he hustled to arrange their hasty lodging, at a saloon yet! Why not an inn, perhaps, a proper English inn… Apparently not here in—what was this place? Oh, yes, Wylder. And a wilder country she'd never experienced. But really! Surely there was an hotel! Why would Mortimer affront them with such a crude establishment in which to lay their heads?

She watched her daughter, equally slim and aloof, Lady Audrina. Tears before bedtime. She glanced uneasily at an uncouth male on Wylder's station platform not more than ten feet from herself and her toothsome daughter, the dregs of their wardrobe arraigned fortress-like in hillocks of hatboxes and steamer trunks. The plethora of scrappy, tattered, leather-bound boxes did not bespeak luxurious travel to exotic locales, but simply age. How long without a lady's maid or proper closet would have her fluff and feathers resembling molting hens, too? She fretted.

Lady Daphne Greville made herself small, unnoticeable, a difficult endeavor as she was still a handsome woman most resembling John Singer Sargent's portraits of divinely willowy, elegant females, despite approaching age forty-two. She had a dread of the state in which Marie Antoinette made her way to the guillotine.

She next eyed the tall flame-haired youth accompanying Lord Greville with a moue of distaste. Hugo, of course, resembled nothing more than a great stork, with his long legs and gangling arms, seeming with more joints than needed. She glanced off, biting her lip as if the very sight of him offended. Hugo had hovered over them in his tediously responsible manner until she shooed him off, now wishing she had not been quite so hasty, as the nearby lout tried to strike up acquaintance with Audrina.

Lady Daphne smirked, watching the trapper—though unaware of his profession—warily eye her daughter as if she were an animal with which he was unfamiliar. She drew her unsuitable lace parasol between them as a shield.

He would just as soon accost an unmarried or widowed lady as call a dog, she was certain.

Oh, to be back in civilized London, she mused. Not that she and Audrina were spoiled for choice.

She exhaled. Keep calm. Must keep it all under her best hat around His Grace, and be thrilled over any accommodations.

"Chance might be a great thing," she murmured to her daughter, checking the odd collection of saloons, domiciles, and sundries across from them, ignoring the approaching storm front clouding Audrina's lovely, sulky face.

Yes, choice would be another fine chance.

She had heard America's siren call a little off-note, thanks to dear Mortimer. More brass than violins. True, his lordship avowed there were gold, silver, copper, and trapper's riches, elegant homes, millionaires as far as Kansas City, even rumored billionaires—an unheard-of figure yet, in this impossibly vast country that took not hours but tedious days to cross. Must they be so brash as to land in the back of beyond, in this raw village?

"I am not feeling top drawer, my dear Daphne," Lord Greville had said earlier, eyeing the saloon across the thoroughfare as a hungry dog did a flat-iron steak. "Perhaps—if you could stiff-upper-lip it for one night, I should fancy alighting there."

Lady Daphne's eyes had narrowed.

The younger woman beside her sniffed. "Why not a hound kennel?"

Lady Daphne turned with a warning glance. "Oh, come now, Audrina, my dear. You did say adventure would be a fine thing, one denied so many young ladies with another boring Grand Tour," she wheedled. "Same dusty museums, same high teas in the same grand hotels. Me…chaperoning."

"Italy and France have been 'done to death,' I believe you mentioned." The older man attempted a smile ending in a grimace Daphne did not miss.

"Oh, but this is most inconvenient, Mortimer. You drag us all this way, and you feel faint! What about us?" Lady Daphne rashly ventured, "Mayhap you, my Right Honorable Lord, have regrets?"

She pursed her lips to show it as jest. He did not see the knuckles of her hands gripping her reticule.

"Regrets. Nay, my dear. Only fatigue from a ride with more jolts and jumps than a steeplechase. I might have caught the ague. It will pass. One night in this colorful heart of the West in that quaint establishment…" He made light. "On the morrow I shall be right as rain and sort better lodgings. Now for a soft bed, a light supper…"

When Lord Greville, her dear step-uncle by marriage, suggested travel might be broadening, Lady Daphne leapt at the chance, even if it meant only a journey to Haymarket. Deep down, she was humiliated by Greville's courtly ploy to ignore her poverty without being overt.

She despised him for it.

Truth was, she and her daughter were on sufferance wherever they went. Why did Cecil have to pass so ignominiously after that spectacularly bad investment? She'd managed to keep it secret, even from her beautiful spoiled daughter, who would have immediately fallen into fainting hysterics.

Ah, Audrina, Audrina!

The figure of her thoughts intruded. She pouted charmingly, kicking her portmanteau. "Why are we here? What about the Season in London? I won't have a chance at a proper dressmaker, even if we flew there now on the fastest steamer."

Oh, how willingly blind were the young.

The duchess twanged like the string her nerves were strung upon. She rounded on her. "Did I miss the hordes of suitable, eligible, handsome, youthful, titled admirers cluttering up our threshold, begging to sign your dance card in the past? Nor do I see many dressmakers in our future."

Her temper, stretched fine as silk thread, snapped as she watched His Grace Mortimer enter the Longhorn across the way, trying to ignore Audrina's protruding lower lip.

"*Maman*! Please don't be crude! That was unkind. The coming-out ball! I distinctly remember Lord Sotheby eyeing me last Season."

The duchess looked away. She'd not wanted to mention Audrina, at twenty-three, was fast slipping from eligible and toothsome to slightly tarnished with age and, moreover, with debt.

"I dare say Lord Sotheby is nearsighted as a goose. Handsome he may be, but he was most likely eyeing the debutante next to you," she said, unnecessarily acerbic. "In fact, I heard he was engaged. My dear, perhaps if you were a little less—"

"Honest?"

"Cutting."

"Fiddlesticks! Honest, to me. I must hide my mind? I must hide thoughts?"

Lady Daphne was decidedly "commonly" hungry, as a noise from her stomach indicated. A rare state in her world of twenty courses plus course-appropriate wines. Or as her world had been.

"Of course you must hide your thoughts, you ungrateful child! Especially if they are cruel, even if they are clever. Or too honest."

"Such a bore. Perhaps I shall only speak behind my fan."

"Best if you did not speak at all," she answered her daughter waspishly and searched the raffish establishment across the way for Mortimer's return. Gilt-inscribed windows, a plank walkway fronting a broad veranda with benches, banker's chairs, and spittoons, swing doors, a balcony fronting the top floor proclaiming, above, *The Longhorn Saloon* in tarnished letters.

After the Atlantic crossing, hellish New York travails, endless train rides over featureless stretches of prairie and mountains, all on Mortimer's whim, she was beyond weary, bored, and in no mood for Audrina's airs and vapors.

"Where *is* Mortimer?" She stamped her foot and then, sighing in relief, spied her benefactor performing a schottische betwixt a lumbering hay wagon, a surrey, and a mule-driven cart. His top hat was, as at home in London, apparently an irresistible target for two boys in an alley between the Longhorn and—Heaven forefend—the Five Star Saloon right alongside on the other edge of the narrow alley.

She squinted at his approaching figure.

"You ken, Audrina," she murmured, as he retrieved his hat, "his lordship is not so very old, and yet quite an adornment for his age."

Audrina eyed him too, hiding her mouth, but could not help sputtering laughter. "*Ma mère*! Uncle Mortimer has at least thirty years on you, if what I suppose you are suggesting—that's something vile!"

"Oh! Audrina! Not a real uncle. We will speak

later." She looked off in an embarrassed huff.

"Indeed, *Maman*. Much later, when I am in my dotage too! Until then, I'll do my best to understand why we are here, and find my own beaux, but I must say, I expected better."

"Didn't we all?"

A slight crease formed in Lady Daphne's as yet unmarked brow as she gazed across the splintery platform at Lord Mortimer hustling toward them. What on earth? Mortimer seemed red in the face and perspiring like a commoner.

****

"Quarters! Our room!" Lady Daphne couldn't hold back her irritation. The three arrivals stood in the gallery that served as a hall above the Longhorn bar, with all its attendant noise and beery vapors.

"Audrina and I need share—a bed! Mind you, in this—this dismal, rustic place—"

"My dear Daphne. You needn't stay tending an old codger." The duke spoke rather too eagerly, considering his appearance. "Continue on, perhaps to San Francisco, or if not there, the—what was it—the Vincent Hotel, right here in Wylder?"

"Alone in this wild place? Or unaccompanied on a train? I think not. Oh, very well, one night!" She bit her lip. "It—it is a rather romantic escapade. Where are the porters?" At that, Dingy Watts, late of Longhorn's kitchen, roughly grabbed trunks, portmanteaus, and hatboxes, and without a word dragged them, banging, upstairs.

****

The Lady Daphne, getting ready for what she hoped was an edible morsel, paced the small room large enough

12

for one but not two. Getting dressed for dinner was her last shred of a civilized life. The drab back room lorded over by the duke, she had ascertained to her distaste, was a hand-me-down from a doxie named Flora. "We are in a brothel!"

Audrina knocked her shin on a trunk. "Why not the hotel?" she demanded crossly.

"You know why. We can't leave him alone for a second. Who kens who he might meet?"

The Lady Daphne had checked her toilette one last time in the flecked mirror, more a formality than a necessity. For whom, pray tell, did she need impress? The answer, of course, as always, was Lord Mortimer Greville. She must bolster her pride and appearance if she and Audrina had a last slender hope.

****

As the two ladies descended into the saloon proper, now to serve as dining room, the duke could not help but compare the disdainful wraith, Audrina, slim to the point of emaciation and pale as linen, to the rosy-cheeked wench with a mass of curly locks who peered from the doorway leading presumably to a kitchen.

We should take up breeding as we do prize horses, he mused. Lady Daphne looks as though she were weaned on whey milk and curds, without a drop of blood in her body, no matter how blue. He laughed, irritating the woman in question, as she fiercely wiped a spoon on her handkerchief.

"Might not be a bad idea to mingle," he proposed. "Get to ken the common folk, keep one's ears keen if we are to find a viable mine." Lady Daphne swallowed a sigh. Hugo speared a chop. "But, milord. Surely overseers, or mine supervisors…?"

"A different country, lad. Not like India, or Brazil—almost as intractable as Wales," he muttered in seldom-heard jest. "In America, a man is what one makes of himself—not having his great-great-grandsire heft a fat king's backside onto his horse sideways, and thus made a duke, or a baron, for that matter. I suspect I shall need to take on that task myself," he said with satisfaction, checking the kitchen door for another glimpse of the striking face but finding disappointment. "I rather fancy this place."

Lady Daphne and Lady Audrina blanched even paler. Moreover, eyeing the Longhorn's interior, they had not spied a single specimen who looked as if he owned more than one good suit or pair of shoes.

*****

"Girl! You'll never amount to anything, mooning about. Get on with you. Customers are languishing out there for clean china!"

Cat turned her head to Madame, in all her swollen glory, hand on belly, scowl on face. "Yes, ma'am. I'm after drying the last and all."

"See that you are!"

Cat heard her mutter, with the swish of skirts as she strode off, "What I get for taking in strays. Too softhearted is what I am…"

Catriona thrust arms up to her elbows in her tepid, greasy dishwater in Longhorn Saloon's lean-to kitchen, thinking wicked, sinful thoughts about Mrs. Levi Gruenwald, lady and mistress. Fell pregnant at her age. Almost forty, and here she, a girl of fourteen going on fifteen, well, maybe thirteen, and would love to be in her place, though not fallen with child, and not that she fancied old Levi. Yet 'twas better than pearl-diving through bits of fatback and smashed taties.

She sighed. And didn't she now defiantly tug a lock of hair from her ugly cap?

Earlier, Madame had sailed in with the greasy, egg-stuck breakfast dishes, ordering her to "tidy up and stick all that messy flyaway hair back proper-like," and declaring that she looked like she belonged in the Wylder Social Club, whatever that was. Cat wondered who'd see her from Madame's fine dining room stuck in a corner of the Longhorn and separated by ferns and tacked up archways of fancy fretwork from the card tables, small stage, and raucous bar, with its loathsome spittoons and all. She didn't ken, now did she?

"Humph," Catriona grumbled to the cup she vigorously dried to within an inch of its fine china life.

"Starched table clothes, too. Polished cutlery—another of me chores, mind you—a single flower on each fancy table. Yes, and I will do the ironin' too!" Madame was trying yet to outshine the Vincent House with all its fancy chandeliers. *It still be the Longhorn, no matter how many silk purses she stitches.*

Oh, Catriona was in a fine state, she was.

****

Before going down to supper, Lady Daphne had stood at the side window between the Longhorn and—God forfend—the Five Star Saloon across the narrow alley, catching a glimpse of a train chugging in and squealing to a stop amid a blast of steam.

Oh, how she longed to be on that train. East, west—it made little difference now. Moreover, San Francisco, fabled land of dreams, New York, or even Chicago were almost creditable replacements for London. There, they might meet someone of worth.

Americans were entranced by titles. They might do well on the charity of New York's Four Hundred.

Staring at the few passengers pacing the slice of platform from her slanted view, she recalled when she and her daughter had walked that same length, still nattering over tedious arguments earlier in their nightmare trip across the states, such as when they were at her cousin Edith's home in Chicago…

"My dear girl, please settle. You must think, as I am worried sick! I fret for your future. For my future. We have none unless we play our cards exceedingly cautious."

"*Maman*! Such a bore." Her lovely daughter once again affected French and an attitude.

"Patience, my girl. We must be extremely shrewd. Not a false step!"

"Very well! *Ma mère*, what must we do?" she asked with the patience of a saint.

"For one thing, be more gracious to our hostess. You know we are here only on sufferance. Just because she's my third cousin does not mean she wants to keep us in bed and board until I'm in my dotage or on my death bed."

"Don't be morbid! So off-putting! You've quite spoilt my morning. Now I am most melancholy."

The duchess had cast an impatient gaze at her spoon-fed daughter.

"I've apparently shielded you from the harsher facts of life far too long, Audrina." She spoke with the bitter dryness of a green walnut. "But true, we might stretch this out until the benevolent season of Christmas, and of course the balls have some possibilities. Yet you see, from there, where do we find our next perch? We're running out of relatives—"

"Is it really that important, *Maman*? Why are we going on this dreadful trip? I loathe the Americas. Rude, classless people. Why, they don't have titles at all!"

Daphne watched her daughter sadly.

"My darling girl, if we do not come into some fortune soon, all we have is our title to keep us warm and fed. When the duke mentioned the trip might broaden you, I jumped at it. Cousin Edith is getting fidgety to see us gone. I see the signs. 'Closing the house, Dear Daphne,' " she mimicked. " 'So, dear, I hope our servants are up to the extra work…' "

Lady Daphne made a face at the recollection.

After her cousin left with that warning, Lady Daphne had checked her daughter as if buying a horse. "—and you, my dear, are running out of gowns. How you do grow! Get the height from me," she had continued ruefully.

True, tall and slender to the point of aristocratic boniness, Lady Daphne gained a certain attenuation as she aged. Firm arms now held strings where flesh had once the firmness of an unripe peach. To her vexation, she needed to cover more of herself each year until she resembled an Egyptian mummy.

"So we will be going with the duke," she continued. "And thank providence he invited us in the nick."

"That stuffy old yawn? All he does is prattle of mines and railroads." Audrina feigned a boredom that, if real, would have surely brought about her death.

"He's old and probably smells." She sniffed. "Most older persons do," she announced from the safe perch of youth.

"Audrina! We shall travel with the duke, even if he

goes to the second circle of Hell, until I can think of something. Besides, we will be with an eligible man." Daphne said with such triumph one would think she'd pulled coins from Audrina's ear. "Hugo will be along too."

"Ugh! Hugo! I would be society's laughingstock. He's a worm! A ginger-hair! A beanstalk. A rag man to scare ravens. No one pays him mind. Why, even the homeliest, most desperate wallflower eschewed his request for their dance card last season!" Audrina tittered, crowing, "And they were empty!"

"Audrina!" Daphne hid a smile, yet she had been angrier with her child then than she had ever been.

"Besides, I was rather thinking the duke might be a suitable match," she murmured lightly as if an afterthought, daubing a dot of perfume on each a wrist.

It had to last. The perfume. She had no more.

"You are young and tender. A perfect foil and sweetmeat for an older titled gentleman in perfect health and temperament—a cultured man of seasoned age and aristocratic maturity. And wealth." She ended heavily.

Fifty thousand pounds a year, three estates, and, more fortuitous, no heirs. Lady Daphne smiled to herself. "*Maman*!" Audrina's horrified outrage entered her consciousness.

"Don't give me that look! A duchess's tiara on your pretty head would not go amiss."

"Please, *ma mère*, surely you jest." The look on Audrina's face foretold storm clouds.

"Oh, do quit sounding like a bad melodrama!"

****

Lady Daphne sighed. Lovely Audrina was one of the few cards she had left to play from up her tattered sleeve.

Now she must go down to the table with an ace in her bodice, if she could find one.

Raising a perfect brow, she straightened elegant shoulders and turned to face the Longhorn rabble rumbling below like one of the famous cattle stampedes for which she kenned the West was infamous.

"Dear Mortimer," she cried when seated. Her laugh was the tinkle of an upper piano key. "We are ensconced with the hired help—the servants' quarters, judging by an odd creature with masses of unruly hair passing us and heading apparently to the attic. What a romp," she ended lightly. "Audrina and I need share."

Lord Mortimer Greville was not fooled by her lightheartedness. He sighed inwardly.

"And Mortimer, my dear man, you seem peaky, and insisting on the back bedroom," she reproved. Not even the front bedroom.

A tremendous, hideously fashioned female called Little Mae apparently resided in the best front room, apparently attached to it as a barnacle on a rock, when questioned. The duchess had dark suspicions regarding the Rubenesque figure queening it over that front boudoir, but she put that minor disappointment aside.

"I would relish the quiet for now, my dear. I appreciate your concern."

The crease in her forehead returned. Such a bother, if Mortimer were ill. Audrina and she might be stuck. Here! In this shabby hostelry of sorts, sharing it with scullery maids!

Chapter Three
Yellow Satin

Cat glumly eyed her grubby work dress, her only dress. If it had a color, one could not define it after so many stains had been scrubbed out. Its length had been added onto with patches until she resembled a fool or a jester at a faire.

There were supposed to be toffs dining at the Longhorn tonight. She hoped to have a peek, even though she had a small opinion of British nobility, didn't she now?

Earlier, she'd eyed the yellow tent-like hand-me-down Little Mae had nicely offered. Cat had timidly attempted cutting it down and stitching it back together. The sides shirred, the neckline drooped, and sleeve holes would shelter two arms in place of one. Cat decided she resembled melted butter in it. The dress now hung shapelessly swagged and rippled in pride of place from a nail in her garret. Her eye caught the pale blue of ma's wedding gown on the next hook. Dare she? Outdated, half an eye could tell that, just by what the Wylder town ladies wore, but the material was good…

Cat smiled, even with her hands deep in cooling greasy dishwater, at Little Mae's comments.

"Well, you look like you been pulled through a hedge backwards. What's that long face for?" Little Mae filled the attic doorway, shook her head, and lumbered across, making the floor boards bounce. "Now, what do you call that there?" Mae twitched the sleeves and plucked a swag of skirt before Cat tripped on it. "Looks like that-there dress is a-wearin' you."

"I ken." Cat's chin wobbled. "Made a proper muck-up of your pretty dress." Then it all poured out like sour milk from a cracked pitcher. "Nothing I do is right. Madame doesn't take to me. Works me like a mule and keeps piling thing on. I will be meetin' meself waking up, sure."

She suddenly found her face crammed to Little Mae's bosom, near suffocating in warmth and lilac water.

"Ahhh, there, there," Little Mae crooned. "Plenty left over. Let's figure what we can make of this mess." And whipping the yellow taffeta back over her head, eyed Cat's handspan waist. "Need to put some meat and taters on those bones. Bosoms not bad, though." She snorted, running hands over her own ample shape. "No hips at all."

Yellow was not her best color. It made her fair Irish skin sallow. But Cat was grateful. Now maybe she'd have a Sunday-go-meeting dress to be proud of, with sleeves puffed and a V waist and flowy skirt over a cut-down petticoat of Little Mae's. The neck might be too droopy, she thought, but beggars and all that…

"I been thinking anyways, ever since you come here," Little Mae mumbled through a mouthful of pins. "Wonderin' if maybe you might be more welcome at the Wylder Social Club. Gal purty as you is wasted here. Me? I'm my own madam." Little Mae chuckled. Her breast heaved like a foundering ship. "Make my own rules, keeps my own hours and my do-re-mi." She rubbed thumb and forefingers. "How-some-ever, this here's about you."

Catriona screwed her face. "I don't have time for a social club. Tea and talk. I need work."

"We-e-e-lll, ain't exactly work." She winked, making her eyes merry brown crescents. "Sometimes kinda fun. Let me take you to Miss Adelaide, and you kin meet up with Ruby, Opal, Pearl, Amethyst, and Emerald, if they ain't sleepin'. Wonder what they'll call you? Maybe Agate? Or Topaz."

Cat just laughed, not liking either name. "Thank you, Little Mae...maybe I'll just keep my own name for a while," for she kind of kenned what Little Mae was on about.

"Okey-dokies, suit yer own self, but if you ever..."
****

Cat looked over her shoulder, conscious of her arms plunged in cold gray dishwater. She hastily wiped them and tugged out a few curly locks from her ugly cap, for wasn't she hearin' now Levi's son, Aaron, with eyes blue as cornflowers? Couldn't believe a dried-up cornhusk like Levi could have a boy like that, or his twin, Arabella, with goldy hair in a high pouf like a yellow dandelion gone to seed. Or that Levi had the get-up-and-go to make Madame fall with child either, and wasn't he makin' her as nervy as if she'd stepped on a goose? But he be kind— Old Levi was, not, to her dismay, Aaron, the song of Catriona's hungry heart.

Swiveling like she did not ken Aaron was there a-tall, a-tall, didn't she now throw Aaron her brightest smile? Cat kenned she had pretty teeth. "Little pearls," one wag had said, back in Londonderry County. Tugging her cap, Cat let down a mass of raven ringlets to hang heavy to her waist, and leaned against the zinc sink, fanning herself.

"How do, Aaron. Are they a-workin' you fearsome hard, too?" She asked all saucy-like and looking slanchways under her lashes.

Toting a tray of crockery, Aaron only grunted. "Don't look at me with those witchy eyes. Never know which one to look at, whatever your name is."

"It's Cat. Catriona! As you well ken," she said hotly, regretting her bad temper.

"So, now I can forget it."

He soured his face, tossing dirty plates in her dishwater, scraps and all. A flicked chop bone splashed her with cold greasy tears that runneled her cheeks. She backhanded them, plunging her hands back in the water so he could not see.

Aaron was so beautiful and fine. So tall and golden, he rightfully thought work beneath him. He should be an actor on a stage, or a prince.

Didn't she now dream of Aaron gazing adoringly past Catriona's grubby tattered state to see how fine her eyes were—though odd, she admitted—and her hair glossy as patent leather boots, her waist tiny with no boning in sight? He would be bussing her, and be so overtaken with love they'd seal their troth on the spot.

He'd find her so pleasing…he'd forget she had one eye as green as May apples and one blue as a starched cambric shirt.

They'd be wed, banns read proper-like, and she wearin' ma's wedding dress and out of the kitchen and having tea with Madame and…

That vision burst like an oily lye-soap bubble. Cat flushed and spun back to the zinc sink, allowing tears to add to the water.

She would like to show him her fine Irish temper, but not again. Too many surplus daughters in need of supplementing family wages would crave this job. She might end up as Little Mae in the front bedroom, but without a pot or a window.

Yet, if she didna set her sights high, who would do for a girl without kith or kin?

Aaron swept past, dragging out his tobacco pouch and papers to grab a smoke out back, and if she hadn't stepped aside, he would have knocked her over.

She heard a snort of derision behind her. Arabella had been pressed into service too.

It was Dingy Watts, who made moony eyes at her, who told Cat they had real toffs out front. "Some muckety-muck out dere," he sniveled, wiping his nose on his sleeve. "Madame sez to me not ta show me face, so I showed me backside," he said matter-of-factly, taking his usual perch on a turned-over apple crate by the firebox.

Arabella tied on a long, starched apron with real Battenburg lace, gave Dingy a cuff, and eyed Cat slantways. "Think you'd learn. Aary doesn't want a girl making cow eyes, even if they are blue and green." She smirked. He doesn't care a fig." She snickered as if reading Cat's mind and flounced out with the heavy burden of a handful of spoons.

Folks didn't take note of Cat's eyes after they kenned her a while. Least they said so. Why couldn't she be like other folks?

As she dried the last cup available, her gaze followed Aaron's slender, broad-shouldered figure as he swept a shock of golden hair from his forehead, even that a graceful move, before re-entering the saloon, trailing the scent of tobacco. She was savin' herself. For Aaron. Catriona sighed to her toes, not allowing her thoughts to stray into sinful territory. Her face flushed to match her chapped hands. If only she had a decent gown. Aaron would see her different. Like a real lady.

Cat, groaning beneath her breath, awoke from her daydream to a familiar clatter.

Didn't now Madame herself tote in a load of dirty crockery? "Now what are you doing, slow poke! We have important guests in the salon." She said salon, not saloon.

"Yessum. I'm washing fast as I can, ma'am. The water is cold, and Dingy…"

"Never mind Dingy! If you need water, go fetch it! Put the kettle on! Must I do everything?"

"No, Madame…" Cat hesitated, drying her hands. "You said, important? May I be askin' where might they be from?" Even secondhand excitement was a treat.

Madame, torn between airing her exalted status and being the formidable taskmistress, bridled, finally muttering, "Titled, if you will. Now get on with it, lazybones." She made shooing motions, warning, "I can always find dishwashers. And stay away from the salon. I won't have them gawped at, as if we are unsophisticated country bumpkins."

Cat eyed the sink. She was chained to teetering stacks of dishes and stuck food and taint of garbage for the rest of her life. Still, she could not lose this job. Where would she go? She had safe haven in the attic. Enough to eat, finally, the most in a long while. Leftovers, not plentiful but enough for a scrap like her and Dingy. And she was savin' up. Not much, but a penny here, a penny there, chucked in Ma's red lacquered Chinese tea chest.

And she had hopes of Aaron.

But first, fetch water. Dingy, spied as usual wiping his nose on his bedraggled sleeve only a second before, had disappeared apparently from earth itself. Cat snatched up the bucket…and hearing the tinkling, fluting laughter out in the saloon.

On impulse, she dropped the bucket and peeked out to see what all the foofaraw was about. She'd never seen royalty, as Cat reckoned most titled folk were. Madame stood behind her. Cat froze.

"Indeed, they are something, aren't they?" Madame murmured, wistful.

"Oh. Yessum." Cat's eyes feasted on the three dazzling creatures descending, and one tall gangly soul topped with hair red as a coxcomb, rather drably dressed compared to his exquisite companions.

"And who might the tall skinny man be, then, with the lord and ladies?"

"Not for the likes of you to ken. Mind your knitting. Don't want you pestering them, I said." Madame relented. "Levi says a secretary, or somewhat. I hear these folks have valets. Can't dress themselves, apparently. Need other folks tellin 'em which foot to put in which trouser leg. Or how to button a dress proper."

Madame humphed and waddled off.

"Hear tell they can't even comb their own hair!"

****

Catriona, captivated, tarried, holding the swing door a crack. The first ambrosial creature, taller than most ladies, her head—a perfection of high pompadours and elegant swirls with peeps of tiny jeweled pins—stuck high on a willowy white neck, swept in fanning the skirt of soft yellow confection behind her.

Cat sighed, feeling the scratchiness of her crude dress, and hungrily drank in the visions, turning to the equally willowy younger creature with hair like shining wheat in soft curls and tendrils about a heart-shaped face. The hair was designed, Cat perceived, to make her look younger—although an expression as if smelling something burnt quite spoilt the wide-eyed innocence which her virginal yet lowcut bodice wished to convey.

The lovely creature, making Cat feel like a slattern in the stews of Cork, swept the room with a gaze cold as moonlight, halting stonily at the door, where Cat huddled, before moving on. Her gown was muted moss, expensive for its odd color alone, softly rustling and complimenting her wide-spaced jade eyes.

Cat shrank. Yet it was all a mime, filled with color and drama. She had to see more, tarrying despite Madame's injunctions, again noting the tall drink of water with hair the shade of a scorching sunset seating the elder goddess. Not a stitch nor drape of the two women's gowns escaped Catriona's thirsty gaze. Starved for pretty things, she was. Though she'd attempted—in her cracked, spotted mirror on the shelf in the attic—to tame, corral, and batten down wet unruly ebon hair, each tendril was an overwound clock spring escaping the strongest trap of nets or pins. Besides which, she'd laid her dress under the thin mattress to press it, but she was still a drab sparrow against these peacocks.

Catriona now owned two dresses, though, she conceded. The hand-me-down from Little Mae—that would make two gowns and a nighty, if she kenned how to hem, and a hanky. Plus her grimy work dress that never came clean, growing grayer and tattier by the hour and lengthened with odd patches like Saint Joseph's coat. Clashing bands increased the hem—one band red plaid from a shawl with a burnt hole, and one a dry goods remnant: yellow, sprigged with tiny clovers, plus a band on each sleeve yet to reach her wrists.

The chest was stramming tight, it hurt her so; a too-tight bust-binder could be no more irksome. Cat did manage a new kerchief and secondhand shawl for Sunday-go-to-meeting, from her miniscule wages. Not a proper church, mind you, not like back in Londonderry County, with the priests and all, and all. Still 'twas church, even if the pastor did speak plain English in place of proper Latin. She tried to be around Aaron when so presentable.

Difficult it was, for he perched in the front pew like a proper saint, with Old Levi and Madame, his eyes the shade of a robin's eggs fixed on the cross. Catriona was content to watch his gilded waterfall of hair reaching his collar in waves, fancying her fingers ruffling those waves.

So far, nothing dented his disregard for her. Perhaps, when she saved enough for new dress goods, she mused, her mind far off the homily the itinerant pastor offered.

Catriona lied to herself. She did have Ma's wedding dress. Fine blue muslin it was, with tiny white flowers. Saving it for her own wedding, wasn't she? The only thing, beyond Pa's long clay pipe, that Cat had salvaged from the rough camp by the water tower before others carried off anything of worth, beyond the red Chinese painted tea chest from the old country. Cat had hidden that under her skirts while they dug the graves.

Chapter Four
How Deep the Water

The younger creature made an annoyed face at the ginger man, waving him off as he attempted to seat her. They were trailed by a tall, bony-shouldered man with a lovely silver lion's mane and high-boned nose, in tweeds and hose up to his banded trews. He looked kind. Catriona just made out an embroidered crest, shaped like a shield, on his jacket. She wondered if he truly was a prince or somewhat.

These three mortals were from fairy tales. It was only way later Cat noticed the discreet patching and hem-turning, the switched lace.

****

Cat started and hastily turned back to the dish pan. Here she was, moonin' about, when she should be working, and no tellin' when Madame might swoop in like a sharp-eyed hawk. In a rare burst of misery, tears once more joined the murky water with its islands of peas, ham, and butterbeans floating about.

Why'd Pa and Ma have to die? Both so cheerful, full of song. Long on plans and dreams, rushing to this lush land of plenty, paid back not in pelts or copper but by typhus carrying them off one after the other to rough graves out where Wylder gave way to scrubland…

Catriona did not often dwell on that which could not be unraveled. Only in her attic room above the Longhorn would she show sorrow.

Long faces gathered no rosebuds, she lectured herself.

She must put her shiniest face forward to make do even in a raw place like Wylder, where everyone was keen as mustard to make a go. Shiny new beginnings dangled before their noses, before dreams tarnished under the harsh onslaught of mines, cold and sickness, and never having the food bodies craved. Cat would not be one of them. She would not be Ma and Pa following a pot of gold. Work hard as a ditch digger and Madame would give her more important duties.

Solange indeed swept in, carting an overloaded tray. Her sharp voice cut through Cat's reflections like a hot knife through butter. Cat started, dropping the cup, swooping red-faced to clear it under Madame's accusing eyes.

"More broken china. That comes from your pay, girl. What's keeping you? Christmas? We have three tables with not a saucer nor a spoon! Quit lollygagging, or you will be out on the street in the time it takes me to untie this apron!" Shrieking, "Where's Aaron?" The kettle hissed the last sputter of steam behind them. "And Cat, you were fetching water. Are you all intent on sending me to the madhouse, when I have honored guests? Cat! Get a move on!"

"Cat" heard, in a fractious mood, pressing her lips together and clenching the sea sponge to keep from tossing greasy water at the woman.

"My name is Catriona!" Cat was a name without respect—a far cry from the elegant specimens ogled a few minutes ago. She had to quit daydreaming. This was her lot. Not the high-borns out there, not for a moment believing it as she warred with herself.

"Catri—ona!" Madame mocked. "An Irish gypsy with enough airs to wallpaper the Longhorn is what you are. Now git on with it before I take my hand to you or tear my hair out!" Solange slapped the work table. Not waiting for answer, she swept out with hair awry.

"Aaron's always missing," Cat wanted to snip after her, grinning despite herself. Aaron could spirit out back whenever work was awaitin', faster than a ghost, and just behind him went Dingy, the overlooked waif she kenned nothing about and hadn't asked.

She looked forlornly at the kettle hissing its last gasp, eyeing the cistern by the old stone sink. Empty too. Cat looked, helpless and appealing, at Aaron just sauntering in after Madame vanished—as appealing as a five-foot-tall girl in a grubby pinny and bare feet can.

"Please?" She gestured with wet hands toward the buckets.

He stared at Cat as if a mongrel dog had wandered in speaking in tongues.

"What you take me for? Your servant? Your water boy? Think yer one of them muckety-mucks out there?" He chucked a thumb at the doorway, casting Catriona looks that if she were white bread would turn her to burnt toast.

Cat sighed deep—another mark against her. Should have saved that mountain to climb until he kenned her better. She had so much to give. Would she never learn clever words? She was too blunt. Aaron wanted a colleen, pink and sweet as peppermint candy, with skin as white and unblemished. Soft spoken, demure, not a freckle-faced, wild-haired scullery drudge. In vain, Cat searched the kitchen, spying Dingy, the slop's boy, conveniently disappearing in the direction of the outdoor privy.

Nothing for it. Hastily drying three cups and setting them out prominently, Cat grabbed two buckets...

"I say! Pardon me—ah—miss. Perhaps I have wandered too far afield..."

Cat froze.

The high, fluting tone was the voice of British landlords and toffs.

Her face heated.

Hideously aware of the slops bucket with its overflowing mess of peelings and coffee grounds and eggshells, grease-filled cast-iron skillets and dirty linen on the work table she had yet to get to, she realized one of the lofty creatures from the "dining room" had wandered into her poor lean-to kitchen.

Cat wiped her forehead with her forearm, gaping at the scarecrow in gentleman's array—the carrot-topped young man who had escorted the two ethereal ladies. His plain gray suit she had noted before was far from inelegant, with the sheen of fine wool so as to resemble silk. Longing to run her chapped, scratchy palms over it, she settled on trying out expressions, finally fitting on a scowl.

"I do beg your forgiveness. I—I have interrupted your—ah, duties, yet if you would be so kind, is this the way to, ah—" He looked about, bewildered. "The gentleman's lounge? I mean...the smoking room?" He stammered. His long, pale, earnest face bloomed color. Perhaps the proprietress had meant the other direction.

"You mean the porch! Does this look like a smoking lounge?" Cat snipped, unbearably aware of her appearance even before such as he. She could not see his eyes behind the thick glasses, but his wide mouth murmured yet another aggravating apology as he knocked over the coal scuttle in place of just leaving.

"Oh dear! Please allow me." He stooped, accidently kicking the scuttle. More coals rattled across the floor as he crushed a few with his large feet.

"Leave it!" She snapped, imitating her mistress, and groaned, as she eyed the sooty mess. Mulish, she cast her gaze about the kitchen in exaggerated fashion. "Of course, sir! Just clear that table off there, and I'll be fetchin' one of Madame's good saucers with the rosebuds and gilt trimmin' for your ashes, won't I?"

"I do say, I have been intrusive."

" 'I do say! I do say!' Cat scowled. "Just spit it out. What is it with you high and mighties? Think we poor serfs have time to listen to your long-winded highfalutin palaver? If you crave a smoke, out there's a place for it, if you've a mind!"

From the doorway Cat waved a bucket at a large roughly-shaped triangle of beaten earth out back where she headed, too late recalling the laundry lines flapped flags of ladies' bloomers and Levi's long johns, plus the pungency of chicken coops, a scrubby garden, and the privies at the pointy end.

"Do allow me." As he fingered his glasses straight, the red-haired man leapt awkwardly past Catriona. Banging his elbow, knocking her buckets with a knee, he held the door wide. Cat hastened out, uneasily aware she had just insulted Madame's toffs, and stomped off to the new stone well, lined proper as it was with brick, at the other end of the yard, muttering, "Ta," as she balefully watched him wander the other way stuffing his pipe.

There was a small gate by the privy. Maybe he

would smoke out beyond.

Cat shrugged the buckets, but before another step, Aaron emerged from shadows between the drain pipe and rain barrel, blocking her way. "You might clean up pretty good if you didn't smell of ham fat and sourdough." Trying to match Hugo's cultured tones, Aaron achieved Lady Daphne's haughtiness, but not her grace. Despite his smirk, a lightning bolt nailed Catriona's feet to the earth, and before she kenned it, Aaron pressed her against sun-warmed wood smelling half-burnt and spicy from the day's heat, his mouth roughly on hers, teeth grinding against Cat's, his tongue sliding in. Grabbing her bottom, he lifted her to him.

She relished his hard body against hers and pressed closer, buckets and well water forgotten. Aaron. Beautiful Aaron wanted her. Then Aaron grabbed her hem to hike it and, at the same time, hefted her roughly to the rim of the rain barrel and with his other hand fumbled his trews.

Cat froze, pressing her hand on his chest and slid off, heart thudding like a band playing "The Star Spangled Banner." She wanted him. Oh, Lordy, she did so want him, too. But the toff was here somewhere, and besides…not like this!

It took him a moment like a galloping horse, to settle. Half-mad, breathing hard, blue eyes glassy and wide, he crushed Cat's face between his hands—soft and moist, not hard as a man's touch—and rammed his mouth on hers. "Not like you're not watching me all the time. I ken what's on your mind." She cried out, pulling away. He thrust his fingers roughly through her curls— as usual a thick, scrunchy tangle, his ring catching a nest of ringlets. Cat grasped his hands to disentangle as strands pulled, but Aaron shook her and, knotting his fingers deeper in her hair, drew her close and kissed her harder.

Cat pulled away, fingering bruised lips. "Please, Aaron. Not like this."

Staring into her face, he laughed harshly, yanked his hands free along with strands of Catriona's hair, and darted a mad look up.

"Aha. Rather make the two-backed beast in your wee garret." Checking her small window above, he showed teeth. "That can be done. More private. Old snoopy-drawers won't get the wind up—just climb this old barrel…" He smacked it. It made a wet thud. "And…"

The horror in her face must have shown.

He could so easily get in.

Part of her wanted that—the romance of Aaron climbing the rain barrel, then the drain pipe, and slipping though her attic window at midnight, when the air was soft with the call of nightbirds and moonbeams. They would laugh, because the window was so small…

But a stubborn part wanted to decide—not just lie there wondering when.

His eyes turned to blue chips at her hesitant look.

"Why, you tease. You trollop! You led me on!"

"I'm not. I—I do want you, Aaron."

Cat's tongue ran away with her thoughts before she could stop.

"I want you to kiss me that way, and—and lie with me." She blushed. "But only after the blessings and proper words and banns read and…"

Aaron stared aghast. "We? Wed? Is that what you're thinking? Hah! Me? Yoked to my stepmother's kitchen grub?"

"I was not always as you see me! Pa and ma died, as did your ma."

"Funerals scarcely give us equal footing."

With that, twisting his face, he thrust Catriona back into the shadows, penning her between rigid arms. "Now Lady Audrina, for all her pretty nose in the air, is the star I'd hitch my wagon to." He dragged Cat out, tossed her aside, kicking the buckets away, and strode off. Audrina. So that was her name. Though tears sparkled her eyes, making her vision swim, Cat wouldn't cry as she tottered blindly across the yard in the direction of the well.

****

The rim was bosom-high.

Cat groaned, letting her pails drop with a dull clang. Oh, no! She looked dully at the pull-rope, which had slipped off the hook and pulley and now dangled into the well. She'd have to lean over to snag it. "Mother Mary and Joseph!" she blasphemed. She'd need to secure it firmly around the pulley, then haul up the wood bucket now hanging slanchways halfway down the well.

Standing on tiptoes, the rim scraping her unfettered bosom, Cat banged her ribs, then her midriff against the rough outer stonework as she strained to reach for the rope, tantalizing inches away, almost fingertipping it.

"Judas Priest!" She cursed again.

Catriona lunged for the rope drooping coyly right before her nose.

One more inch.

Her forefinger finally tipped the rough braid, sending it swaying maddeningly away. The bucket dropped another foot. She stared up at the pulley. The dratted thing was unwinding the rope as she watched.

She stretched harder. Her dress ripped at the waist; stone grazed her ribs.

Suddenly, the rim pressed her belly instead.

She flailed; her wet apron, slick with grease, edged her farther over the rim until Cat was staring into Hell—if Hell was a dank, dark, green-with-moss hole dwindling smaller to a black watery bottom with the moon winking slyly up from what seemed a mile down.

"Hellooo," the man in the moon winked from the stirred surface, as pebbles plummeted down. "Coming to visit?" The moon twinkled slyly.

Madame would be waiting. She had to try!

Cat lunged one last time…she was going in…over-tipping! The stone edge scraped a knee. She flung arms out, pinwheeling them, grabbing for the rim, now behind her, flailing, kicking a foot down, striving to touch blessed ground—and felt nothing but air.

Catriona's heart-stopping terror had made her balance over-waver like an assayer's brass scale with a copper nugget on one end and a feather on the other. She reached to grasp the rim on the other side, anything, waving for the wildly swaying rope, as she sensed through the coarse weave of her dress that her hips were grinding farther over the stone, helped by the grease-slicked apron. She stared face down past the narrow, round brick walls, thick with velvety moss, clean to a winking black bottom fully reflecting a placid moon.

As she gawped, Catriona had the oddest feeling.

'Twas as if the moon was sayin'…*Come. Join me…no more pain. No more fear, sorrow, or longings…look how beautiful I am.*

That's when Cat panicked in earnest, hooting down the well, "No-ooo! Help!" Flinging her arms, striving to

37

throw her weight back, Cat felt her apron snag. Now balanced on a straight razor's edge, she was going in! She felt a sickening slide of counterbalance—sensed her head and torso now weighed more than her fanny and legs.

Cat tried to remain motionless. Thrashing did not help. Too late. Her scream got cut off as she tumbled in head first. Flinty stones struck her shins, and then her feet banged hurtfully against the stony edge. She grabbed at air, striking the brick wall, fingers skimming the slimy mossy sides, digging desperately to reach the rough red brick. She had presence of mind for that, in the split-second of free fall, nails scraping, breaking, sliding off velvety sides, before her head struck and she saw nothing but white flashing rick-rack.

"Ow-ah!" Cat's hip struck the heavy wooden bucket halfway down, and she snatched it onehanded, as if that gray bleached pail was the Angel Gabriel himself and this was the last chance into Heaven—near yanking her arm from her shoulder in the bargain.

The wail shot from the funnel of damp brick to the stars and to nothing and no one else. The swamp-scent of moss and well water, deep from the earth, surrounded her in cold murk, stealing breath and voice, if Cat had any left.

Catriona desperately clutched the bucket at an awkward angle, hanging with her back to it, elbow straining, toes dangling into nothing. Sucking a deep breath, she swung her body around—for one breathless time, both hands slid off the wood rim. Grabbing at nothing, she barely hooked the splintered bucket with the first joints of fingers of one hand. Twisting, grasping the other side, she painfully drew herself up and, stomaching it, finally clambered aboard the wildly swinging staved thing, thanking her stars it wasn't a slippery metal pail.

Her perch immediately plummeted with her weight, jerking to a stop, fully ten feet down now, closer to the water than to the top.

She glanced up in horror. What was holding her? Then, Cat saw a snarled knot above the pulley. One knot between her and plunging to bottom. She checked the tarry, winking circle of untold depth below her toes—and wished she hadn't.

Trembling, Catriona hugged the rope, trying to stay very still, hearing her own short panting breath. Surely someone would heed? Dingy, if he wasn't sneaking a dried corn husk smoke behind the outhouses, or that toff. *Please! Someone come!*

Cat winced at a whining overhead—her bucket spun, jolted and dropped; the pulley ratcheted. Cat leaned carefully back; her gaze tied to the bucket's handle traveling up the rope—watching terrified as the line, spitting and hissing, stretched, untwining from its hitch-knot, the ends fraying thin as string near snapping even as she watched.

Abruptly, the bucket plummeted again, with her slight weight straining what was left of the strands. "Help! Help! I'm in the—" She glanced down, terrified, and the rope whined and sizzled louder as it spun over the pulley. Her perch lowered with a sickening fast drop.

Cat was blind save for the small dim circle far overhead. Her toes were inches from depthless blackness, near pitch black, that far down. She unstuck her tongue.

"I'm in the well! Dingy! Madame! Help!" Her call echoed up steep walls.

Her voice was a ghost-echo bouncing off brick, muffled by moss. She kenned all that in a split second. No one could hear her, this deep. How long could she keep her head above water? She hated the thought of her mouth gulping in…Lord alone kenned what! How long could she tread with naught to hold on to? Weighted by a petticoat and heavy dress, she'd drown. How deep was it? Over her head? What lurked beneath? Black snakes?

A late spring. Gully-washers. Cloud bursts. Laden heavens opened up day after day. Ground water aplenty. They'd all watched the diggers, cheering as the well plunged deeper and deeper into the earth.

All that flashed through her as quickly as a lightning strike.

She wished she'd said her prayers last night—

The knot slipped past.

The bucket hit the water with an echoing splash, half-filling it as it tipped, with Cat hanging onto the slack rope as if it were formed of iron links, her skirts billowing over her head, dragging her down, and her face plunging under icy water that closed over her without a ripple. Only the moon would ken where she drowned.

Water filled her mouth.

Unfasten buttons…rip the petticoat off.

Legs numb from chill.

Her feet did not touch bottom.

Then they did…mucky marl, sharp bits of stone…

Desperately, she swam up with great floundering motions, kicking wildly, willing herself up, blind through chill water black as onyx. Her head broke surface. Buttons ripped off. Petticoat floated away. She overturned the bucket, gripping it as a lifeline in her arms, bobbing unstable and offering poor flotation as she released great gulps of precious air. Kitchen empty. Dining room, saloon regaled with the clink of cutlery, laughter, ByJingo's piano. She could hear faint tinny sounds even thirty feet down… She sank lower. The wood-bottomed bucket now barely broke surface. Fear froze muscles and numbed her mind. Tiring fast. Was this the end? Down here in the evil blackness? Her hands slipped off. The bucket bobbed away.

"Help!" Water slopped in her mouth. Choking.

The rope jerked with a sharp backlash.

The bucket slammed her side; her hands jerked free from the rope.

She snatched at it blindly and caught it as she looked up desperately at a face far above, framed in the circle of the well and dimly recognized. Cat's scattered brain realized it was only a short time ago… The tall gawky man in the gray suit, an unattractive angel, Heaven-sent, leaned over the rim. His face was a pale, unreadable oval behind thick glasses, far, far up there. His mouth pressed together grimly as his long arms reached down, grasping the rope end straying from the pulley and yanking hand over hand as Catriona hung on for dear life, urging him to go faster.

"Don't let go. I am good!" she rasped, as if Saint Antony of lost souls would deem her worthy of rescue from a watery grave.

Thick glasses, like the bottoms of Madame's best crystal, hung all cotty-whompered from his ears, dangling perilously close to falling from his long nose into the well. Fiery hair lolloping messily over one eye, a wide mouth pressed to a thin line from the effort of hauling her.

The face she gawped as she got nearer was long,

lean, and very ugly, even allowing in her ungrateful wretched soul that she wisht it were Aaron savin' her. She was clasped to his body and warmed in the shelter of his arms as he hauled her out and murmured fervent prayers of thanks to all the saints that she was safe and...

She gritted her jaw hastily, swallowing wicked thoughts.

She should burn in Hell.

This man was Gabriel himself, with shiny halos radiating about his wild reddish hair. What a wretched creature she was! As if reading her wicked mind, the bucket lurched, dropping inches as his arms tired from him leaning in such an awkward stance.

"Please, sirrah, don't let go!" she shrieked.

"Then stay still!" The voice was vexed, commanding, high-toned. She had heard little of such speech. Almost a foreign tongue, yet the same plummy tones as heard in Ballygawley, her old home village, when British landowners stomped over their poor rocky fields come for ruinous rents and tributes, and she, little Catriona, peeked out from her ma's skirts.

One toff had offered her a bag of either barley sugar or humbugs.

Catriona was too shy to accept, but that was long after the Great Hunger, when tatties rotted in the fields.

She still regretted that small stubbornness.

Cat looked up desolately through dripping curls, taking in her savior as she jerked upward, dropping inches to rise again, lurching with agonizing slowness to the top as she held her breath, then sobbed with relief when her head reached the stone rim.

Hand over hand, ever so slowly, the tall thin man dragged her up, chilled and half-drowned, her thin scrappy bodice clinging in an unladylike way, her poor skirts twining her legs like a lover and ripped to one knee from scraping the coarse brick.

She mourned that dress. Her knees were cut and bleeding. One more stain. One more band to sew on, she thought, heedless as the ginger-haired man grabbed her elbows to drag her over the last stone. His daddy-long-legs and her weight over-tipped them backwards. Scrabbling for balance, he knocked over the rainwater barrel, managed to get one long foot tangled in a coil of frayed rope, and snagged two pairs of Little Mae's bloomers from the washline, snapping the line as he fell and allowing clean laundry to drop into the widening pool of muck while she, adding to the bemusement of others, who'd come out hearing all the foofaraw, tumbled out with the bucket, sprawling face first in mud on top of him. She stared down, nose to nose, through his muddy glasses while he blinked up at her.

It seemed the whole of the Longhorn had decided to take the night air, use the privy, or smoke a pipe. Cat propped herself up, scrambling backwards off her savior and showing her gray-bloomered bottom for all to see.

Slipping again, Catriona stared balefully at her rescuer, who had managed to regain his feet. Why hadn't he caught her? Her whole front and pinny were now hopelessly filthy. She hadn't a tinker's chance of escaping Madame's eye of wrath. Cat wept from anger and frustration.

Aaron leaned against the doorframe with an unreadable expression. All was lost. He would never think of her as pretty, pink, feminine, or delicate. Though she didn't cry, water runneled Cat's mucky cheeks. Her hair swung in heavy wet clumps of mud and gravel.

Her rescuer, meanwhile, flung flaming hair from his eyes and, like an unfolding yardstick, unbent in stages, disentangling himself from both rope and clothesline, righted the rain barrel, hopped one-footed from water turning the yard into a churned quagmire, retrieved a shoe big as a gunboat, and brushed slurry from his fine gray brocade waistcoat and suit.

"So sorry!" He patted her awkwardly. "I went in search of a lucifer match. I didn't see you fall!"

Her rescuer blinked at the sodden mess of Catriona behind glasses coated with a brown wash, helpfully reached his forever-long arm, and, clumsily leaning, used one lengthy hand to raise her up and the other to brush her down too, succeeding in rubbing the dirt in. He eyed her, embarrassed, through thick dirty lenses, blushing like a rose when he touched the no-man's-land of her small bosom.

Aware of Aaron's unbridled laughter, she smacked at him.

"Oh! I am ever so sorry!"

Cat swatted him away. His plummy toff tones scratched like thistles. "Never you mind!"

This sort would always carry humbugs.

And sure, wouldn't I refuse if he had?

Crossing arms over her chest, she wished she could vanish in a puff of smoke.

Cat tucked into the back of her mind that, at odds with his appearance, the flame-haired man's arm was hard as an ax handle when he held her, miserably aware she should have said, "I thank you, kind sir, for savin' me from certain drowning in a watery grave."

Instead, the devil in her found resentment aplenty, hellbent on digging up more, too aware Aaron still looked on, snickering with onlookers at their clownish display. Even now Catriona and the red-haired man danced side to side, stepping on each other's toes. *We are a right spectacle. We belong in a mummer's show. All we need is a monkey.* Catriona fumed, attempting to sweep past him to the kitchen. "Get out of me way!"

Even his wide mouth was set straight to keep from grinning, but his eyes crinkled. as he removed his dangling spectacles and wiped them on his coattail, the only clean spot of his ensemble.

Cat scowled him down, then stared, unabashed, forgetting onlookers.

The irritating man had unexpectedly fine eyes.

Never mind that.

Large, slightly slanted, as if of Cornish blood, silvery like rainwater or a sparkly mountain stream, the irises, dark-rimmed, dark-lashed too, so opposed to his fiery hair.

White skin.

Red hair.

Mercury-gray eyes.

The combination was not displeasing.

Spectacles replaced, his eyes narrowed, taking in her scowl. Now the hardness of two flat gray pebbles behind the hastily jammed-on glasses studied Cat, catching her derision, before her befuddled state over the change in his appearance.

He watched her as if familiar with that look. He set his chin and looked off. "Wouldn't let a dog die like that," he maintained coldly.

"Oh! You wouldn't, would you now!"

Cat continued glaring, trying again to stumble round him to the relative privacy of the kitchen, away from the entertained crowd, looking for somewhere she could clean off. In her room she could, and recalled she had yet to haul water, with dishes stacking up, and she was dribbling muck on Madame's clean floor. And there from the corner of her eye, the blue one, she spied Arabella newly arrived, also archly amused, smirking with Aaron, her beautiful twin double, to make Cat's day perfect.

Cat spied the broken meerschaum. The lovely carved clay pipe lay sullied and broken. She was an ingrate. The man had left the fug of the dining saloon to make more smoke on his own. Thank God for it, too. She would have been meeting her maker sure, wet as a mermaid, not encrusted in drying mud.

"Sirrah!" Catriona stammered, lowering her voice to a whisper. "I wish I could replace your fine pipe and all…yet I have no—"

"Hugo!"

Cat had scratched a window once with a flint. That is what she thought of the voice behind them. Cutting glass. What a *scritching* it made down the pane.

They both jerked their heads round.

The last female she wished to see her thus. Not Arabella but the diaphanous young noble lady. Would she have no peace? Was all Wylder drawn to this mucky back yard to see her shame?

"Whatever are you doing with this drowned rat! *Maman* has been wondering. And here you are, in odious flirtations."

The lovely lady—amusement curling her cupid mouth in a leer, took in their filthy appearance.

"Lady Audrina," Hugo stated without inflection. "I'd rather you not tale-bear to Lady Daphne." He glanced back, winking where the lady could not see. Cat smiled back before she recalled she was scowling at him.

"Oh! Don't be a fool! Stop this buffoonery with scullery maids, or Lady D. will have the vapors. And just look at your clothes and your lovely waistcoat! Don't even think of making an appearance until you cease resembling a chimney sweep."

She cast a disparaging glance at Cat.

"Ah. I see you finally bathed."

"Yes, of course. Where are my manners. May I present—?" The man, Hugo, turned to Catriona.

"Please! Hugo! Don't be daft! I do not intend to be introduced to those beneath us in every way!" The Lady Audrina snorted with sour grace; spinning on beribboned slippers, she wafted off in a cloud of mossy green, lifted above the chaos of slowly draining muck.

Hugo turned to follow after a clumsy smile and half bow in Catriona's direction. "I will leave you to your own devices." He sourly eyed Audrina. "No. I shan't do that. I'll clean up here a bit."

"See that you do!" Audrina slung over her shoulder.

Hugo flipped wet red strands from his eyes. "Never mind her. Bit of a snob. You know. lord's daughter and all that?" He smiled sympathetically.

"And yourself?" Catriona boldly asked, wondering all the same if Aaron was yet in the kitchen. She'd nip up the back way.

The flame-haired man merely grinned lopsidedly. "I would have your name, if I am to be your champion." Cat could tell he was making light to ease her and perhaps even trying to jest. Cat was not feeling charitable. Wet, itchy, chilled, feeling a proper fool, Catriona erupted. "I need no champion, sir! And it is

Catriona!"

"Cat!" He gave a short laugh of genuine humor. "Yet cats despise water, I am told."

Cat scowled. "Cat it is," she said, and sighed deep. "When I'm ta home."

"I won't ask where that is. A female must have some mystery. But here, you are shivering."

He swung a flaming curtain of hair and removed his jacket, offering it, unsure whether to drape it around. Moreover, he kept looking at her eyes, darting like a hummingbird from one to the other.

She'd had that before.

"Some call them Devil Eyes. I ken they are strange. So don't be after starin' at them!" She lowered lashes to shield her odd eyes and looked up slanchwise at him. "So, one eye's green, t'other blue. Like I was tryin' to be two people, 'fore I was born, sure!"

Another too-familiar voice cut the air like a rusty scythe.

Cat winced, pulling her shoulder blades together as if hit by a blow. "Oh, no," she breathed sharing a moment with Hugo. "Yes, Madame, I fell in—"

"Oh, there you are! What is this tomfoolery? I heard all the ruckus. What are you doing, lazy wretch? I send you out hours ago and what do I find?" Madame Solange sputtered to a halt, not sure what she found. "You are all wet and—and filthy!"

Since she'd drained half the well into the puddle now at Madame's feet, that was undeniable. "Yessum, Madame," Catriona offered. "Since I fell in the…" She gestured at the toff and the well.

"And the rope was— and I nearly—"

"Oh! Don't blame him! Oh, my!' She swiveled, too

late. "Ummm—sir?" Undecided how to address him, Madame dipped an awkward sideways curtsey and swiped at his waistcoat, smearing it worse. In her confusion, Madame spun on Cat.

"I shall have this wretched girl clean that for you…"

"I'm sure." He cut her off, backing to the gate all elbows and knees and knocking over the stacked woodpile. Hastily righting it, he murmured, "Now, madame, if you please, allow me the freedom to enjoy my pre-prandial stroll."

Madame looked struck, with no more idea what he meant than Cat did as they watched him pick up pieces of broken pipe, forlornly checking them and stuffing them in his pocket.

"Of course, I leave you to your leisure, your, ah—sir."

Rolling a look at him that said, *You see what I have to put up with, in these uncivilized backwoods?* Madame swept to the kitchen, sparing a glacial glance at Catriona that would freeze the pygmy folk far south of there, Cat heard tell.

"Get back in here!" she hissed. Glancing at Hugo's retreating back, Madame continued in genteel tones with gritted teeth. "No matter what you were up to, where is my water, dear? And folks are clamoring for ice."

She was proud of the ice house, so she pretended it was ice she'd sent her off for, though Catriona had little truck with it. 'Twere up to the boys, Dingy and the lot, who hauled the kindling, kept cream and butter and cheeses cold, or ice buckets full for the rare bottles of wine Madame ordered, clean from Kansas City or Chicago, packed in straw.

Ofttimes bats fluttered in the cool dark, supposing it

a cave. 'Twere a favorite chore in sultry Wylder, Wyoming summers, when black flies and mosquitoes bit, but not for Cat, as she was afeared of dark, shut-in places.

"Yes, ma'am." She backed, sorrowfully contrite—in a pig's eye—to the lean-to kitchen.

"And fetch a fresh apron," Madame grated, peering closer once they were both safe inside. "Oh, that one's ruined. I will take it out of your pay, mind you." She grabbed a fresh one from the hook. "Clean yourself and get back to work, as if you ever do anything right!"

Shivering, Catriona rinsed off as best she could. Dingy, bless him, hauled in two buckets of water, one of which refilled the stove cauldron. From the corner of her eye, Cat could see Arabella loitered, eager for new slander, fresh, pretty, pink as a newly cut rose, and nibbling an apple.

Madame pushed Cat to the sink as she tied the apron. Arabella flounced into the dining room with the heavy burden of a bundle of spoons.

"Quit dawdling! Do what you can, and hurry. Pots and pans don't wash themselves." Catriona gazed with dismay at teetering mountains of greasy, crusty, burnt roasting pans, iron skillets, and stew pots amassed since her misadventure, plus a messy pile of dinnerware and bar glasses dangerously tilting. If that lot came from her pay, she'd need to pay Madame.

"Dingy!" Madame shouted. "Fetch more wood."

Dingy, back from the privy, about-faced as if shot from a cannon. Cat hesitated, hating the thought of plunging arms back in cold greasy lye suds, looking up at Madame through lowered lashes. She must have seemed so forlorn and miserable and shivery—Cat caught her blinking, as if she really saw Cat for the first time that evening.

"Oh, I see. Very well, then." The fresh apron bloomed damp patches. She moistened pale lips. "You are all wet."

Cat bit her cheek to keep from gritting, *I thought that plain as the nose on your face*, waiting while Madame mulled.

"I-I might have a gown that should do, since I am…" Madame drew thin lips together in a simp, smoothing hands over her loosely corseted belly.

"A moment."

Returning, she held a mud-brown dress before her and as if already regretting her generous offer, thrust it at Catriona. "This will do. Go behind the stove. Strip and dry off."

Cat clutched the ugly dress to her.

"Don't get it wet!"

"No, mum, thank you, mum."

Though it be doin' her no favors for a blue-green-eyed girl, still, 'twas clean, and though a cottony, linsey fabric, 'twas the finest Cat had ever had, with its high neck and a row of tiny winking brown buttons like bird's eyes. The waist was loose, and it was over long, but the bodice fitted her like it should. She could breathe.

"If wishes were horses, we'd all ride," Cat had heard her ma say. She'd wished for a new gown to impress Aaron. He would only see his ma, now. Cat morosely buttoned the last button.

Madame tapped her lip. "Not too shabby." She cocked her head. "Hummm? You could even serve."

Oh, how grand. One more chore and shan't I meet myself coming? Still, pleased. *A step up!* Though she wouldn't show it.

"And when would I be doing that, ma'am? When washing up, carrying out slops, or before?"

Madame was undecided if she was being pert. "Don't be smart-mouthed."

"No, ma'am. Thank you, ma'am. Swellest gown I ever had." She thought truth wouldn't hurt, even if she hated the tobacco-mud-brown shade.

"Yes. Of course it is! I would think so, for shanty Irish! Don the apron. I won't see that dress sullied, or I shall regret it." She already looked as if repenting the gift of the gown.

"Am I to be keepin' it, then, ma'am?"

She studied the dress. "Hmm, yes. I suppose so. Might need to take it in here and there," she grunted.

Here and there? 'Twas a furlong too long, and the waist sagged.

Cat's heart beat faster. A new position. A step up. Like Arabella, wafting about ordering Rattlesnake Jake and Dingy in a clean starched apron and a cap.

"Yessum, after tonight, I'll put it out for best."

And she would, next to ma's wedding dress, where she had her cot and small tea box of trinkets in the privacy of the attic. She'd been awarded private quarters after Madame saw how she was defenseless in the kitchen at night, with gents going to the privy, and Dingy sweet on her and all, and all.

Madame looked with horror at the cookstove. Cat caught the whiff of scorch. Madame fluttered over, poked the firebox, basted a goose, and checked the hot water cauldron.

"Arabella! Where is that girl! First you, then her. Go wait tables," she ordered Cat. "Dingy! Tend to the washing up! I must look to the cooking, or all will be fit for the pigs."

Cat knew Arabella's business, like Dingy's, was being scarce when work raised its heavy head. And Aaron had been sent to beg a few kegs of Five Star's best whiskey. Rye it was, but p'raps the toffs wouldn't notice.

The saloon and dining hall got rowdier, what with a pile of drovers storming in, perishing for drink, slapping the bar, and loudly hailing Rattlesnake Jake.

Peering through, Madame shuddered a long sigh as she checked how her illustrious guests were faring. Cat, too, peeked through the swing doors. Taking a deep breath, she smoothed her fresh starched apron, patted her hair in place, and headed out to her new duties.

Chapter Five
Pestilence

The toffs, whoever they were at home, had airs bouncing off the ceiling they were so lofty.

Of the ladies, the older woman—whose age had not dimmed her comeliness, save for a sour look—Catriona later learned was "the Duchess, Lady Daphne" or somewhat. The younger one resembling her was "Lady Audrina." She'd already crossed cudgels with her, and watched as she eyed a certain cowhand at the bar with less than dislike as they sailed past, when her ma wasn't looking.

Cat had to laugh. She knew Levi's daughter Arabella didn't find that cowboy particularly unfavorable either. Let them fight over him, she grumped.

Hitching a shoulder, she hastened over with a tinkling pitcher of iced well water—to which she'd nearly added her personal flavor—marveling over her swift reversal of fortune.

She wanted to drink in every sparkly bit of them, carefully setting down the pitcher, arranging the cutlery, shifting glassware, sneaking looks at the elegant, handsome older man with the silvery wings of hair swept from a widow's peak spearing a high dome of forehead.

Cat wanted to say something smart and cultured. All that came out was, "Your water, sir." Catriona studied him with a frightened gaze and bit her cheek.

"Are ye feelin' well? 'Tis hot in here. P'rhaps 'tis right to remove your coat, and all. We ain't…"

"Enough!" Lady Daphne stood up so fast water sloshed on her beautiful gown. "How dare you address his lordship in such a vulgar manner, unless expressly spoken to? If we wish advice, it shan't be from the help."

Oh, Lord, help me. Already I've stuck my foot in.

"Oh, *Maman*, do don't be awkward." The Lady Audrina, made a moue. "The poor thing can't help it, most likely," she sneered. "Feeble-minded, like most in this miserable misbegotten backwater, or she wouldn't have fallen in the well."

The last declared as if she did not care if she wounded all of Wylder.

Cat was conscious of her own still-wet hair.

The elder man darted a look of displeasure at the Lady Audrina, eyeing Catriona with rheumy eyes and a faint smile stretching parched lips. "I appreciate the concern, child. What is your name?"

"It could scarce matter!" The younger lady snapped.

Cat paid her no mind, for the gent's eyes were red-rimmed, seeming to swim in the sea of a flushed and swollen face. Her heart seized like a fist, for had she not seen such back at Ma and Pa's poor camp by the water tower? "Catriona, sir."

Her knees weakened under the brown skirts braced against the table, and the water pitcher sloshed again as she shakily finished pouring the elder lady's glass.

Lady Daphne eyed it as if Cat offered her arsenic.

"Sir, you seem poorly," Cat stubbornly continued, setting down the pitcher.

The Lady Daphne deigned to glance at him then,

with an oh-how-tiresome look. "Of course he is! Scarce concern for you. Just an extremely tedious journey. Now shoo!"

Yet the look the grand lady cast the older man shivered Cat. The highborn lady was interested in an odd manner. Not concern so much as a hawk eyeing a plump mouse.

Lord Mortimer rose jerkily, wiping his forehead. "Perhaps I should go to my quarters, dear Daphne. A nice sponge bath…" he murmured.

Catriona sighed despite her concern. No doubt another chore before her…hauling water upstairs, unless she could coax Dingy.

He began to reach for the grand lady. She pulled away without seeming to. The poor gentleman would have fallen had Cat not slipped under his shoulder, belatedly throwing him an anxious look because of her impertinence.

The older woman narrowed an inscrutable gaze at Cat and roved the room for more suitable help, bypassing Rattlesnake Jake tending bar with a shudder. She finally flapped long narrow hands.

"Oh! Continue! See that he is settled down proper. And no familiarities." Whatever that meant. The Lady Daphne hesitated. "I shall look in on him—later."

"Shall I tell Madame Levi? Should we fetch the doc?"

Lady Daphne merely stared in the distance while the Lady Audrina looked off, bored, tapping her toe and pinching off bits of bread roll.

"Sir," Cat offered, "if you will lean on me, and all, perhaps I can help you upstairs. A few days, and…"

"But we weren't staying here…" He muttered. Even

sick as he was, he spoke with the impatience of the toffs.

"Indeed not!" Lady Daphne slammed down her wine glass, the one Madame had hastily purchased at the mercantile.

Audrina stared at her ma as if she had two heads. "Here!" Her voice rose an octave. "I would think not! In a saloon! *Maman*, if you allow this creature to help him up there, we might be imprisoned Lord knows how long."

Ignoring the performance, Cat led the gentleman away.

The elder toff, leaning heavier, mumbled, "Yes, child, mayhap they are right…" They hobbled to the stairs.

"Yea, I ken, sir. But I fear you're ill, and 'tis only for one night, sure," she soothed. If he did have the typhus, maybe 'twere best she handle the gentleman as well as she could.

"One night, p'raps two…" he gasped out, lapsing. He felt hot over her supporting arm. She glanced back.

The highborn lady held a curious expression. Conjecture, irritation, pique.

The younger lady looked off, embarrassed. Neither, frozen in place, attempted to rise.

The duke, leaning on the banister on one side and with Cat under his shoulder on the other, took the long flight up, turned at the landing, and reached the gallery overlooking the saloon.

He headed the wrong way.

"No, sir, 'tis this way. It's the—" She started to say best room, but Little Mae had that one in front, and Cat didn't think she'd fancy sheltering a sick duke in her bed, though she often had many others, well, under and over her coverlets.

"Sir, the last bedroom. 'Twould be best—the quietest." And closest to her, she thought belatedly.

He groaned a muffled answer. His large bony frame was ever heavier. Cat passed the middle bedroom. She kenned the highborn lady and the younger were ensconced there. Fearing she couldn't make it down the long hall to the last room, she yet struggled on, sensing the dread fever through his heavy tweed, as she one-handedly opened the door and heaved him half onto the bed, struggling to haul his legs atop the coverlets, for he seemed done in.

"Should I—?"

She gestured to his clothes, him needing to be out of the tight-fitting trews and vest, and under the quilts. He made no answer. Cat was unbuttoning his coat and satin waistcoat when he awoke, staying her hand.

"Where's…valet…?"

"Sir, you haven't no valet—whatever that creature might be. 'Tis only me. Let me help you out o' your coat and breeches." He seemed to swoon, whether from her comment or from sudden weakness, she couldn't say, could she? That was his last utterance.

She stared at the poor man, pondering and listening for his companions, and finally eased him out of his clothes, leaving him in fine lawn underdrawers and vest. She covered him lightly. Catriona knew she should sweat the fever, but she didn't have the heart, what with the duke a far cry from the elegant gent of an hour ago, his face red and glistening, hair plastered with sweat, and flesh hot as an iron on a cookstove.

Cat's heart leapt, troubled.

"So like Pa…" she breathed, biting her tongue for

summoning the devil.

The patient sighed deep, a sound like an ox cart over gravel.

****

The highborn lady swept in after Cat had sat with him, afraid to leave, fearful of staying when not appropriate and of Madame's wrath, wondering where she vanished.

The grand lady held a flimsy kerchief to her nose.

"Where are the physicians in this filthy town?"

Expecting to answer in her ignorance, Catriona stopped placing cool clothes on the sick man's forehead. "Why, ma'am, out visiting t'other sick folk. I hear Mrs. Ledbetter at the feedstore is ready to—"

"Did I ask you to speak? It is 'Milady'!" she said in a near shriek, as if other ill folk might as well be vermin in a trap, with no right to mercy. "Oh, don't look at me with those off-putting eyes. Turn your face from your betters!"

Cat stared at her a moment too long. She had had that reaction too many times, but not like this. She would have none of it.

"Madame—milady, I mean—he's been to look in, and dead weary he was and all. He should be at his own bedside."

"Do you have any idea who we are? Of course, you don't! How could you, in this rustic outback? Are there still untamed savages? Oh, don't bother." Looking smug, she gazed right at Cat. "One untamed savage is right before my very eyes."

Cat thought that a might strong.

The older lady looked as if she wanted to come in further. Itching to do it, Cat felt safe to sass back some.

Again, in her ignorance, she answered. "Yessum, milady. I ken who you are. High muckety-mucks and greedy landowners you are. Least by what Pa said."

The lady turned crimson, then white as a starched pillowcase.

"Muckety! She raised a ridged arm down the hall. "Get out!"

Cat, torn, fidgeted with the poor man's covers.

"Do not put your filthy hands on his lordship again," the woman shrieked, heedless of the saloon below.

"Yes, milady, but…"

An idea crept up like a sly cat. "You be wantin' to tend him, then, I 'spect." Offering her the damp cloth, Catriona indicated the basin. "'Tis dead easy, and if he needs…well…" Catriona motioned with her foot to a covered basin from which an unwholesome odor emerged.

"Oh! How dare you think I—I…!" Words failed the lady. Her expression said she would rather muck out pig lots. Knife-blade cheekbones flared red, and pale eyes burned holes in Cat. "What impudence! You filthy, unwashed trollop, speaking to me in such tones and expecting me to…to…"

"I am not filthy, and since I just fell in the well, nor am I unwashed. I mean no harm, me." *Yet everyone seems to find me dirty and wanting.*

The duke groaned and rolled his eyes beneath the lids. A tiny smile stretched his cracked lips.

Faint, the fine lady banged out into the hall. "Audrina! You won't countenance what—"

Then Cat heard the younger lady, Audrina. "As I told you, *Maman*, I shan't stay in this pestilential swamp one more hour."

****

Hearing footsteps pacing agitatedly next door, Cat waited for the next outburst, but she was weary, having been at her various posts since before the cock crew, and yearning for her own bed. She heard Lady Daphne murmur something, which of course made Cat listen.

"You will, my pet…"

Lady Daphne's words were spoken in a hard and indisputable tone.

"You will if you want your reward."

She said it with such quiet menace, Cat shivered and turned back to her patient. His breathing drew harder. Squinching her eyes shut, Cat kept the memory of Ma and Pa's sad passing, days of tortured breath, through throats so swollen only a thimble of air could pass, and chests sounding as if they dragged rocks up a mountain. They'd be drenched and shivering, then so hot their flesh burnt like embers.

Cat looked sorrowfully at him. Same as this doomed gent here.

How Catriona didn't catch the near-morbid disease, she did not ken. Yet she might have had a pinch of the typhoid. Some say some folks are touched by angels and never get the dread pox, nor typhus either. It would be several years before a good doctor invented a cure whereby they thrust needles in your arm with the same pestilence they vowed could knock you dead as a doornail but could cure you anyways, even malignant quinsy, or the scarlet fever. But not then.

She sensed by a fresh breeze the door once again opened.

Madame, aged tenfold, stood with an arm full of quilts, not that this poor man needed them.

Dingy, beside her, carried another wash basin and towels. Haltingly, Cat told Madame what she feared.

"What is to become of us? You will stay! The good doctor asked if any of us have recovered from—this."

"Yessum, I did, indeed."

"Thank God, one good reason I took you in. Then you shall nurse him." She cast an evil eye at the duke, shuddered, and nudged Dingy. Dingy hastily set down the tray. "You will have your meals here. Dingy or Jake will fetch you a cot."

There went her chance of advancement.

Later, Cat found ham, greens, taties, and even a tiny wedge of apple pie under the cover.

****

Catriona yawned and stretched her neck. "What now?" she grumbled. A stampede of cattle rammed the door.

Between candlelight burning her eyes, long hours, and the heavy meal, Cat had nodded, chin to chest, until her eyes blinked open at the ruckus. "All saints preserve us! What now?" she grumbled, darting a look at the poor gent she hoped was sleeping.

Holding her breath, she waited till his chest rose and fell, spinning when the door popped open and releasing a sigh as the ungainly carrot-haired man fell crashing in, one knee and both palms striking the floor. He stammered, rising, "The—the door stuck," and peered at her through spectacles hanging off one ear as before. Recovering himself, he jumped up and swept his flaming hair from his eyes, asking anxiously, "Have I awakened him?"

"If not, you have wakened the dead."

He knuckled his specs back and, knocking over a

vase stand, half bowed an apology, then stopped dead before her, seeming not to ken what to do, waving his hands helplessly. "Here, miss. Don't cry."

Cat wiped her eyes. Should she laugh or cry? She decided to laugh.

Hugo looked behind him as if performing a furtive act.

"Sorry, sorry, most terribly sorry. I've come to see—um—how—is he?" To his credit, he looked proper worried behind the round rims.

Hearing disgruntled shouts from the women's room, both held their breath, letting out groans of relief and a shared smile, though Cat's barely broke the ice.

"Well, come on over, but not too close, or you'll be catchin' it too, and then I'll be havin' Saint James Infirmary all to me own," she growled fiercely.

"Is he—in pain?"

She softened and studied her patient. "Not now, but when he wakes, 'tis hard for him to catch a decent breath, and him being so hot and all. Would you be raisin' the window, sir?"

He didn't question but rushed to the sill, ramming into a chair, barely catching a fussy figurine on the table beside it and replacing it sideways while righting the chair, but he managed to raise the wooden window frame with his other hand.

Clean brisk air blew away the sickroom fug.

"Don't be tellin' anyone."

He nodded gravely and took the duke's hand without fear, gently squeezing. "Milord?"

The older man fluttered his lids. "Hugo…" The smile was faint as a butterfly flapping its wings.

****

Cat groaned. Dawn slanted through the windows. First checking her patient—his breathing had coarsened to a ragged whistle during the long hours—she then wrung out a cool cloth to place on his head and neck and eased her back. In doing so, pretending she was not startled, or annoyed, Cat spotted the highborn Lady Daphne just inside the doorway as if an invisible line were drawn on the floor. The lady dipped a toe in but hastily withdrew her foot, looking frightened.

After clearing a rusty throat and tapping fingers on her arm, she demanded, "Will he survive?"

Here, now, and her ladyship be asking me? Cat looked down to hide her expression. "Many do, milady." Cat expected a fresh deluge of scorn and wasn't disappointed.

"How many in your—illustrious experience?"

"Ma and Pa both passed on to their reward with this, milady."

"A dubious recommendation. Yes, yes! But of what?"

"Why this dread affliction, milady. That be why I be caring for the gent."

"His lordship," she snapped.

"Yessum," Cat muttered. "Yet many in our camp did come out the other side; thin and poorly, but alive and glad for it."

Oddly, the fine lady seemed disappointed, and about to stamp her foot in aggravation.

Catriona watched her closely.

"Turn your filthy gaze, girl. You pollute me with your sight."

Which Cat thought a might harsh too. Her flashpoint flared like an old musket.

"Why do both your ladyships suppose me dirty? How could I look decent with gruel splashed on me bosom—" for she'd attempted to spoon some into the gent "—and eyes feeling like hot pebbles from no sleep at-all, at-all?"

A silence dropped like a stone. "And how does his lordship seem?" the woman asked in a grittier tone. "On—on the side of the angels, or one foot still—on earth?"

"That I could not say, ma'am."

"Of course you can't," she spat. "I must be mad."

"Yessum," Cat murmured.

Lady Daphne eyed her for contempt. Unsure, she huffed. "Fetch a servant to inform me, if he worsens. In fact…" She tapped her lip. "You may leave us—alone. I feel a tenderness. It is only fitting, after all."

She made irritated shooing motions, raised the cobwebby handkerchief to her nose, and tentatively stepped a foot in, watching the floor as if a pit of vipers opened under her.

A chill prickled Cat's arms in the fetid room. The look Lady Daphne threw the older man was not one of mercy but the blank stare of a hawk about to dive on a helpless rabbit.

"Thank you, ma'am."

"Lady Daphne!"

Cat nodded, contrite. "Tea would be a treat." But as if an angel pressed her cold hand on Cat's midriff, holding her back, she halted, not wishing to think what she was thinking.

"But no, milady. I would not be havin' you fall ill too—'tis very catchin'. Just being here, brave as you are and all. The very air is—is—" *What is that word?*

"Pestilential!"

Daphne stumbled back, clutching the knob for support. "Oh! You should have said!"

"I thought any fool could think as much," Cat blazed, fearsome tired, for the clock had just knelled seven strokes, and she awake in the chair till the clock knelled after one, earlier.

"Your insolence will not go unreported."

"Then you must do just that. Madam Gruenwald is still in the kitchen, most likely."

Lady Daphne eyed her with killing frost and swept out, slamming the door. Catriona heard no more from the tiff but kept tending the man drenched in enough sweat to fill a washtub, his handsome face made even thinner and finer, more fetching in a way, as if he were turning into an elder angel, or a faerie king, with his long silvery hair spread across the counterpane—if Cat were to be fanciful.

****

Cat did not relish sinful thoughts against the Lady Daphne, though she could not shake them, nor forget her watchful eye from the doorway—waiting at the mouse hole with a tail twitching metronome-fast, while Cat fed the duke spoonfuls of Madame's special broth—rabbit it was.

"Be sure to inform his lordship it was made by my own hands, you hear?" Madame Solange had admonished her.

"Yessum, I did," Catriona vowed. But after the good gentleman had closed his eyes.

****

Cat made a dash down to visit the privy and to give a brief report to Madame before returning to her duties, halting on her way back, caught in a snare of words from behind a cracked door. Intrigued by the hushed whispers even though the speakers were alone, Cat again tarried, putting her ear close.

"But if he made a will, might he have included—?" Lady Daphne was speaking, but the rest of her whisper was muffled.

Then, "You could have been more…"

Audrina let out a long sigh. "But what more can I do, *Maman*? Besides, it's too late anyway… He's dying! That Irish cow can't save him."

"You'd best hope she does, my girl! We might have one more chance." Silence. "Either way…" She allowed the subject to drop, then exclaimed in apparent exasperation, "Oh, I wish we knew more. Do you suppose Hugo—?"

"Fiddlesticks! Hugo would not be privy to his will." Lady Audrina spoke in scornful tones.

A rustle of skirts sent Cat rushing to the duke's chamber.

As Cat lay on her pallet that night, a shade moved across the lamplight and then across her eyelids.

Squinting from where she lay, there stood the fine Lady Daphne still as a statue at the end of her patient's bed. Holding a kerchief to her nose, she scanned the duke with eyes glittering in the moonlight with such intensity Cat almost sprang up.

Lady Daphne, holding back something fierce, gripped her skirt till her knuckles popped. Her hands opened and closed, opened, and closed. Breathing a lurid oath Cat had heard only on street corners, the lady swiveled, easing the door closed after giving the patient another hard stare.

The next night, the grand lady performed the same, approaching the bed on the other side, but not before Cat noticed she carried a small armchair cushion.

That's when she saw Catriona sleeping in the chair. Cat opened her eyes and pretended to yawn.

The highborn lady did not flinch. "I was just seeing to the duke," the duchess announced, chillier than the ice house. "I want to assure myself he is getting proper care, the right care." She had the grace to allow a slight quaver in her voice. She looked at the pillow gripped in her hands as if she had never before beheld a pillow.

"I thought I might…see to his comfort," she muttered haughtily as if previously Cat had forced the sick man to lie on a bed of spikes.

His everlasting comfort? Cat wondered, studying the soft plush pillow. She placed herself half in front of him. "He is restful now, ma'am," Cat spoke softly. "He needs no extra pillow."

Awkwardly, Lady Daphne threw Cat spiky smiles like heat lightning. "I'll make that decision. Stand aside." With distaste, she tucked the pillow behind the gent's head, cautious not to touch him. Yet to Cat, she watched the gent as a starving man did a platter of roast pork, greedy for his pain. On her way out, she cast a withering glance at the open window. "What are you striving for? Consumption?"

A strange look passed her eyes like a ray of sun hitting her face. Then her face turned flat and gray as if she were tucking this knowledge away for further use.

"Yessum." Catriona rushed to the window and closed it—for now. And she puzzled over why the woman hated this poor man so and pretended she did not. After that, Cat fibbed about the duke's recovery, to stay longer than needed. But why should she feel the need to defend him till he was able to protect himself?

She removed the hard pillow, feeling his forehead. "Yes, sir, I will care for you. Let the devil take me, if I do wrong." She brushed his fair silver hair and took the liberty of letting her gaze rove his face, the noble nose and mouth of a warrior, the fine high forehead with the springing silver widow's peak now slamped with moisture. He felt cooler. His breathing had eased to a rasp.

He had been kind to her, something rare as hen's teeth in this place. Cat felt tears of gladness welling up, angrily brushing them aside.

She stayed on still, fearful of leaving the room.

The duke's fever broke three nights later.

****

"Don't you be leavin', sure." Cat pointed at Dingy, even then edging away.

Dingy Watts was not the shiniest spoon in the drawer, yet "a genius at vanishing when work was near," Cat grumbled as she tied on the apron, symbol of renewed servitude, and stared in resignation at the towering clutter of baking tins, skillets, and crockery. She cast a sour glance at Dingy's disappearing back. He apparently had anticipated her stepping back into the role of dishwasher, because he'd let several meals' worth pile up.

Chapter Six
Desperation

Lady Daphne stood silently at her stepbrother's doorway. Maps and surveys, letters, reports, and anecdotal tales in yellowed newspapers littered and surrounded the table he'd transformed into a work station. He peered even now through a large magnifying glass. The aggravating man seemed to be burrowing in here like a hibernating bear!

She bit her lip, uncertain how to approach him, and tapped lightly on the door frame.

He did not stir.

"Mortimer dearest, I do hope I'm not interrupting? How hard you work." She made a moue of sympathy.

He looked up, startled. She studiously noted spots of red on his cheekbones—otherwise, he had turned from hale and pink to the hue of a dying rose since his recent illness.

"Of course not, my dear." Reluctance dragged on the heels of his voice. "Just contemplating. Researching." He blinked.

"What? May I ask?" Mayhap, she could put an end to this fool's errand!

"Nothing you'd be interested in, my dear."

"You have that right," she muttered almost without sound.

"How is my dear Audrina?" he asked belatedly.

"Ah, strange you should ask. Audrina is much on my mind. Dear Mortimer! You know girls of that age. Restless. Endlessly infatuated. They mature so fast. I fear she may even be losing her second Season." She left unsaid, *If we don't leave this pestilential hole soon.* The dratted man looked confused.

"Did she not have a first one?"

"Of course," Daphne cooed. "Men do not keep track of such things," she trilled. "Audrina is not getting any younger—the dew is still on the rose, but a young bud quickly blooms and fades. Plus, I fear my daughter is not the most tractable of girls."

She threw a rueful smile. "Quite, ah—saucy, betimes. She dreadfully needs another Season—she did not make a match, as you well know!" She added that last bit more waspish than intended.

"Oh. Right. Perhaps there is a suitable swain here," Lord Mortimer answered with the vagueness of a professor of ancient archeology.

She could not believe he actually said that. Aristocracy? Here? Canada was the closest possible source of a random duke, or earl, even a baron! She wondered if there were mines in Canada.

Lady Daphne was speechless from anger and disgust. She trembled, reining in her desire to hit Lord Greville over the head with his Waterford crystal inkwell.

"There is no shortage of suitors!" She laughed gaily, adding airily, "yet not a title amongst them. And Audrina at such an impressionable age… I fear her purity—" she didn't blush "—her honor might be, ah…breached."

"I'm sorry to hear that, Daphne…" She saw him thumbing through, completely absorbed, a book of squinchy type and tightly-packed statistics, or some such rot. He wasn't heeding.

"Suppose you will be winding up here soon, dear Mortimer?"

"Ummmm," was his reply.

"Think we shall be here long?" Acid ripped her throat.

The wretched man finally looked up, blinking, beyond his pince nez, letting them drop. "Oh, I expect so, dear Daphne. I find the weather quite pleasant here—the air bracing. Do us all good to be out from under London's pea-soupers for a change."

She said through gritted teeth, "And have you found suitable prospects?"

"There are several, yet to examine, my dear. I suspect I shall be visiting many more. I must weed the contenders from the ones fobbed off on clueless aristocracy." He coughed jovially. "You would not understand these things."

"Never mind, dear Mortimer." She laughed before she could say more. *...and my daughter is turning into a spiteful unwed spinster. What to do, what to do...?*

****

Lady Daphne stared out at the muddy streets of Wylder, Wyoming as dreary rain tinseled down. They'd been here a month. Precisely twenty-nine days longer than desired. She groaned and swore, "God's garters!" in an unladylike Daphne way.

"He will tire of us, even if he did survive." She washed her hands as if worrying the skin off. A commoner's habit—forcing her hands to clasp before her fine bosom.

"*Maman*! Please. Not again."

Lady Audrina crossly picked the hem of her last petticoat—a tedious, odious job—with a frown that would have scorched the material if it could. Letting it down to its utmost, so the wretched thing at least hit her shins, she stabbed the needle viciously into once-fine lawn. "Thimbles hurt so, but no less than pricking one's finger within an inch of one's life," she grieved. "This chore!"—she spoke as if asked to embroider the entire Bayeux Tapestry—"is fit for a lady's maid. That's what I deserve! If Uncle Mortimer hadn't been so mean, we'd be in London."

Daphne cast a weary eye, forgetting her plea to return. "Doing what? Cadging off third cousins once removed? What do we say this time? 'Just passing through. Here's our calling card and baggage'? 'Mind if we tarry a year or so?' No, my spoiled poppet. This is our only chance. To stay close to Mortimer until an opportunity arrives. Any opportunity. At least he puts food in our bellies!"

"Must you sound so lower-class?" Audrina shot her mother a jaundiced look. Their close proximity was trying both of them. Snipping at each other was turning into a finely-honed game with game pieces traveling the same routes with the same outcomes every time they played it.

"He's so keen on exploring damp, dripping mines! They can be quite dangerous, you know, especially after his last brush with death..." she murmured, scarcely aware she spoke.

It was too tedious to quarrel. Her mother was already in a fine fettle. Still, Audrina could not countenance what was so odiously hinted at. Might as well bludgeon her with a crimping iron.

Heedless of her daughter's delicate nature, Lady Daphne continued, almost dreamily, "Lord Grenville owns five estates. One in the Hempsteads. A town house in Belgravia…" Her voice trailed.

"And what, *Maman*?"

"His Grace Lord Mortimer owns entire villages in Shropshire and York! Cotton mills, railroads, but this passion is mines! Many mines." She smirked as if His Grace had taken up breeding cats.

"How tedious." Audrina sucked her pricked finger.

Her mother smiled bitterly. "It is rather humorous. A Brazilian diamond mine, or was that emerald? Maybe both. Even a platinum mine in Russia, I've heard." She sighed. "Along with sables, and Lord knows what else he imports. I must be discreet when I query him." She tapped her lip to recollect. "Welsh tin mines in Wales, South American gold mines, and now, for whatever reason, he yearns for a copper mine." She looked off, thoughtful. "So indulge him, take an interest if that is the only way to gain his favors. He seems to be rallying. Tell him, 'Oh, how clever you are.' It can do no harm."

"But *ma mère*! He is *très vieux*! Old enough to be my grandfather."

"My girl. My dear spoilt child. Wake up! Wealth is young. Riches cover a multitude of ill features. In time you won't even notice because you'll be so bedecked and bejeweled, making appointments with your dressmakers, dining at Claridge's or the Grosvenor, traveling the continent in one's own train car like the bloody Queen. How I envy you! If only I weren't so close in kinship." She cast a mournful gaze at the rain. "Though not real blood lineage, appearances would seem so, or I would set my cap for His Right Honorable Lord Duke, I assure you."

"Rather you than me," Audrina answered waspishly, recalling this same contention yesterday and last week, if not the week before.

"Come." Lady Daphne lifted Audrina's small pointed chin. "You won't notice his age—"

Her daughter interrupted, looking down and unexpectedly blushing. "*Maman*. You never told me what happens—when a—a man—a man and a maid—are alone." She glanced up and away, scowling at Lady Daphne's blush.

"I always had a chaperone. You know what I mean. Don't make me say it. After the vows, and the church and well-wishes, what happens when we are alone? Alone in the dark? My maid wouldn't tell me, my acquaintances say I might get with child if a man kisses me…"

"Oh, my dear, time for all that…"

"But he's so old!"

Lady Daphne chortled in a most unladylike way. "Yet all cats are gray in the dark, and I'm sure that in the middle of the night you'll find him most attentive. Now, no more about it! Besides I extremely doubt any child will enter into it. However…" She tapped her teeth. "You might offer the possibility, as an inducement, whether he, well…miracle or not…" She snapped her fan in a way Audrina knew ended the debate, but not for her.

"Make sense, *ma mère*. Oh!" Audrina tossed her sewing basket aside, tumbling out snarls of thread and scissors. "I am tiring of this room. Must you take up so much space? Our quarters, miserable as they are, are even more miniscule when you flap about like that."

"I do not flap! I'm saying that he intends—yearns—to send us back." The handwashing again. "Why he even mentioned we'd be more comfortable in London. We'd have more room!"

"And you refused?" Audrina's face turned the ugly purple of her gown. "*Maman*, we would be in London for the Season!"

"Must you go on about that? You have no Season! We have no place to lay our heads there. No gowns. I sold most of the jewels. Why cannot you grasp that?"

She knelt at her daughter's feet. "Audrina dear…" She exhaled. "Mortimer only mentioned it because of your drawn face and histrionic sighs. We have to act as if we absolutely adore this place."

Audrina wadded the petticoat and tossed it messily in a corner. "We adore living in a pigsty?"

Lady Daphne gazed at the puddled petticoat, raised a brow, and plucked up the offending garment.

"Promise me you won't show discontent tonight."

Lady Daphne suddenly found her nails to be of intense interest.

"In fact, I want you to go out with him, now he's keen, on some of his…excursions. Say anything. Say you find the air bracing! Say you've developed an acute interest in mines, since you have known him. They are intriguing. Romantic! I don't care how distasteful."

"*Ma mère*! I'll get consumption. Mines are dank and—and dangerous. You can't want me to go climbing over Lord knows what, in a dark, wet, hideous place! There's bats and bears and…"

"Bosh! Do be sensible! Bats, bears, or tigers, I don't care. Sprain your ankle or pretend to. If he won't wive you, perhaps the old fool might fancy a surrogate daughter—a sweet, loving puss who relishes adventures with her dear friend, or her beloved step-uncle, and she cannot bear to have him from her sight, and further more…"

She tapped her teeth. "Furthermore, you're cold, and could you not…?"

"That shouldn't be too difficult," Audrina interrupted the avalanche of her mother's words threatening to bury her. "But it would not be you stumbling through a slimy mine."

Her mother continued to ignore her. "…and won't he put his arm about your shoulder? Snuggle up, get close."

Daphne swiveled, brushing her skirts like a silken rose wave over Audrina's lap in the tight quarters.

"Imperative we make him interested in us—beyond a burden. We are barnacles on a boat hull, useless, slowing him down," she announced bitterly.

Audrina shivered. Judging from the frosty look her mother shot out at Wylder's rain-swollen streets, her thoughts, if not morbid, grew chillier, overhearing her mother murmuring, as if forgetting Audrina's presence. Her mother's face had turned into a death's head, all high alabaster cheekbones and dead gaze, looking farther into the future than did Audrina.

"Yes. Mines are dangerous places. Filled with pitfalls, explosions, rocks falling. Anything could happen… I'm surprised something has not already befallen dear Mortimer. One can get lost in a mine," she mused. "And if Audrina is a favorite? There's more than one way to inherit a fortune."

Lady Daphne swiveled back. "Besides, my love, I hear there is to be a ball right here at the Longhorn!" She tinkled it, a brittle sound, as peace offering. Lady Audrina, of course, groaned.

****

As a bright star on Cat's horizon, there was to be a dance! A Harvest Festival, in two weeks' time! Right here in the Longhorn Saloon! She mayn't be able to attend, but she could share the hooley from the kitchen, and all the comings and goings—the fiddle-playin' and drums, like a real *cèilidh*.

Just maybe, if she asked proper, and the yellow satin could be…

It seemed a good deed should never go unpunished.

Madame was going through provisions with a fine-tooth comb, with Arabella taking notes, judging how much flour and eggs, how many hogsheads of whiskey. "That is Levi's department," she muttered.

When Cat asked if she could perhaps serve…

"Catriona, keep to the kitchen for a while longer. Some of my guests are fearing you might be—soiled." Cat didn't ken why, if she were that tainted, the dishes were somehow not.

"How much longer, mum?"

"How would I ken!" Madame snapped while Arabella flashed a smug look.

Banished. No dance for her.

The typhus had vanished from Wylder unlamented. Thanks to Madame and Catriona, it had been kept contained. No one else fell ill with the petulance. Evidently, the good duke caught it on the train, and the train whipped right through. He frequented the smoking car, apparently contracted it there, and therefore it left his ladies unsullied.

"Put a bright face on, girl," Cat muttered. "This be

your lot. Not being with the fine gentleman, or fancy dreams, or dances. No time for fretting and all."

Scrape the dishes into the slops pail for the hogs. Scour the sink, draw hot water from the woodstove's water box, shave yellow strips of lye soap into the pan, put more hot water in the rinse basin, look about for clean towels and scrubbers.

Catriona snagged Dingy for drying duty.

Chapter Seven
Temptation

She didn't mean to take it, Cat fretted.

Cleaning she was, in the highborn ladies' bedroom behind Little Mae's. There, under the dresser. Winking at her. Catriona drew the shining bauble out as she stooped to chase the dust devils with the broom.

The sweetest little oval locket, fat as a baby's fist—gleaming gold, warming in her hands like a living thing, soothing rough palms as she cupped it, nestling perfectly, as if it belonged. A tiny blood-red ruby, bright as a blood drop welling at the end of one's finger, sat square in the middle of the heart.

The chain was gossamer light.

Before Cat kenned it, she had it up to her neck, then slipped it over her hair, where it tangled for a panicky second. She thought she'd lost the chain in a snag, and the more she worked and twisted the fragile links, the more it became one with her snarl of curls.

She'd be caught red-handed!

Somehow, the chain untangled and fell, weightless as a whisper, around her neck, glinting a gold skein against her white skin that scarce sensed the smooth gold locket nestled between the heat of her breasts. Then it warmed and became one with her heart.

Footsteps, rapid and clicking, approached.

Catriona yanked the chain. She could never get it

off! It was near snapping. Her hair tugged. She heard stomping footsteps. She tossed the locket down her bodice and, blushing, bent to lift the young lady's chamber pot.

Audrina eyed her as she swept in, as if catching her in a detestable, unmentionable act. Then, pretending she did not notice, she made a moue of distaste and waved her out, not wanting to admit the ruder, natural part of life, not that Cat would have minded forgetting them too.

So that was how it happened.

The guilt was overwhelmed by reason. She was getting back some for slights her family had endured, but that wasn't it.

She kenned better. Had not catechism classes and her own ma drummed into her all the "Thou shalt nots"? A whole string of such, with "Thou shalt not steal" being a big one right under "Thou shalt not kill."

A venal sin, sure.

The small heart alternately burned and throbbed against her flesh. The chill metal scorched a thin line into her neck. The hefty locket thumped in time to a guilty heart. Cat's sleep was troubled the first night, with one eye open, and during the day one ear open for a hubbub from Lady Audrina, or her ice-coated ma barging into the kitchen with an accusing finger.

****

That Sunday, Cat temporized all through the long homily. Perhaps it had lain there forever; it needn't be Audrina's. She could hardly give it back now. She might find her in the room when she should not be. It had no initials. *It could be anyone's, so why not mine?* 'Sides, they had so many baubles. After all, who kenned how long the locket lay kicked deep under the dresser? It might well not belong to the haughty ladies. Wouldn't they have missed it by now?

Conscious of the locket's weight both in her mind and in her bosom, Catriona's mind twirled on and on like a many-striped top. Moreover, if Catriona did ask either lady, she was certain sure either one would snatch it faster than a dog did a platter of roast beef claiming it whether or not it was rightfully theirs.

No. Better say naught. Yet she could not keep it where it burned guilt in her breast with a red-hot poker. Cat stuffed it, wrapped in cotton wool, where the rafters hit the walls.

Lady Audrina never noticed. Or supposed she'd lost that locket. Or perhaps it *was* from another unfortunate traveler. Cat never kenned for sure. Did they hang one here for thievery, as back in England, or cut off their hand? She trembled and got precious little comfort from the pretty thing she could never sport. Yet Cat affeered it began a deeper hunger.

Then, Cat spied a lace handkerchief, so fine a linen one could read a book through it, abandoned on a pew after the homily and last prayers. She tucked it up her sleeve. It had an initial K. She wondered if she could find the soul who dropped it, but no one professed it when she asked round. Or that silver hat pin stuck between floorboards in the saloon.

Yet she sorrowed as she dawdled to the yard goods shop for Madame. She did crave pretty things—gowns of fine lawn, or silk, with handmade lace or buttons that resembled tiny rosebuds—but that was the fairies talking.

She placed her treasures in the small painted tea chest with the locket, and stuck it behind the rafters. For comfort, she would take them out and study them in the moonlight streaming through her small attic window. The locket with the blood-red eye glittering in the pale blue light seemed to mock and blame.

She would burn in Hell's fire.

****

Cat could not keep the locket, hers or not, and worried the direction her sinful actions led. Cat looked both ways, slipped into the room, and toed the lovely locket back under the dresser, and who but Audrina swept in.

Cat leapt up. Guilt scribbled her face with red ink.

"What are you snooping about in here for? What is that?" Lady Audrina pounced on the bit of gold at the end of Cat's toe. "Were you taking that?" she shrieked.

"No! No! Is—is it yours, ma'am?"

"Lady Audrina to you! And what if it is…or isn't? It is now!" Her smile was a thin slice of cold moon. She grasped the gold bauble in her fist, so tight Cat wanted to rescue the plump little gold heart.

"Yes, ma'am, I'm glad 'tis yours and I found it for you." Cat said, feeling the fool.

Audrina curled her lip. "Of course you are!"

She stopped her as Cat rushed out.

"I hear there is actually going to be a ball in this godforsaken village. Imagine that! To have something approaching culture… I wonder if that handsome Aaron is to be attending," she said, idly swinging the locket.

****

It was the day before the Harvest Festival.

Tying her apron, Catriona pounded down the hall to get to the kitchen before Madame sent bloodhounds after her; cakes to ice and ham to slice, piccalilli to spoon into dishes and biscuits waiting for the oven, when she felt a tug and, spinning round, vexed, to snatch her apron from whatever snagged it, was astonished to see Lady Audrina with the corner of her apron string tight in her fist.

"Where do you think you're going? Not too far, I'm thinking. I'm also thinking I'm well in need of a lady's maid." She narrowed her eyes. "We had to leave mine in London." The way she darted her eyes away, made Cat think that statement was not true. Frowning in confusion, she re-tied her apron.

"What do you mean, lady's maid?"

"I shall need attending before the ball. Help with my hair and dress," she announced loftily. "I mean you, dunderhead. You could be more than a scullery maid! I mean you shall spare an hour or two with me each day. I need mending. My hair needs washed and brushed. Oh! You know! Other chores that ladies' maids do. You might need some training." Audrina curled cupid bow lips. "After all, I cannot expect you to ken a bustle from a tea urn! So. Two hours before the dance, I shall be expecting you."

Catriona stammered in her haste to be away. "That'll work so, will it? I'm fearful I cannot. Madame takes all my time." Lady's maid indeed, as if she had two minutes to rub together.

Audrina grabbed Cat's arm. "Tosh! Oh, yes, you will." Catriona jerked away. "I don't have two minutes to brush me own hair."

"Who cares? No one looks at you anyway." Audrina swayed hip to hip, taunting. "Besides you will make time, all right. I will tell them all about you stealing my locket and pretending you were putting it back. You won't last two minutes. If you think to even try to find another position, I'll tell all of Wylder you're a common thief and they should lock up their silver." She slapped Cat. "Who do you suppose they will believe?"

Cat stared, feeling her Irish blood steaming, hot as soda bread fresh from the oven. "Even if you did your worst, I have no time. Madame keeps me busy. I scarce get to bed before midnight."

Audrina, stamping her pretty pale blue leather shoe—which perfectly matched her baby blue gown—venomously spouted, "Very well! But, I expect at least an hour." Cat noted the torn scuff mark on one toe.

She groaned. There went the afternoon break when she could put her feet up on the stove and have a cuppa, or venture for a short stroll.

"Late again, lazybones," Madame scolded from the doorway. Cat exhaled and rushed to the stove.

****

"Ow-wuch!" Audrina's hands flew to her head. "Mind what you are doing! You aren't carding wool in whatever miserable hovel you came from." She smirked at her mother, who, Cat noted, seemed less than amused. "What can one expect from shanty Irish?"

Catriona gave her hair an extra tug. "Sorry, miss."

"Lady Audrina!"

Cat bit her cheek. "Lady!"

"After this, wash my stockings and underthings. Make sure they are dry!"

Catriona looked in the mirror in despair.

Where could she go? What could she do? She hadn't money to get on the train even to the next stop. Somehow…

She stared at her white face over Audrina's head. She couldn't bear leaving where Ma and Pa were laid to rest, and where she placed flowers on their graves and talked to them—all she had left of the old days, besides the tea chest, Ma's wedding gown, and Pa's old clay pipe.

As if reading her mind, Audrina smirked back in the looking glass. "Better count your lucky stars that I don't report you, so don't spoil my good mood with your sour face."

Lady Audrina looked sideways for her mother, who had slipped out, before whispering to Cat, "I'm going to see that handsome, rough, backwoods chap tonight. Aaron. A girl must have some frolic before she is wed."

Aaron! Audrina was pretending they were girlish chums, sharing confidences.

Catrina longed to smack her.

"Ow! I said gently!"

Her heart flipped. Audrina made light of her news about Aaron, as one girlish gush to another, but she was bursting to tell, Cat saw. Nevertheless, Cat's heart stopped beating.

"You can't! You mustn't."

"How dare you!"

"Lady Audrina. He cannot mean anything to you." Cat crossed arms over her chest as if to say, *He's mine*.

Audrina slanted a jealous eye. "You? What, pray! Take him from you? He doesn't know your name! You are dirty. Your hair resembles a squirrel's nest! And your red rough hands and broken nails are a disgrace to womanhood."

"He does know me!" Cat's blood boiled over. The slap rang like a gong. Her handprint reddened Audrina's cheek alarmingly, Catriona thought with savage pleasure, feeling no remorse. That hurt. But not as much as the pain in her stomach.

Audrina narrowed blue eyes to slits of ice. "Oh! Oh! I will have you whipped! *Ma mère*! Where are you?" Audrina bolted up, green eyes blazing with rage. "I will have you horsewhipped! Back in England, you'd be hung for such effrontery."

Cat doubted it, whatever that was, but one could never tell with the English.

Nothing came of it.

****

Arabella pouted prettily in the kitchen looking glass, turning her face this way and that, while she absently stirred apple butter.

"Mama? If that ragamuffin will do for the grand ladies, why not me? I could use a lady's maid, like they do in civilized societies—like in London! A hairdresser and someone to help me don my dresses and keep up my wardrobe. Besides, I want to look my best."

Madame Solange watched her stepdaughter with an irony not lost.

"Well, why not?"

Madame gave a last pat to holly berries, late mums, and pine sprigs to set on the bar. "A passel of petulance, laziness, the I-wants, airs, and lifting oneself beyond one's means is not our way. And just when is that girl Cat going to have time, between serving, dishwashing, scrubbing, ironing the linens, plus looking after the high-and-mighties?"

Arabella pouted. Cat would pay!

Chapter Eight
One Jest Too Far

Squinting, with fists balled on hips, Arabella eyed Catriona leaving the hallowed room of the Ladies Audrina and Daphne.

"I want you in my room each dawn or—or whenever I awaken," she hissed. "And especially tonight!" Catriona kenned some storm brewed behind that poufy blonde hair and smooth white forehead. "And fetch me tea, like you do those two." She pointed savagely down the hall.

Cat groaned. "Aye," she answered faintly. 'Twas a new chore added on, but as she was brewing strong Irish tea first thing for herself anyway, 'twas a small one. Still she protested, "But you do not drink tea."

"I will now, stupid! And while you're here, I wish you to do my hair in the manner in which you fix that snip's, that Audrina's, for the dance." She curled perfect lips. "With the two coils above the ears, allowing the rest to hang free. You will need to set it in curlers for me."

Cat looked at her with a face bland as oatmeal, kenning the only way round Arabella's castle in the air was to ignore her orders. Catriona's orders came from Madame or, in a pinch, from Levi, though he usually tended to the bar side—or rather hid behind it.

****

"I wonder if it is best, milord, to be on such a

strenuous excursion so soon? You mentioned 'tis twenty miles or so off?"

"Nonsense! I have tarried far too long," the duke proclaimed. "Time I built back my strength and focused on important endeavors."

Upon leaving the road proper, Hugo looked askance at the rough trail winding into the hills. The duke, though still handsome and looking even more aristocratic astride the half-wild horse as if born to it, after many a fox chase with hounds braying, was noticeably frailer.

"Twenty—thirty? I could eat the miles! That old miner mentioned somewhat past the next little settlement, or farm." He waved vaguely. "Ah, Hugo, grasp life with both hands, as if one were starving."

"Whenever I do, something typically shatters beyond repair," said Hugo with rue.

The duke companionably clapped his shoulder, chuckling. "Cannot naysay that! But you have heart." He laughed. "You are a fine lad! Smart as this whip."

Hugo flushed. He did not mention "fine looking."

Aaron, who had not waited for an invitation— "allow me to show you some of the local flora and fauna"—tagged discreet paces behind on the stable's next-to-best mare—the duke had claimed the best—and did not hear the exchange. Yet if he seemed to listen closely and mimicked their speech and gestures, it was not accidental.

He desired to insert himself as much as possible. To intrigue Lady Audrina by ignoring inviting glances, flatter the duchess by pretending to be a smitten schoolboy—not that he wasn't half in love with the aged beldame. She was admirably fine-looking. And did not older women have youthful paramours, without castigation? He smelt money, too, and if he could be attached to a cool aristocratic female just waiting to be plucked, well who was to argue? Indeed, he would stick close as a tar baby to these two dandies and their ladies.

The older man, glancing at Hugo, shook his head.

Hugo thought himself carrot-haired, fumble-footed, socially incompetent, and ham-fisted. None of that was true, poor lad. Well. Mostly. Hugo had talents. The lad thought before making a decision. And when impulsive, his intuitions were spot on. A copper-bottomed friend. With Hugo, one never sensed cold fingers of unease on the back of one's neck as one did with Lady Daphne, or—he quirked a lip—that jackanapes following them like a hound.

Aaron would not be amiss in fashionable salons, he mused, with polished nails, reeking of cologne and hair pomade, yet to his seasoned eye the lad seemed more a prowling tom with a harem of willing kittens.

He spoke aloud then. "One hears the Pale Horse galloping ever closer on one's heels, but I feel strong as a bull." The duke, consulting a scrap of map, galloped ahead, not showing how each bounce rattled him from his bony rump on up his spine to his skull.

"Keep up," he hailed back. "I hear there is to be a Festival of some sort tonight. Can't miss that!"

Aaron groaned. "Twenty miles!"

****

Cat, sweeping the main saloon floor, pointed upstairs. "Madame, 'twas I what was wonderin' if I could be watchin' from the gallery tonight, for a wee bit?"

"Certainly not! The idea! You will be busy enough, my girl. There will be dishes to fetch and wash. Food to bring in. What are you thinking? Do I pay you to lollygag?"

"Then, Madame…" Cat leaned wearily on her broom. "Might I be having a few hours off to meself today? I've scarce had a wink, what with the ladies…" Cat trailed off. "I am dead on me feet, sure. I've done all the cleaning, and I will be here on time to do the ladies' hair and all."

Madame glanced up quickly, narrowing her eyes. Rarely did Catriona make any request. She did look frazzled and frayed. Perhaps a few hours might do her good, and she'd be fresh for the evening. Cat scarce heard her acquiescence, thanking her and untying her apron before she hit the back door for the stairway.

****

She hastened, putting distance between her and the saloon, the two English *cailleacha*—witches, she giggled—Madame Solange, and the dread dishpan. This mild winter day seemed almost springlike. Even a few apple blossoms were coaxed from their buds.

Skipping the mile down the rough trail, spying piles of boulders ahead that looked tumbled in giant's play half-surrounding the U-shaped pond, already anticipating bracing water and sun on her face, so long denied by her punishing hours. Cat couldn't wait. After a week of redding up for the Festival, ironing a boatload of serviettes, pillowcases, and sheets, baking of all kinds, and scrubbing down the kitchen, she had felt weary to her toes. But now she ran for the freedom, shedding her clothes even as she ran. She plopped on a bed of fern, struggled out of shoes and stockings, and waded past reeds until her toes drifted off the pebbly bottom and into cool marl.

"Aahhhh!" She laughed out loud and sank down, the water a nippy kiss loving every inch of her, finding her secret parts and making her small breasts bob on the surface. Lazily, Cat paddled almost to the sharp bend demarked by an enormous boulder lording over all, where she turned back, much preferring the more private, shallower end.

****

The duke studied the rude opening in the craggy hillside framed in rotting timber, brushed a sagging plank aside, and peered in.

"Take me for an old fool," he said, not meaning a word of it, "yet the old scallywag told me it was a working mine." He booted scattered frames and raised a rusted pick with a broken, bleached handle. "When Moses was a mere sprat, mayhap," he muttered, tossing it.

"A pity," Hugo murmured, not meaning a word either. "Suppose we should meander back, then…" He intuited the old rogue had kenned it all along and merely yearned for the jaunt, mayhap away from demanding kin.

"Faint heart and all that never won anything. Whatever that saying was."

"Fair lady, I think," Aaron muttered under his breath.

Hugo cantered closer. "Are you certain we cannot save this for another outing, sir?"

"Stuff and nonsense! I'm going in."

"Might have to bend ourselves like a folding yard stick." Hugo patted his head, it being fully six feet five inches above the ground.

"Piffle! You young folk!"

"Allow me to explore then a bit. Don't want the roof

falling in on you."

The duke grumbled, "Don't dillydally!"

Aaron sighed, already bored. The outing was apparently to be wasted exploring a damp cave!

"No, sir, merely a reconnoiter. Allow me to be your batman." The duke huffed and made a shooing motion as if to say, "Well, get on with it."

Hugo crouched, waving dead vines and webs from his eyes. The derelict mine opened up inside. The roof had indeed fallen, twenty feet in, but the rest was under solid rock. No trouble the duke could get into. To treat the old gentleman as an invalid would make him one.

Hugo emerged, brushing cobwebs and dirt. "Looks safe enough, milord."

"Of course it is! Now off with you. I need no amateurs dogging my heels asking silly impertinent questions." Hugo bit his cheek, watching the old gent with concern. His manners were usually more accommodating, even gracious.

"We promise. The souls of discretion."

Aaron groaned, again under his breath.

The duke dismounted. "Phah! Who says? Not in my dotage! I need to build strength in these old bones or I shall grow rusty as grandfather's sword from the Napoleonic wars. I don't need a baby minder. Now, scat! I will meet you on the road, if I am not returned before you."

Hugo eyed the duke. He knew this mood. The more he protested, the more he would dig in.

"Well done," he said mildly. "When you return, you must tell us all about it."

The duke, fiddling with arcane measuring devices, a small pick, and a kit of stoppered bottles, merely waved him off, irritated. Hugo waited a second, then motioned, to Aaron's relief. The duke would grow bored and, saving face, wait a full hour before catching up.

****

"Want some fun?"

Aaron withdrew a flask, waving it in invitation. "Know a spot, if you don't mind roughing it, City Boy. Go for a swim, have a drink, wait for your old codger"— he turned that into a cough—"er, gent to return." He nodded. "Not far. See those rocks?" He pointed a mile to a jumble of boulders. Hugo had noted, on the way out from town, the range of buggy-sized rocks scattered about a weirdly shaped pond.

Aaron smiled. *Let's see how you do, City Boy.*

Hugo was flattered. Till now, Aaron had been off-putting, and male chums his age were thin on the ground. He nodded agreeably. Aaron looped his horse to a tree, beside Hugo's mount, in a copse near the boulders, and both laughing young men shed their clothes on the way, tossing them on bracken and running naked to the inviting sun-sparkled pond.

****

Cat's undergarments and stockings, stretched on a warm flat rock, steamed gently in the sun. Time passed in blissful oblivion as she relished the cool clear water on her naked body, washing away a week's worth of smoke, grease, and food spatters, ducking under in preparation for sudsing her thick mass of curls; she'd be fresh for the night. With that movement, she missed the small splash on the other side of the pond. Wading to fetch her kit bag, Cat rummaged soap, comb, and a scrap of linen for drying after her bathe.

Those laid out, Cat closed her eyes and held her face

to the golden disc of the sun, spreading her arms as if inviting flight. At a slight sound, she blinked open, shielding from the dazzle.

****

Lazing nude, perched against sun-warmed rocks, Hugo and Aaron passed the flask, and Aaron sullenly eyed Hugo when he wasn't looking. He'd supposed strong drink would make him "go blind." Instead, it seemed mother's milk to the redheaded fool. And did he need to be, with his milk-pale existence, so amply endowed?

"Come, let's swim a bit." He tossed the flask. *And wrestle you under the water.*

However, to his pique, after Hugo outswam him, Aaron was amazed to spy him nimbly clambering the tallest boulder, which demarked the bend separating the larger pond from the smaller. Was he pretending to be king of the hill?

Hugo did not want to say he was watching out for Lord Greville when he reached the top.

****

Catriona gasped. The image did not seem real.

Standing on the tallest boulder—a nude man caught in a gleaming rosy nimbus—the impossibly white creature seemed to glow in an unearthly manner from the sun. Cat had never actually seen a man unclothed before, but she had viewed pictures of marble statues—one called David, from the Bible, that some artist sculpted long ago, for instance. She saw that in a book in a rich house in Ballygawley where every week ma had cleaned and scrubbed.

That David fellow from the Bible had come to life.

She placed her hand above her eyes to ward off the

dazzle. She couldn't break the spell, if that was what it was…unconsciously admiring long slim legs, smooth, tautly muscled, and seemingly carved from hard stone. The buttocks firm, round, shoulders broad, divided by a deep cleft of spine leading to a finely muscled neck.

The tall sun-burnished figure, one hand behind his neck, the other outstretched, appeared to glory in the warmth as had she. Edged in rosy light, the male seemed aflame. The perfect head a corona of fire…

****

Then, still gazing out to the far distance, the figure slowly revolved.

Intrigued despite herself, Catriona noted all his manly attributes. Moreover, they were astonishing, nestled in a dark crimson briar patch with a silky red feathering leading to his navel.

Snapping her mouth shut, Cat heard her teeth click.

It wasn't a blazing halo but the locks themselves, visible after the sun blunted its fire behind a wisp of cloud.

"Hugo!" She gasped, clapping her hand to her mouth, struggling backward, forgetting she too was as God made her, to deeper water. David, or Hugo in all his earthly glory, tall, godlike, topped with fiery hair picked with gold, lowered his startled gaze to Catriona.

Catriona's speech returned. "Sir! Sir! I am beggin' your pardon for starin'. And truth, I know you are a gentleman…"

Hugo dropped unhurriedly down on the rock, still above her, perched with feet dangling. He threw a cheeky half-smile that unexpectedly lit up his homely face, making her scowl back.

"Unfortunately, yes. Otherwise, I would be sorely

tempted. And you are forgiven, for it is I who should be more—circumspect."

"Then, sir, if you wouldn't mind turning your back. I would like to be leavin' the water now, sure."

He laughed. "Very well, and where are your garments, so I may direct myself appropriately in the opposite direction?"

He was flirting, she realized. He seemed not a bit put out, or awkward that he was naked as a babe—as was she, though she had ducked to her neck.

Hugo grinned and ostensibly turned his face.

Defiantly, Catriona, fist on hip for the very devil was in her, half-rose, pointing to where her miserable collection of rags lay.

To her consternation, Hugo jerked forward, almost going into the water from his perch. However, he seemed more pushed, and at the same time another voice hailed from nowhere and Aaron's handsome angel face suddenly appeared behind Hugo's.

Cat stood like a statue in a fountain. She had waded to the shallows as Hugo's head was turned and was now cold and wet—the air making rosy nipples turn to hard little blackberries—and caught twixt the shore and deeper water, she did not know what to cover first.

She ducked instead.

"Go away! What are you doing here?"

"Whatever concern might that be of yours? Don't you know how to address your betters?" Aaron sneered, as if he too had arrived with the titled group weeks ago, rather than being Madame's stepson.

Cat sank to her knees, looking desperately at the shore where her small kit and drying laundry lay.

"Had to show our snooty chum here the sights,

didn't I?" Aaron thumbed at Hugo studiously staring at the trees at the far shore. "Who knew one of the sights would be our grubby little kitchen help?" he said nastily.

"I say, Mr. Aaron, the jest has gone far enough."

"Oh, but Hugo! The fun has just begun." Aaron's golden face lit up.

As the sun faded, Cat was all chattering teeth and goosepimply arms. Inside, she raged hot over her own inexperience, Aaron's mockery, and the fact she was caught in such a distressing position, or rather the flame-haired Hugo was, and he did not seem put out a bit.

"Please, sirs, I wish to get out."

"Then do so." Aaron giggled. "We won't hinder. Will we?" He nudged Hugo. "You rogue."

"You are no gentleman."

"The titled never are," Aaron announced loftily, assuming the same position in society as the saloon's aristocratic guests. "We don't need to, you see." He spared a glance at Hugo. "You are titled, aren't you?"

"I've had enough fun, as you put it." Hugo flashed a look of apology at Catriona before scrambling down the far side. Still, Aaron and Hugo were in the only spot where she could gain her clothing, the rest of the shore being marshy or ringed by boulders. And she'd need to climb out without a stitch.

Cat gained a deeper spot, sinking to her chest and calling, "You won't go about your business, then?"

Aaron smiled, as triumphant as if he'd won a great bet. Cat saw he would remain if Hell opened up beneath him and scorched his bottom to cinders.

"Very well, I ken what you're all about. And ye don't affright me. I had six brothers! Now will ye do me the favor of handin' me my clothes?"

Aaron vanished the way of Hugo, reappeared, and prodded a stick to snag Cat's underdrawers—clean they were, scrubbed to mere threads, but gray and shabby. Catriona's face heated with chagrin.

"Oh! Are these yours? Do you want them? Never did treat poor old Hugo there for rescuing you from that cold and lonely death in the well, did you, you ungrateful tart?" He nodded back at Hugo. "Not even a bit of snogging? Perhaps, now, he could take his payment in kind. Perhaps we may all enjoy a good ducking." Aaron smirked.

Cat kenned nothing good would come of this if Aaron or Hugo, or both, came into the water. Aaron checked behind him. "Hugo? I say, old chap, where have you got off to?"

Hugo appeared, hastily buttoning a shirt.

"I'm fetching the young lady her clothing," he said in a way that bridged no argument, as he stalked the perimeter to Aaron.

"Oh, no, you don't, deserter!"

Aaron leap-frogged over small boulders strewing the shallows, holding her rags aloft with a broken limb, waving them tantalizingly over her head—Hugo was still feet away, making his way among treacherous stones.

"Please, Aaron!"

"I, umm, I think this has gone far enough. She's— ummm, is cold." Hugo looked uncomfortable, like he yearned to have a bout of fisticuffs.

"That I am!" Cat snapped.

Aaron just waved her rags over the water like a flag at the end of the stick.

Catriona's eyes flashed. If her frock was wetted again, she would never get back in time, to Madame's certain displeasure, already late for redding up the saloon as promised.

She had had enough.

Brazen as brass, Catriona rose, fists on hips, glaring them both down, let them have a good ogle, then strode forcefully for the shore, water rushing back from her legs, ready to repossess her dress and druthers, mayhem in her witchy eyes.

Both men seemed transfixed, gaping at Catriona as if they saw a mermaid, Tatiana Fairie Queen, or Odysseus's siren on the rocks, with her wild flyaway hair quenched and covering her breasts, reaching past her tiny waist, matching the darkling soft patch below—Hugo averted his eyes, but late—where it joined the sweet swell of Cat's thighs.

"Oh, all right!" Aaron sulked, tossing her things after her when Hugo did not react but glared him down. Her bits and pieces fluttered, scattered on a lower rock. He appeared not to care if they struck water or not.

"It takes sophistication, I suppose, to learn the art of a jest—the nuance involved," he muttered aside, yet she felt this was for Hugo's ears.

"I ken a sick joke well enough!"

Cat snatched up her things and stepped behind reeds, swiftly donning bloomers and petticoat, and lastly her shift, little aided by the dunking in the water, but it felt fresh. Fuming and sorrowing, she pulled on stockings, rolled garters, and lastly fitted feet in boots in order to pace off without a backward glance down the long road to the Longhorn.

Cat had misjudged Aaron's angelic face.

Her heart shrank to a cold lump. Would she never love again?

Without hopes of Aaron in her dreams, what had she? What could she have done if indeed they had carried off her things? A movement cut off these dark thoughts.

Hugo clambered down the road side of the rocks after pinwheeling long arms like a broken windmill.

She scowled.

Aaron needled, "What, pray tell? You are aiding this wench? Hah! Creating a bad habit of rescuing 'maidens' from the wet." He smirked.

Catriona walked faster. She wasn't running from them. She wasn't! Partly true. She really needed to get back, hating every step.

"Come, now. Don't be like that. Can't walk all the way. Come, a jest only. No stiff necks now." Sensing a horse's warm sides, longing to press herself to its flanks, Cat scowled up, catching Aaron's face, blue eyes beaming down as if there were holes in the sky, golden hair haloed in the sun. He held down his arm. "Come behind me, wench." He made it a love word.

Cat glanced back at Hugo and defiantly stuck her foot in the stirrup Aaron vacated, not wanting to show her appalling need, and with his arm to aid, managed to hop over the saddle behind him, relishing the warmth and contact with his strong back, struggling not to lean her head against his shoulder or to clasp his waist.

Aaron glanced back at Hugo with a questioning smirk.

"I'll await his lordship." Hugo spoke stiffly. "You'd best go."

Cat felt a pang of repentance.

Hugo avoided her eye as if she were not there.

"Suit yourself." Aaron wheeled the horse, calling back to Catriona, "Don't be angry. I only wanted to show our fine guest—that weak-wristed toff, to see if he had blue blood or manly blood running through his lily-white veins. My silly joke. Went too far. Just the spur of the moment. And you, my dear, would stir the britches off any real man."

Cat could not trust herself to speak. What could she say?

"Forgive me, Cat? I did not realize the water was so cold. Only showing up Hugo—the odd thing! He is rather silly. I near lost my balance too, when he almost went over. Funniest sight since that pig got loose from the stockyards and ran into the ironmonger's store."

Cat giggled in spite of herself.

"Aaah, there. That's better! That's my Cat!"

She hated to admit—her heart thumped harder at his expression "my Cat," hoping he did not detect it through his coat, and that this troublesome episode might be a fresh beginning with shared confidences.

They reined in at the Longhorn, and Aaron handed her down. For a delicious moment Cat was chest to knees against him, reveling in his animal scent, his wicked blue eyes, his hand on her back branding her through the cloth.

****

Lady Audrina coldly watched the tender display from her slanted viewpoint, upstairs. Nevertheless, it was enough. Her pretty face turned to anthracite as she eyed the double-mounted horse canter into view with Catriona huddled next to Aaron's back.

Torn between racing down and confronting them—or at least seeing more—or remaining rooted to the spot, she stayed. She might miss something in the interim, and she did not intend to forgo a single tender moment.

"So. They are courting! The hussy is after him. What else could the two of them riding in so intimately mean?" she muttered with a look that sent chills down her mother's spine. "We shall see about that! How dare he choose a fatherless kitchen drudge over me!"

Chapter Nine
Cat's Cradle

"There you are!" Madame greeted Cat with a smile stretching her thin lips—all teeth, she noted, like a wolf eyeing a lamb. Was she in for a drubbing?

"Ah! I see you are all fresh and clean. Just right for the special treat I have for you this evening!" She clapped thin hands. "Before the dance, as you know, there will be the feasting, and perhaps all through. Tonight, you are to fetch and carry," spoken as if conferring a great honor.

Cat's heart lightened.

A step up. She might see the swells, and hear music…

Madame broke in. "And you have my dress—so suitable…"

"Yes, ma'am," Cat ventured. "Who—who does the washing up, then?"

"Oh, that!" She waved airily. "Perhaps Dingy can step in."

Catriona tried to look grateful, sweeping her hands to her wayward hair to neaten it.

"Mmmm…yes. May have to do something with that. Perhaps we should trim it now."

Cat yelped, clapping her head.

"Oh! Very well. Perhaps I have a comb or two."

Later, Cat learned her advancement was because

Arabella claimed a fussy stomach. Dingy did a runner, so she needed to wash dishes after the frolic was over.

****

In her attic, Cat eyed the drab brown dress, muddying her face miserably and making her off-color eyes more obvious, while complimenting neither.

Yet earlier, Cat had plucked out the ball of butcher's string saved with Ma's words ringing in her ears, "Waste not, want not…" Still had Ma's crochet needles, too. She was always a deft knitter. Catriona had hooked a simple trim about the drab neckline and wrists. True, not exactly white, grubby from handling, but holding the gown at arm's length, a definite improvement. Cat ran out of string halfway around one wrist, but if she kept her arm close, no one would notice. Pleased, she ran down to make her grand entrance with her new finery.

Little Mae stopped her at the head of the stairs, or rather, she stopped and Cat plowed into her—somewhat like colliding with a purple silk pillow, soft, comfy, and jasmine scented.

She flicked a finger at Cat's new cotton-string trim. "What's that dirty cat's cradle?"

"Just—a little something. I didn't steal it. No one wanted it. Just old string."

"And looks it, too." Little Mae chortled deep in her throat.

Cat's shoulders drooped. Of course it did.

"Looks just like knotted up old string!" Little Mae reasserted, eying Cat skeptically. "Might have somethin' tucked away. My fi-an-say is a tailor, 'tween you and me."

Ah. So that tiny little fellow, who made her gowns and all, thought Cat.

"Here." Mae dragged several yards of lurid pink lace out of her sewing basket that to Catriona's eyes looked no better, but nothing for it but to accept, vowing to stitch it on after tonight.

****

All eyes were on her, it seemed, when Catriona importantly entered the dining room with a tray of silver and tea things, hair neatly corralled under a cap. Madame widened her eyes over the change in costume, pursed her lips, but did not interfere.

Arabella, arranging more of the Harvest-themed bouquets, smirked at the knotted string trim, already unraveling as Jake's bar cat tugged a loop trailing from Cat's sleeve.

Audrina sat with her mother over the tea that they insisted was life's blood, that they needed to engage in a ritual with daily at four on the dot, never mind preparations swirling about them. She eyed the crude lace with raised brows like commas.

"Who is your dressmaker? The slops boy?"

She snorted through her nose, making Lady Daphne raise brows and sigh deeply. She meant Dingy, of course, even now aimlessly sloshing dishes in her place, Cat hoped.

"Oh, do look, *Maman*. It must be the evening's entertainment," Audrina hooted as the spitting, snarling, leaping cat snagged the string trophy no doubt still scented with butcher's paper, batting and rolling in the unravelling string, bouncing on stilted legs, clawing the tablecloth, dragging a cup off—which shattered noisily on the floor—and generally making a nuisance.

The wretched man Hugo, who had joined the ladies, watched her through thick lenses that seemed to fill his eyes with so much pity they looked underwater. Cat wanted to shrink within her dress and scuttle out, crawl beneath the tables, vanish in a puff of smoke—anything but be chuckled over as a traveling pantomime.

Madame's face seemed pinched at the sound of their laughter and the cat's snarling bedlam as she rushed in, apologizing overmuch, to Cat's mind, for "interfering with your tea," and casting furious looks Cat's way.

Cat's heart sank. She wanted to gag. Scooping up old Whiskers, she ran with the dratted cat to keep the damage down, more lace trailing, as he spit and clawed, until she tossed the mangy yellow tom out the back door. She angrily yanked at the rest of the crochet and returned to her duties, the drab little brown sparrow that she was.

Beyond a few arch sideways looks, with stifled giggles on Audrina's part, the dining room remained quiet save for the sipping of Madame's tea.

****

Cat rushed in.

"It's about time!' Audrina thrust the hair brush at her. *Must she be so close, with all that fly-away hair?* Audrina enviously noted Catriona's thick glossy ringlets tumbling freely and looking adorable without any aid at all.

The Lady Audrina resorted to little clumps of curls and fringes resembling dead animals that she insisted upon pinning. For tonight, a perky fringe just touching her brows, lending her a very French look, she thought, as Cat experimented with one style after another.

Audrina rounded on her as Cat's own ringlets tickled her forehead.

"Do something with all that. You look like a gollywog!"

Cat admitted her coal-black hair had a disobedient bouncy, wayward way…try as she might with water and pins, it sprang back in scrunchy curls, sprigs, waves, and coils down her back and over her shoulders unless pinned tight under her cap or snared in ribbons.

Audrina's hand strayed toward the scissors. Cat yanked Audrina's hair, and swatted the hairbrush.

"*Maman*, did you see that! This drudge threatened me!"

"My dear," Lady Daphne cast an annoyed, long-suffering glance at her daughter. "It is too late to train another, and where would we get a dresser this close? Do you intend to pay and keep her in our spacious quarters?" She snorted in her unladylike fashion. "Catriona will have to do, as needs must."

"Oh, very well," Audrina snapped with poor grace, glaring in the mirror and throwing Cat a nasty look. "What may one expect from Irish trash?"

They spoke as if Cat were a picture on the wall.

Chapter Ten
The Fated Blue Gown

Dingy was fairy dust—a poof of steam, when he wished it, and he waved that wand often.

"God's bum," Cat blasphemed, eyeing the overspilled slops bucket for the chickens. She sighed and slipped out. She'd enough time, before bed, to nip out for a cup of tea of her own on the back stoop and watch the stars wheel overhead. That was her entertainment, it seemed. She had been banished. The groaning board was laid, with platters, napkins, silver, and condiments arranged. Sprigs of holly, pine, and cedar greenery festooned the antler chandelier. Spittoons and bar were polished, glasses gleaming. The fiddlers and banjo player had just arrived. Rattlesnake Jake had trimmed his beard, secured his pet snake, and BiJingo was poised above his keyboard with a glass at his elbow.

All was ready.

Not Catriona.

The dance, it seemed, was never for her.

****

As Cat loitered, downcast, to the coop to fetch an egg for her supper, she couldn't help spying out a spot of bright blue.

The bright blotch was so out of place in the drab brick and dirt courtyard that her eye was drawn like a magnet. On the way back, eggs stuffed in her pocket, she poked the old trash barrel and wonderingly plucked out the lovely thing—like a silken whisper. Yards of it—the finest she'd ever seen. Familiar, somehow. She knew then—it was Lady Audrina's, who apparently didn't want it! "Ohhhh!" Cat breathed, imagining the possibilities.

Cat quickly wadded it and tucked it under her apron, scurrying the back way to the attic, lighting both candle and lantern to get a good gander. A rip under the arm and a wine stain on the hem. The arm could be stitched, and the stain—well, no one would see it down there!

Lady Audrina was thinner, so Catriona's bosom over-spilled a bit, as she couldn't wait to put on the pretty gown. She had no proper petticoats or corset. Nevertheless, her waist was slim and her bosom firm enough without.

Cat dashed water on her face, pinked her cheeks, disentangled her hair—there was nothing else to do for it. "Where is that ribbon!" She knew she had a blue ribbon saved back. "Oh, well, let it loose. No one will see or notice me." She vowed to keep well in the shadows behind the curtains concealing the lean-to kitchen.

Her carping demon spoke then: "If that is the case, why not wear the brown dress?"

Cat ignored the argument.

It was hard to reach behind and fasten, but she managed it. The dress skimmed her ribs like blue satin skin. She shimmered! Her bosom looked smooth as cream sprinkled with specks of cinnamon above the low neckline. Bits of fine lace edging it, too. Certainly better than dirty string.

True, the dress was frayed here and there, and the

lace yellowed, but worlds finer than any she'd ever dreamed of, marveling how anyone could toss such a lovely piece of fabric, when there were so many ways one could fix it, and she would, later, for she had no other place to wear such a fine gown, she thought, with the first sense of unease… Lady Audrina might want the blue dress, late in the day.

"Oh, well, t'would not be wanted, after being tossed in with eggshells and such." She chuckled, holding up the mirror.

"Don't be breakin' a shin on a stool that's not in your way yet," she scolded herself.

****

Cat stood by the archway betwixt kitchen and saloon, peeking through the hastily added velvet drape. The music, bouncy and twanging—the fritz of a harmonica, the fiddle's melodic whine, ByJingo's chirpy piano, and a tambourine's thump and rattle—had her toe tapping along with the floor vibrations as revelers bounced and stomped, twirled and skipped. Oh, 'twas so lovely to see the whirling patterns of skirts, chaps, Sunday-best trews, and coattails whipping by, and she so longed to be out there, but this was better than the kitchen.

Then Cat's traitorous stomach felt the first rumbles of hunger.

In the hurry-burry of getting the feast laid out on the long bar, Madame forgot the help's supper. Catriona supposed they were to forage leftovers. Good enough for her! Yet her mouth watered now. The pitiful egg had been poor substitute for the glorious bounty spread along the bar's whole length.

The variety of comestibles on that long slab dazzled

the eye and palate. Ruby and apricot jellies and jams glowed like jewels under the staghorn candelabrum, and the breads—rye, corn, sourdough, scones, Irish soda bread—pickles, an enormous turkey, a crispy suckling pig, platters of crunchy fried chicken, and a beef haunch, with mustards and horseradish, sausage from the smokehouse still skimmed with green, cabbage slaw, pickled beets, and eggs, German potato salad…and the pies! Chess pie and apple, mainly, with a few sour cherry, wild blackberry, and gooseberry thrown in. Platters of sugar cookies, ginger bars, and molasses jumbles, jugs of sarsaparilla for the few kiddies or teetotalers, and a paying bar set up at a table for the grownups where Rattlesnake Jake also collected admission for such a feast and the merrymaking.

Cat spied the duke enjoying the festival atmosphere with his party of three at a table close to the sea of dancers. The ungainly Hugo wore a gray velvet waistcoat and jade green sateen jacket, the lovely Audrina seemed a vision of pale pink, and Lady Daphne was in muted periwinkle that matched her lavender-ish eyes.

Usually, they dined on the small stage, in vaulted position, or behind the fretwork. However, tonight it was lorded over by the deafening band.

Cat fretted, tearing away from their perfection. Judging by how fast the bar was being attacked, she pondered if there would be a dry biscuit or a crumb of butcher's cheese left for her and Dingy. Her stomach nagged her, ever more insistent, grumbling like a bear and reminding Cat that she'd had no victuals since noon, save for that one boiled egg…

"Too long for a growing girl," she muttered,

112

covetously eyeing the bounteous bar between bobbing couples. If she could just edge over without being seen, or go outside and come through the front—but no, Madame was watching Jake and the collection like a hawk eyeing a hare.

It seemed her feet, connected with her wayward stomach, had their own mind. Catriona edged out, hugging the wall and the small stage. No one was looking. Cat ducked behind dancers till she was at the end of the bar, near a platter of cheeses and zwieback. Not her first choice but…

She checked again. A potted cedar tree concealed Madame, who greeted paying guests, and old Levi would not care. Cat laughed when she spied Dingy's hand reaching from behind the bar, snatching whatever he could reach, cookies, pickles, cake—it didn't matter, taking it back to his lair among the barrels and bottles.

Seizing a plate, Cat began loading anything she could too, before Madame spotted her, one atop the other, cake on top of sausage heaped on potato salad nudging a square of peach cobbler, stabbing a thick slab of roast—an unheard-of treat in the Gruenwald kitchens for her and Dingy. She grew dizzy with choice. Besides—her bosom swelling with pride, she looked presentable. Her hair might not be styled, but soon she'd be safe back in the kitchen anyway. That is, until a man beside her widened his eyes when Catriona's small mountain of food threatened to topple.

"Why, ain't you a strong strappin' gal!"

She felt like an eejit. Why did she and Dingy need to skulk? Had they not been a large part of the preparations? Cat felt like flinging the plate. Either way, she needed to scat before she mortified herself further.

Looking like he'd like to take a bite out of her too, Cat sidled off, unsure if that was a compliment or not, defiantly snatching a few ginger bars on the way, but she somberly conceded this was a sign to leave. Casting a mournful eye at the array of pies, she wended past frenetic dancers with her loaded plate, animated by the smell of delectables, not quite seeing where she headed.

Balancing the heavy platter, Cat nipped awkwardly past the more boisterous prancers—but the dance ended abruptly with the fiddle's last skree-skraw, and the sweating dancers vanished—like kitchen mice when the lamp's lit—toward the edges of the room, fanning themselves and making excited noises.

Catriona stood in her found blue gown in the midst of nothing, clutching her mountainous plate to her bosom.

It seemed all conversation, laughter, and eating halted. She was an island in the midst of a wave of eyes.

Unfortunately, Madame turned at the quiet and spied her.

Lady Audrina too, unfortunately.

"*Maman!*"

Cat heard the screech, wincing her shoulder blades together as if a knife had been thrown and she the target of Audrina's cutting words.

"*Maman!* You see what she is wearing! Do you see what that tramp has on? My gown!"

Cat swore Audrina's voice made dust leak from the rafters.

"Audrina…"

Cat heard reproof in the duchess's highfalutin tones.

"*Not* 'Audrina'! She is not getting away with this!"

Cat froze with her wobbling plate. With big grins on

faces eager for entertainment, all eyes were on her, a target in the midst of the floor, holding a plate filled to running over. Her feet itched to be in the kitchen. Cat's soul itched to be dead.

Soft slippers pounded behind her.

"You sneaking little thief! Stay right where you are!"

A blur, the room a carousel, and she the dunce in the middle. Her body swayed.

Cat had little choice.

Her feet were as rooted as a dead tree. Yet her knees threatened to turn to gelatin and she'd melt into the floor, food and plate flying.

Before Cat could unlock and scramble, flaming, to the sanctity of the kitchen, Audrina grabbed her arm and spun her around with surprising strength in her willowy body.

The plate and food went flying as promised.

The throng screamed with exaggerated horror as the entire mess—roast beef, cobbler, and all on her plate— flung messy missiles, striking clothing or splatting on the floor.

Why could she not die?

She heard muted giggles, raucous laughter, and comments too garbled to hear yet too easily imagined.

'Did she really steal that nice dress?' and the like, as some looked from Cat to Audrina.

Cat heard a ripping as she felt a ferocious yank, and Audrina pulled a puffy blue sleeve hard enough to separate it from the shoulder, the rest shriveling down her arm.

Audrina, face twisted with outrage and perhaps pent-up disappointment, grabbed the bodice next, in a fury of motion, clawing it, apparently in a frenzy to disrobe Cat in the midst of the dancers.

The room spun with faces. Lady Daphne's venomous visage ballooned up, whether directed at Catriona or her willful daughter, Cat couldn't tell. Madame, distraught and uncertain, wrung her hands and looked askance at Levi.

Jake stood blank-faced and unjudging.

Dingy continued gorging behind a potted cedar, with blackberry juice and a pumpkin grin on his puss.

Aaron was leaning against a post, smirking over a tumbler of whiskey.

And Arabella, with her eyes for once not on the handsome range rider…

Then Lady Daphne laid a firm hand on Audrina's shoulder. Audrina's rage melted like spring snow at her mother's touch, leaving her panting with a trail of ripped lace and clutching a snatch of blue silk, shuddering and weeping.

"Oh, *Maman*!"

"Come, my dear." She patted her shoulder and whispered, "It is only a gown. This spectacle is unseemly. You would not want it now anyway, my darling." She cast a disparaging glance at Catriona. Though in a whisper, nevertheless the hushed room heard every word.

Now the spectacle subsided, and Madame hovered. "Do forgive us, your ladyship!" She spoke in a low and desperate tone. "I don't ken what gets into girls of this sort these days. I try to get good help. She will make up for it, I assure you."

Madame Solange tossed Catriona a look that said, "Come with me!"

Yet Cat, watching Daphne lead Audrina reluctantly off, was aware she was still the object of pity and derision, and she wondered bleakly if punishment would be endless favors for Audrina.

If Madame even allowed her to stay.

She saw Madame hesitate, looking at someone over Cat's shoulder.

Hearing cultured words, Cat detected a soft touch.

"I say, may I be of assistance? Allow me to refill your plate. These dancers. So crowded! Quite knocked you about, I fear. Take my arm, miss—Let us both renew our repast and have a quiet chat."

Hugo smiled innocently at Madame, nodded, and invited a stunned Catriona to the bar still adequately laden with comestibles. Silvery eyes twinkled behind thick lenses. The wide mouth stretched in a smile. She saw pity there—at least she thought 'twas pity. A blob of potato salad slid off her skirt at his feet.

Cat's dam broke.

"Oh! Leave me be!"

Hugo, outside of the brush on the shoulder, had not touched her.

"Just go away," she hissed. "Please! Everybody's looking."

Catriona glanced up quickly, then away, wanting to dampen the hurt in Hugo's eyes, too aware of Audrina with her narrow jealous face blazing contempt, burning holes in both her and Hugo, and even Arabella, her arm hooked in the handsome cowboy's, smirking by the bar.

That's when Cat's contrary devil decided to poke pitchforks into prudence.

Her limbs and mouth unfroze.

She pivoted, addressing the kibitzers.

"Leave me! Let me be. All of you. Just leave me alone! I did not steal this dress." She lifted the blue satin skirts. "This was thrown in the rubbish! I found it! She is lying!"

Lady Audrina's pale face turned an unattractive scarlet, contrasting rudely with her pale pink gown. Daphne sniffed as if something was burning, looking down her nose at Cat. "Really! The arrogance!"

Cat spun, gathering up the hated blue dress's skirts with as much dignity as she could muster and bee-lined for her refuge, the kitchen and her attic room, where she would tear off the gown as if it seared her flesh.

Cat once again heard soft-slippered feet pounding toward her.

"Oh, no, you don't! You are not running from me! Filthy thief!"

"Please, Audrina," she heard Hugo soothe. "Haven't you caused enough, even for you?" Audrina gasped, choking back anger, rounding on Hugo.

A small smile played on Catriona's lips despite her resolve to hate Hugo.

Behind her, Madame Solange drooped with despair, not appreciating that most of the throng quite enjoyed the fracas. Meanwhile, fiddlers started up again. Dancers scuffled to the floor. Hubbub returned. Cat reached the kitchen on rubbery legs. It was dark, thank goodness, as she groped to the worktable.

****

"Mistress, I meant no harm. My intention—not to embarrass. You looked as if you needed—" He blushed. "An ally. You—you seemed quite pale," Hugo ended clumsily.

"You're still here?" In the dim glow of a sputtering

kerosene lantern, Cat whirled on him. "Does it give you amusement?" She felt wretched. An eejit. Trying to be someone she was not. Wanting so much… Cat could not put it into words. The loneliness. The yearning to belong—somewhere.

"No one minded or noticed," his voice murmured in the silence save for the guttering kerosene work lamp. "Forgotten already. They're out there, dancing a—what does one call it? A hoedown, a jig?"

Cat ignored his words. "Like your precious Lady Audrina, I don't need you. Not even as a friend. Yes, all right," Cat said grudging, "you—you have been a friend. But—why?"

He gazed, perplexed. "Mayhap, someday you might conjure up the reason," he murmured, looking into tear-glittering eyes, then averting his gaze.

"Well! I haven't forgotten! I see you are still wearing it!" The voice shattered the gloom. Hugo groaned, rolling his eyes upward, making a moue at Cat as Audrina stormed through the drapes, looking first at Hugo and then at Catriona with scorn. "Spare me your maudlin attempts at seduction, Hugo. I don't care what *Maman* says, I still want that dress. I changed my mind. You will fix it!" She stabbed a finger at Catriona.

Cat backed as Audrina snatched the shoulder of the dress, once again intending to disrobe her.

"I will take it off!"

"Audrina! This young lady says she will return your gown."

"I want it *now*! You will remove it from your slatternly body, and be glad I don't burn your pathetic rags in the stove." She marched over to the cast iron stove and opened the lid with the lever. "If you do not wish to embarrass Hugo, I suggest he leave."

Hugo looked from Cat's obdurate face, to Audrina's hateful one, bowed, and said, "As you wish. I shall go, but only because—" and then he, as usual, tripped over the butter churn, leaving the rest unsaid with, "Oh, dear! I am sorry!"

"Leave it!" Cat snapped.

Whey milk washed over the tile floor she had spent the morning mopping.

Cat could not wait. She began stripping the satin shoulders down.

She would need now to mend as well as to clean it. Soon, standing in the rags and tatters of her grubby shift, washed a hundred times to near sheerness, and mended knickers beneath.

Gray and ugly as I am, Cat thought.

"All right. Now I shall have it."

Audrina stomped through the milk puddle, heedless, holding out a ridged hand for the dread gown wadded in Cat's arms. At that point Madame parted the drapes, looking from Cat to Audrina. Marching closer, she shook her kitchen help by the arm.

"Did you do this? Did you steal this dress?" she had the grace to ask.

Audrina, her fists in knots, a vein throbbing in her forehead, shouted in Madame's face. "Are you calling me a prevaricator? That I do not recognize my own gowns?"

Madame Solange glared, unused to being called down or shouted at, but she kept her lips tight. Then all three turned at the sound of thumping and the feeling of the floor shaking as, yanking the drapes aside, Little Mae's tugboat figure approached on heavy feet. She studied each woman with solemn eyes, her gaze flicking over the now hated and wrinkled blue dress.

"No, ma'am. Cat didn't steal that there dress. That there dress was shure nuff stuffed in the trash barrel. I seen it. Fixin' on fetchin' it out myself and making somethin', but Cat beat me to it. I even spied this one"—she jabbed a thick thumb at Audrina—"toss it in. Wouldn'ta fit me none nohows. Don't know why, but Cat here shure didn't steal it or nuthin'. The dang thing had been thrown away, fer shure."

Madame turned to both Lady Audrina and Catriona. "Is this true?"

"Shure nuff, God's truth." Mae stuck her oar in again. "Seen it under Mr. Levi's worn-out boots you done flung out."

"Liars!" Audrina's face turned uglier. "You all stick together like thieving magpies, don't you?"

"Here now! I ain't no magpie," Mae replied. "And I sure ain't wrinklin' up my face till I looks like a old prune."

Audrina gasped.

Madame was torn. Assuage Lady Audrina, or hear out the truth? "Milady." She half-ducked a curtsey. "You shall have your gown back in the morn, good as new. I'm not sure how it got in the trash in back," she said with the heavy flatness of a stove lid. "Yet I'm certain none of us had anything to do with it. Please forgive our backwoods ways. We may not be high class like you, but we are God-fearing."

Audrina did not want to end the humiliation, looking from glowering Little Mae—and if she ever glowered at you, you would think several times over calling her a liar—to Cat. To her everlasting reward, Madame took

Audrina firmly by the arm, forcibly shoving the virago back to the festivities, murmuring, "Now let us leave this behind and enjoy ourselves... Have you tried my syllabub?"

Cat sighed, checking the dress for damage. Upon hearing a snicker, she kenned her humiliation was not complete. There leaned Arabella, sipping punch, taking Audrina's place in her mortification. Cat covered her shimmy to hide mended patches.

Arabella sashayed closer, taking in her dingy underthings. "What would you be needing a silk dress for anyway? Nothing but a gutter-rat. Good for naught but the kitchens. Your pa and ma probably weren't even hitched, like your kind don't."

"Why do you hate me so?" Cat blurted. "I've done nothing to you."

Arabella narrowed her eyes, deciding. "Have you ever looked into a mirror?"

"M-maybe," Cat stammered, wondering what barb was heading her way now.

"Oh, please, don't play the innocent. Under all that roughness, you are very pretty, Miss Sly Puss, as if you don't know." Arabella scrutinized Cat. "Pretty in an odd way. All that hair, and your figure is far from slim. And those weird eyes. But there is no accounting what men favor." She uttered it as if men were from an unknown planet.

She sipped. "I've seen you spy on your betters, and my brother. Think they know you're alive? You'll never be anything but an ignorant drudge to them."

Cat could take no more, feeling her eyes burn. Spinning, she paced to the back door. She would not run. She would not let Arabella see her sobbing.

****

It wasn't until Catriona got to her attic room that she allowed herself to weep. Why! Why? Why could she not be more like them? Graceful, elegant, without even trying, with sleek hair and complexions unmarred by the merest freckle bridging her short nose; not the refined knife blade of any one of them. Her bosom was too large. Hips too wide. Hair too wild to be tamed, and scrunchy to boot. Her accent mired in country, compared to their lyrical tones.

Still, why did they look down upon her so?

Except Hugo.

He had been kind. She had been unkind.

They had no idea who she was or where she hailed from, yet by accident of birth, they were superior. She wiped an errant tear and took inventory in her small spotted mirror. Somehow Cat kenned life would always be unfair and that she had to fight with every simple tool she had to rise above it, no matter what.

Cat lay on her cot, pondering the day. Madame, to her shock, popped up through the trap door. She hesitated, then stepped on up, bit her lip, and quietly, not looking at Cat, laid a nice little lace collar on the wood box used for a nightstand, and left, keeping her face averted. That bit of innocent lace somehow hurt worse than all the rest. Cat held it to her face and finally wept aloud.

****

Lady Daphne paced in her room, which grew ever smaller with two of them forced to cohabit among their luggage, flounces, and furbelows.

What to do—what to do?

"I fear we are close to being tossed out on our ear.

You must cease this constant harassment. I saw the look on Mortimer's face."

Lady Audrina, still smarting from her run-in with Little Mae and Madame, barely heard. An old saw anyway. She pouted.

"But *ma mère*, why cannot you snag Uncle Mortimer? You could trick him or something. Get him drunk…put him in a compromising position—anything!"

"Audrina! What, pray tell, do you know of compromising positions?" Daphne eyed her critically. Audrina sulked and wouldn't answer.

Flopped on the bed, her troublesome daughter seemed to have gained weight. Her face was yet fair, and the added plumpness softened an increasing sharpness of nose and cheek, yet her bosom and hips were swelling alarmingly. Already her stays had been let out to the end of the strings, and her gowns were bursting their seams, even allowing for a growing girl—it wouldn't do.

"Audrina you must quit eating."

Audrina scarcely paused, slipping another biscuit—they called them "cookies" here, for some odd reason—into her mouth, which was already crammed with crumbs. "But *ma mère*, there's precious little else to do. The only nice things they have to eat are the sweets and what they serve for pudding."

"There is walking. There is your embroidery and your crewel work. We were to make new gowns. That is why I sold my last pearls! My choker!" She looked off, bereft. How humiliating to sell one's pearls to a shoddy mercantile. She shuddered to think she might spy them roped on the bosom of some farmer's wife!

Audrina released a long sigh that seemed to deplete

her lungs. "Ohhh! *Maman*! Where is there to walk in this dull place?"

"Wylder might not be so dull if you would stir yourself. There is a dress goods shop. We could have some day gowns whipped up, to save your finery." *And make them larger.*

"What pray tell would I find here?" Audrina curled her lip. "Cheap cottons with appalling patterns? Coarse muslin to chafe my skin? And what trapper's wife would I find as seamstress?"

"Take a buggy, hire a horse! We've enough for that—if nothing else, I may sell more of my jewelry— the ladies here are sadly lacking," she said with some irony.

Knowing the full price of her pearls would send a buyer reeling from shock.

"And, my dear, wedding Mortimer. As much as I would like to make that liaison, that simply could not be, as you well know. The old goat!"

Lady Audrina opened her mouth, allowing a crumb to dribble, brushing her bare bosom. Never had she heard her mother utter such coarseness.

"There is such a thing as appearance, Audrina! Mortimer thinks of me as a sister, as do most in our circle, even though we are not thus related, actually." She eyed her daughter slyly. This would put her wind up. "There's always Hugo. He might have some money."

"Hugo! I would rather die a dried-up spinster! He's a nothing—a nobody! I would rather wed a— a miner, or run off with the next tinker passing through. I would…"

"If you were not so obstinate, you could make a play yourself for the duke," Daphne uttered waspishly. "And when the end, God forfend, arrives… Well?" She flipped her hand. "You would be a duchess in your own right."

Audrina's answer was to slam from the room, stopping to pinch her cheeks and bite her lips. Perhaps Aaron might be below, and they'd worn their arguments to tatters.

Daphne sighed and picked up some stockings. Mending! She, who had had two lady's maids and a full staff. Mending! She who scarce knew how to thread a needle.

*****

She should have been praying for forgiveness for sins of pride and malice, of envy and even hate. Cat fidgeted, watching the plump schoolmistress energetically thump organ keys, pumping through the seemingly unending notes of all five verses of seven hymns, from "Abide With Me" to a rousing rendition of "Holy, Holy, Holy." She put her penny in the collection, noting a few buttons among five-cent pieces and other coins, and skirted past parishioners lining for the pastor's last words of benediction.

He wasn't a proper priest, so Cat left guilt behind.

Madame had apparently forgiven her. She had a second chance. Soon the English would be gone.

And that wretched Hugo.

She hated him.

****

As her daughter schemed ways to disentangle Aaron from the upstart so far beneath her, her mother had stratagems of her own. Desperation and her daughter's wild expositions took on a life of their own. Why not? What did she have to lose? Discounting Audrina's all-too-frequent bouts of moody, sullen brooding, Lady

Daphne rehearsed what she would say.

Even now her daughter stuffed herself with great stodgy blocks of cornbread liberally smeared with blackstrap, a dish she avoided like the plague in London and with the aid of which she would soon resemble the Christmas goose. Her strong-willed daughter was bored.

She must do something drastic before all their wheels fell off.

Lady Daphne approached the duke on the Longhorn's wide veranda, where he enjoyed after-dinner cigars and watched the town of Wylder jolt by. She would have preferred a quiet, velvet-paneled lounge, or a snuggery. Nevertheless, diffidently, she sat next to him as an old chum, who happened to be wearing a deeply low-cut sheer dressing gown, and who was also thrilled by the unhurried parade in silence, until she judged it right to plunge in.

"Dear Mortimer…" Still facing the street, she murmured, continuing, "I put this rather indelicately… yet, we are old friends and acquaintances. I presume on our past familiarity and family connection to hope you will not take this remiss."

"My dear Daphne!" He removed his cigar with a slight moue. "What is so grave you should take such a formal approach? Out with it. Are you, shall we say, as the youth of today so crudely put it, 'smitten again'?"

Lady Daphne summoned a pretty blush, not too difficult under the circumstances, and hesitantly turned. "Dare I say it?"

"By all means." A slight annoyance twisted his mustache as Lord Mortimer's fingers drummed the survey plat map on the table-turned-desk beside him overflowing with charts, arcane books, faded maps, and scribbled notes and ledgers. A lump of copper held down the mass.

"Oh, dear Mortimer, I dare name it! Over the years your friendship and consideration for me have come to be so—so cherished. My affection has over-spilled, I fear, into an—" she dropped her eyes, flicking a look at him, and tested a soft tremulous smile "—abiding love."

Bunching his silvery brows, Lord Mortimer gazed at her with consternation as if she were a new animal or mineral he was assessing. Then he let out a roar of laughter. "Oh, very good, Daphne! And what prank, pray tell, is this about? Trying to wheedle new dress money, I wager." Here, he dug in his pocket and shoved over a gold eagle almost as dismissal.

Lady Daphne ground her molars. She did not want charity. Crumbs thrown to pigeons. However, she managed a dimpled smile, slipping the sovereign into a ruffle without seeming to.

"Oh, Mortimer! You are overly generous! Why, you treat Audrina as your own daughter, imagine that!" She tinkled like stepped-on ice in a frozen pond. Cracked and sharp.

"True." He nodded with some asperity, glancing forlornly at the plat map. She rushed on. She wouldn't settle for one sovereign, now she was on track like a runaway freight train, even if she went flying off the rails, crashing and burning. He would see it her way! Was she not "a fine piece of horse flesh," as a cruder member of his sex had once put it?

"But Mortimer, you do not understand. Though grateful," she hastened to say, clutching the coin tighter, "the truth is, before God, I love you." It was spoken with the blushing shyness of a virginal maiden, after dropping in humble supplication, her fair head on his knee, spoiled only by the gritting of her teeth. And boniness of his knees.

"I realize that and am grateful for your affection, dearest Daphne!" He lifted her up. "As I do Audrina's as well. Why do you need my affirmation? Are you in a state?"

Lord Mortimer looked about as if desperate to lay hands on smelling salts. Mayhap it was one of those female complaints they were prone to, when for a few days each month they went a bit balmy and touchy. *Poor dears.*

His manner grew uneasy. He fidgeted in his chair.

She could feel it in the tension of the arm she so lightly held in supplication. *No! No! Not 'I love you too'?* She could not help bringing her narrow elegant foot, in its equally elegant slipper, albeit with hole in the sole and smudge on the satin instep, down hard on the floor. The desired effect was missing, as the sound was merely a childish slap. Inhaling harshly, she began again. Why was the man so consequently obtuse?

"I mean I have a genuine—a lasting—affection for you, and we needn't let sanguinity stand in the way of true happiness and contentment in, in our…" she hesitated, "golden years."

Faced with his unchanging features, she added desperately, "I would be a good and gallant, even…" again she hesitated, "a passionate wife!"

"Oh dear. Oh dear! You are overwrought. It would be unseemly. Why, I care for you as—as a daughter, or niece, as you well are, I think." He frowned in concentration. "Never thought of it. Family trees are so convoluted. Come, let us put these importunate speculations behind us and"—his eyes strayed to the plat map—"get on with our evening."

"Your evening! Your evening! Audrina and I are dying here!"

She slapped the maps and paraphernalia from the table, splashing the inkpot's contents across the tabletop in chase. "What about ours?" she bawled in unseemly passion. She was instantly sorry. "Forgive me—a woman's vapors."

Mortimer flushed tomato-red, coughed, and groaned. "Of course, of course. You go…ah… rest… these things…these things be best unmentioned."

Daphne's cheeks flamed. He supposed her a weak woman prone to monthly spasms! She had never…and never would now, she briefly mourned. Yet Audrina was quite enough offspring for an entire village of Cossacks.

"I will not mention it again," she murmured with a rueful face. "Passing fancy only. One does feel ennui, from time to time. A jest, actually. How I did get you going!" She gave her brittle tinkle, swatting his shoulder with her fan.

"Splendid! Now what shall you do tomorrow? Put some color in those pale cheeks—a symbol of breeding in London, but here? Get some roses blooming, and who knows?" Mortimer chortled. "Another chappy might strike your fancy," he said, rather awkwardly for him.

Lord Greville never kenned how close he came to having the ashtray beside him make an indentation in his silver mane.

"Naturally, dear Mortimer," Daphne ground out. She must retake lost ground. At the moment, she felt like a hidden fox with the white muzzled hounds of age braying after her. "As always, you've a wiser head on your shoulders than a silly woman such as I could ever hope, and that's why Audrina and I are so grateful to be under your wing."

"Ah—um, yes," he said shortly.

Lady Daphne saw she could venture no further up this path.

"Good night, dear Mortimer."

****

"Well, *Maman*, that went well."

"Sneak. You were listening!"

"I suppose your 'withered wiles' did not sway him." Audrina's curved smile did not quite soothe the sting.

"Never mind," Lady Daphne muttered, looking into the distance. "He leaves me no choice."

While Lady Audrina plotted whatever her latest scheme—her mother kenned the signs—Lady Daphne dressed again before rooting through their jumbled baggage to retrieve from a side pouch a rather frayed deck of cards and slip them into pockets that were cunningly secreted behind a profusion of ruffles. Then she whipped out, heading down to the saloon with a determined face.

Chapter Eleven
Luck of the Draw

The Right Honorable Lady Daphne perched in the Longhorn's quietest corner quaffing tea, and laying cards in a pattern called Grandfather's Clock. Her presence was not hidden but not obvious, as she intended.

Madame had had to make another run to the mercantile to fetch the tea, as the usual Longhorn clientele did not run to Earl Grey. Nevertheless, Daphne made do with rather coarse black China leaf as she sipped, grimaced, and idly spread cards, ignoring random curiosity seekers who wanted to tinder conversation.

Dear Mortimer was off on another quest of the Holy Grail of Copper Mines, dragging poor Hugo along for note-taking, no doubt relieving himself of her own suffocating company.

At length, one brave man approached. He pinched his cowboy hat and kibbitzed, thumbs in gun belt. Daphne, ignoring him, looked confused, as if deep into where to place her black three of spades—on the red four of diamonds, or the red heart?

"See ya like the cards."

Lady Daphne snapped the black spade on the red diamond rather forcefully.

Unencouraged, he plowed on. "Ever play One-Eyed Jack? Now, there's a game worth your time."

"I regret I did not catch your name," Daphne commented with frost in her voice.

The man dragged over a chair and swung a leg over it, facing the back. "Oh, well, now, ma'am, don't mind givin' it."

Daphne did not correct him. He was a boor, but she'd played this bloody game for two days now with no viable takers.

"A popular game hereabout, One-Eyed Jack," he encouraged.

She looked pointedly at his hat.

He belatedly tipped it, only to sling it on the next chair. "Name's Hank, fer Henry. Glad to show ya the ropes. Might be a tad more interesting than whatcha got there—"

"Solitaire," she murmured and bit her lip. Steady on! "Yes?" She smiled gently. "It might be amusing. I thank you for your kindness."

"Think nothin' fer it, ma'am, or is it—" he winked "—miss?"

She couldn't help it. It was ingrained in her prideful make-up.

"It's *Lady* Daphne." She was peeved when he didn't bat an eye.

"Welp! I knew you weren't a lad. Hah-hah!" He gave Daphne's ribs a painful elbow.

Oh, dear gods.

"I got all week, seems like, till next roundup."

"Oh, yes?" she murmured politely. "How exciting, out on the trail, free as a bird. Do show me."

****

He felt his oats. Here he was palaverin' with a miss too big for her britches. *Wait'll I tell the fellas this!*

Expertly the cowpoke riffled cards. "Now, this is how you do it."

Lady Daphne finished her tea, watching him over the rim of the Longhorn's best china.

Some time later, she was heard to say, "I am sorry. I do apologize. Was I not supposed to play this? They look so pretty all lined up in a row like that. Imagine four queens and that nice ace!"

He narrowed his eyes. "Yeah, that'll do."

She twinkled. "Oh, my! Such fun! I do believe you owe me a debt of honor?"

"Honor! Hell's fire, lady. Looks like five gold eagles to me."

Lady Daphne coughed, turning her head. She must wind this up soon before she got miner's lung. That was his fifth straight rolled smoke.

"Well, give me a chance ta cut my losses!"

"Shall I deal this time?" Carefully, after a quick dab to her lips, Lady Daphne dealt. "Three aces and two kings." She studied the chart he had scribbled for her on a cheap pocket notebook. "I do believe that beats your two queens and three twos? Is that right?"

He'd even listed a blinkin' diagram of hands for her, from three of a kind all the way up to a royal flush, aces high. Funny how she never referred to it after the first hand or two.

"Jumpin' Jehoshaphat! that's yer tenth straight pot!" Her opponent tossed down his cards in disgust.

"Oh, dear. I so regret this. I don't ken what to do…" She looked appealingly at him, placing her fine fingertips to her cheeks. "Perhaps, if we play a few more hands, you might recoup some of my lucky ones. Do you think that would work?"

"Hell's fire and spare the matches, no! Luck me inta the poor house!" He stopped fingering his wallet under the table while Daphne patiently waited. "Aye. We'll just do that! Beginner's luck can't hold forever." He hitched the chair closer and clamped a cheroot in his lips, grinding it to shreds between his teeth.

A half hour later, he staggered off, cheroot chewed to rags, tipping the chair over and mumbling something about, "…a gallon of rye whiskey and devils in women's corsets."

Lady Daphne ignored the discreet, gathered crowd as she prettily raked the last pot of crumpled bills and various coins into her reticule, now heavy as a river stone. Upon arising, she failed to note the dapper gent with one polished boot on the bar rail brushing his trim mustache.

****

"*Maman*! How loathsome! I saw you from the gallery, too mortified to descend. Consorting with common rabble," Audrina reproved.

"His money is sovereign, my spoiled poppet."

"Really, *Maman*, what will folks say?"

Daphne lifted an elegant shoulder. "They will note you have new gowns, my pet, to lure the honeybees."

****

The card sharpie speculated from the bar. His own cards burned a hole in his pocket. He studied the grand dame in the mirror, how she bit her lip and studied her solitaire layout—one bewildering to him but apparently called Napoleon at St. Helena, or Forty Thieves—with the assiduous attention a monk gave to the Lost Testaments.

Fingers hovering, laying down, shaking golden curls

in hesitation, finally selecting, and stewing anew. Then he saw her take the dumb cowpoke for every last Confederate wooden nickel. He grinned in admiration, wiping the rum from his 'stache, flipping a coin onto the bar, and rising.

"Time I showed the little lady a few tricks out of the goodness of my heart and the flatness of my purse," he told himself, strolling by as if on the way to another table. He did not view a comely female but a lady's reticule stuffed with cash, perched on the chair.

"Oh, I say! Lovely game ain't—isn't it?"

"Yes, indeed," she murmured, mildly flustered, or so it would seem. Lady Daphne colored, dipped her head, then studied him with a cool gaze. "Have I your acquaintance, sir?"

He smiled to himself. "Well, we ain—haven't been properly introduced, but I won't tell. You play—" he looked askance at her complicated layout spread over the table "—um, anything else?"

"Why, yes!" she declared, warming. "Just a bit of whist with my friends back in—" Dropping her voice she daringly flirted, "Old Smoky. We are," she simpered, "quite cut-throat! You would not be safe, I dare say."

The shark bit back a snort. Good act.

"You don't play with your hubby?" He made it a leer.

"Hubby? Oh, no, I am a single lady, sir. Otherwise, I should not be chatting with you on such familiar terms." Lady Daphne's cheeks blushed becomingly.

"Old Smoky? Ah! Thought you might be a swell from London Town."

"Mmmm…yes." She graciously dipped her head with no other encouragement.

He waited, not showing discomfort save for a twitching mustache. "Can two play that game?" He motioned at the layout.

"Oh, no!" She tinkled. "That is why they name it Solitaire!" *You bumpkin...*

"That right? Well, seems a tad unneighborly, even unfriendly."

He wasn't sure yet what her real game was. Outside of giving him lip.

Lucky beginner, or seasoned player?

By that time, the sharpie had already taken his ease, crossing muscular legs in his tight fawn trews in the seat opposite, amicably chatting. Either way, he could take the stuck-up bitch. "Perhaps, dear lady, I could learn you"—he pursed lips provocatively—"a gambit or two?'

"Well as to that…" She exhaled gustily. "I'm sure I could not teach you a thing." She batted lashes, smiling winsomely.

"Don't know about that," he said easily. "I do have a few games you might take back to entertain your card partners."

Her gaze flickered with hope, then modestly dropped. "And what might those be?"

"Poker, ma'am. Easy to learn, though you have to have a keen mind and a good memory."

"Indeed," she responded earnestly. "My friends say I recall too much."

****

He reached his muscular brown hand across the cards and took hers, giving it a gentle shake. Lady Daphne gazed up all aflutter at the handsome stranger, with her other hand on her breast—after a discreet brushing of her thigh.

"Shall we celebrate our new-found acquaintance with a libation from the bar?"

Lady Daphne grimaced sweetly. "I don't believe they have sherry."

He groaned.

"No. Um, perhaps a tot of their finest whiskey, ma'am?"

She pursed her lips prettily. "I shouldn't mind."

The look he threw her bowed head bespoke, *This will be too easy. She thought she was a hustler. She never met one till now.* He crowed silently. Now he could relieve her of her ill-gotten gains. He grinned, tossed his first whiskey back, and nudged hers closer.

"Perhaps a quieter table, away from the riffraff?" she suggested, glancing quickly at a growing crowd all eyes.

****

They were in a quiet corner shielded by a large potted fern. A large stack of chips toppled near Daphne's elbow as she frowned at her cards. She ignored them, shuffling, reshuffling, as if in a dither of indecision, till the sharpie's eyes crossed as he scowled into her growing pile of coins and bills.

The sharp sipped watered whiskey, sourly watching Lady Daphne rake in her eighth pot to his measly two and sip her fourth tot of whiskey—so far, between the libations she lapped up like mother's milk, and the pots, he was out one hundred seventy-five bucks. How did she do it? She was costing him a bundle he could scarce afford. Wiping a trickle of sweat from his eyes, he glumly eyed the pile of bills at her frothy elbow, beside her towering stack of Longhorn chips.

He narrowed his eyes.

Never saw so many ruffles and furbelows on one female!

And she caught on so blooming fast! Recall, hah! He chewed his mustache. That lady'd been around the block a few times, he suspicioned at last. *There's cards tucked beneath those sleeve ruffles, and somehow in those flounces, by gum.*

He squinted, searching for telltales in her face or form. She had a way of throwing her wrist out, there again, at the last deal, grabbing her hand before she could withdraw it.

"What's up that pretty lace furbelow there?" He trapped her hand with one of his, groping under the flounce covering her wrist and hand to the first knuckle with the other. "Yes-sir-re-bob, hides yer whole hand, don't it?" he slurred, grinning his lupine smile beneath the slim foxy mustache at her frown. "Easy to skin a ace or two outa there, betcha."

"I have not a clue what you are gibbering about." Daphne yanked at her hand, looking past him for Rattlesnake Jake. She was certain he was onto her game, but he would never rat on her.

"That's right, lady, card hustling's a serious past-time."

"Please, sir, you are quite offensive." Daphne spoke mildly, as if he were a minor irritant, finally pulling back her hand from his iron grip.

"Not as 'fensive as I'm bound to be if I find you bin a lowdown lyin' cheat." Before she could rise, he grabbed her arm and scrambled about around her hips, tearing at the lace, as she glanced quickly side to side. The room was quiet, yet Rattlesnake Jake was behind the bar, thank God.

She made a distressed noise.

"Shut yer pie-hole. Be more'n me fired up, if I find somethin'." All his gentlemanly, man-of-the-world veneer slewed off like rotten onion skin.

At the sacrifice of a lace ruffle, Daphne sat down.

She kenned the secret pocket secure in her sleeve would not be found on casual inspection, nor the many pockets in the froth of her dress. All she ever need do was withdraw her hand from her knee, or her hip, or flip her wrist and play the hole card. They all had the same backing. Yet his clumsy scrambling, something no gentleman of her class would ever attempt, might find the secret pockets by force as he ferreted under her wrist ruffle.

"Sir!" She bolted up so fast, drawing to her full five feet, six inches, that she left him blinking. "You are a scoundrel! I refuse to have congress with you in this sorry drunken state! Jake?"

Jake calmly reached below the bar. Before the sharpie could register a rifle, he was gawping at the writhing rattlesnake that Jake held pincered behind its head. Jake turned the snake's snout to himself, whispering—no doubt—sweet nothings to his pet.

Daphne swept the winnings into her reticule, struggling with the hefty bag, and with head high paced loftily to the stairs, giving Jake a nod, leaving the sharp staring after.

Jake would be rewarded later.

Giving her hips an extra switch for Jake's benefit, she glanced coolly over her shoulder at her gambler friend, who apparently did not ken she was used to drinking several rounds of spirits, from aperitifs to the last port before bedtime, and beaucoup wines between courses of not-so-long-ago banquets. She had, to put it crudely, an acquired hollow leg.

****

Lady Daphne swept in. Her daughter lounged by the window, devouring an apple and reading a novel lent by the questionable female in the front bedroom.

"*Eveline. The Amorous Adventures of a Victorian Lady*!" Indeed! She decided to ignore Audrina's questionable reading material, to not deflect from her minor triumph. Throwing her back to the door, she slumped somewhat before hurling the reticule to the bed, where it made a satisfying thump and jingle of coins and rustle of bills.

Besides, she might borrow the novel. Boredom was crushing her like hammers on walnuts.

"There! New shoes, boots, a gown or two, you need a cape, and at very least, a renewal of our undergarments."

Actually, the Lady Audrina had not been reading but gazing broodily out the window, unseeing, at the dull clapboard wall of the Five Star Saloon, her thoughts far inward, deep "in her blackest soul," if she had to put her novel's words to thought.

Audrina raised her brows. "Again, *ma mère*? Really. What riffraff did you manage to—I heard the most amusing quip— 'hornswoggle' this time?"

"Don't look down on me, my fine poppet." She smacked her lightly. "Plus, this might buy us a dressmaker, and even my pearls back. Might yet gain a decent evening dress."

"Little Mae," Audrina waved the book, "mentioned a lady of questionable virtue—a Miss Adelaide, who orders dress goods from San Francisco."

"Mmmm." Her mother nodded, thinking closer to home would stretch the ready.

"Not like the salons. Eh, *Maman*?" Audrina had a waspish side, frequently stinging her mother. This time the stinger aimed true.

Daphne's face changed color. It was common knowledge rashness had led her to gamble what little inheritance she had, after the death of her husband and duties, against cannier players in wealthy salons, all in the name of recalled buying sprees she could no longer afford.

She had been desperate to make a match for Audrina, or herself, which was why she'd accepted Mortimer's invitation with alacrity. Debtor's prison loomed even if she returned, now. She rose, haughtily swishing her long train behind her as a way of fending off Audrina. She still missed her husband dearly. She must not be seen weakening. She could not seem needy! Especially to Mortimer.

Chapter Twelve
Ugly Onyx Brooch

The evening, before, over an unexciting repast of river trout, but with discussion of the latest mine excursion, which both Lord Mortimer and Hugo enthused over, Audrina appeared her usual aloof self, yet beneath sweeping lashes she was excruciatingly aware of every move made by Catriona, who had apparently been drafted into serving. After the dress episode, she supposed wrongly that Madame Solange would have chucked the thieving wretch out. And away from Aaron's proximity.

Cat wore her mud-brown gown, her embarrassing mass of crinkly hair barely tamed by a straggly red ribbon. Still, with the odd eyes, milk-white complexion, and becoming rose-pink blushes, the handspan waist and high bosom, Catriona was still striking despite her hard life or possibly because of it. Even in the darkest part of her heart, Audrina recognized that quality.

She was used to being the most fetching female in the room, with overflowing dance cards and inveigles into dark corners for covert kisses.

Audrina had swayed like a willow tree when she walked, gracefully leaned, or turned her head—at least before she gained a rather stodgy waist. She misted over, reflecting, munching her apple. When she raised her hands, it was as if she lifted lilies. She was tall, with a wealth of glossy, wheat-colored hair and an intriguing purr to her voice which she kenned drove men to distracting dreams of what they would like to do with her out on the balconies or in quiet places in Saint James Park. Was that all a vanished dream, a whisper of a memory?

It posed a mystery why potential suitors, and there had been many, seemed fleeting as the last rose of summer, attentions going from fulsome, overpowering blooms into withered, drooping brown petals within a fortnight. Somehow, she feared in her most introspective cold-blooded moments, she had no lasting allure.

And now, in the back of beyond and a stone heavier, she found no eligible men in sight—scarce as hen's teeth, she overheard one uncouth citizen of Wylder comment.

She must, as they say, level the playing field.

Even now, "the Cat" was making very obvious eyes at the one man who made her very breath seize from across the saloon. Audrina's body swooned with sudden desire. Perhaps because he was the only likely candidate for her favored attentions. Still smoldering over her slanted glimpse of the two of them as he handed her down from the horse, before she lost sight from the window.

Aaron.

Aaron, she dreamed. Tall, dashing as a Queen's Guard. Eyes like the finest summer day. A way of looking at one, as if slowly peeling away layers of clothing, a lingering gaze as if hands skimmed one's body.

No more unfair competition from the kitchen drudges, thank you!

****

Mustn't waste time. And no time like the present, while she is ogling Aaron as he helps the loathsome bartender. Wiping lips daintily on the second napkin Cat had ironed only that dawn, she dropped it on the floor and, making her excuses, slipped upstairs.

Now.

What could she afford to lose if all went end-over-teakettle?

She rooted her jewel box.

That dreary onyx brooch.

She frowned and shook her head.

What if Mortimer died? All that stamping about in cold, clammy, dangerous mines! Must be all of fifty. She must have correct funereal finery. She shook her head, reluctantly replacing it.

Audrina grubbed about the silk lining, discarding a broken strand of pearls, the too-small amethyst ring, halting as she hauled out a dull jade brooch with a broken clasp, holding it up for inspection. Never liked it. Real gold, though, with tiny, dirt-blackened pearls surrounding the center stone.

That should do it.

Audrina snatched it from her frayed, depleted jewel box, clutching it, looked both ways in the hall—no meddlesome Little Mae this time. Skimming to the low attic door, she slipped through, climbed the short ladder, and popped up through the trap to the attic floor. Expecting a grubby, dusty garret, she made a sniff of protest.

"Well! The Irish witch certainly got the grand space. No sharing for you…" Unless Aaron… She banished the loathsome, impossible thought aborning. *Sly like a cat though, aren't you?* Audrina covetously mumpsed, eyeing the lofty beamed volume overhead, a low westering sun turning the moted air into liquid gold and spilling over to aggrandize the neat cot with the patchwork quilt…the broken mirror and small shelf with her pathetic bibelots.

Anyway, not for her the garret!

"Now, where shall I secret this precious jewel!" She chuckled, choking back a giggle. "Not too difficult to ferret out, yet not obvious, either. Hmmm?"

Somewhere a board cracked like a gunshot. Expanding timbers? A foot on the ladder? She listened, tense. Oh, to be humiliated snooping about the kitchen scut's lair. She would rather die.

Audrina tiptoed, listening.

Tomb silent.

As she returned to the center of the lofty space, she caught a faded spot of color—a red tea chest tucked against one of the slanted braces.

Rather nice, that. Quaint. She wished she could take it, but where would she put it? She made a face at herself. *Might spring my own trap.* Sensibly, she put it back, then dragged it out again. *Why not?* She chortled. *That's the sort of thing a stupid country girl would do.*

Grinning, Audrina eagerly unlatched the tiny knob and pulled out first a drawer, then saw the small space in back. Perfect. Yanking out the drawer, she rammed the ugly brooch in. The replaced drawer protruded ever so slightly.

Not too obvious, yet one might wonder why it could not close, and inspect it. She curved a smile, catching an eye tooth and so appearing lupine for the moment, with eyes half-closed, slanted with satisfaction.

****

"I simply cannot find it anywhere, *Maman*!"

Lady Daphne, buttering rich, airy biscuits for which the Longhorn's kitchen was famous, regretted the battle between her waist and her ever-constraining stays. Few enough comforts, she grumbled. I deserve this! She was reaching for the clotted gooseberry preserves when her spoiled daughter came flying down the stairs with yet another complaint. Lord kenned she had enough of her own!

Daphne groaned, swallowing the airy goodness and sighing as she dabbed her lips. "What is troubling you now, dearest heart?"

"Oh, *ma mère*! It has vanished!" Audrina plopped dramatically on the seat across. Audrina was never a very good actress. Betimes, after a particularly dramatic tantrum, Lady Daphne called her Sarah, after Bernhardt, yet now, seeing Audrina with her arm crooked to shield her eyes, was a bit much.

"What, pray tell, my pet? You most likely misplaced—" She contemplated the last biscuit—funny they called them that—rapidly losing its steamy lusciousness, just as she, moreover, was losing her interest in Audrina's latest melodrama.

"My brooch!"

Daphne looked around for an audience. Her daughter had chosen the time when the witch on a broom was peering from the bar, from whence she daily harangued the creature Rattlesnake Jake, and Levi could be seen fiddling with books behind the register.

How mortifying.

"Which, darling?" She asked shortly.

"The jade! It matched my eyes."

Daphne frowned at nothing in particular, mulling

Audrina's declaration, eventually recalling the ugly piece. The dull drab stone did not favor anything, leave alone Audrina's eyes. Positively bilious! She'd quite forgotten the gift from a spinster aunt in her salad days.

Now, every bauble no matter how homely counted, she supposed.

But still.

"That dreary piece?" Perplexed, she set down her knife. *Might as well let the rest get cold.*

"Yes. Gone! Right from my jewel box." Audrina glanced round to her audience. She saw Madame studiously appearing not to listen.

"I've torn our room asunder. It was a gift from… oh, I cannot recall who. But it was my favorite pin!"

The duchess raised her eyes at that, but did not reprove her daughter.

"I'm sure we will find it, my sweet. The room isn't that large." She addressed Madame Solange sideways.

"I saw that kitchen maid, only yesterday! She looked to be leaving our room. She said she was cleaning!" Audrina addressed the remainder of the saloon, and most likely, the streets of Wylder. "All servants are thieves at heart."

****

Catriona stood at the bottom of the small stairs leading to the trap door.

It was open.

She heard commotion, footfalls pounding, racing hither and thither across her dusty boards, Lady Audrina's excited voice piercing the air. Madame Solange too. Cat's nose sensed her clove perfume.

"I am certain, as I am of the sun rising in the east, we shall find it here in this very attic. I saw her lurking!"

Lady Audrina declared.

Cat overheard Madame sigh. "Perhaps, milady, she was merely coming to her room?" Cat flinched at Madame's humble-pie voice. She who never backed from confrontation.

"Oh! Of course, you would side with her! For all I know, you are all a den of thieves here, and we shall be murdered in our beds." Audrina's voice held an hysterical viper's sting.

Catriona popped through the trap in time to see Madame Solange's sallow cheek bloom with outrage as if Audrina had slapped her, yet with the kennage she could do little to stem Audrina's insults if she wished their further custom. She would not give up the old duke's windfall or the reason to lord it over the Vincent House. It would be mortifying to have her exalted guests scarper to Wylder's other place of lodging.

Cat wanted nothing more than to duck. This was no good at all, a-tall.

Mayhap Audrina wanted her precious attic room in place of the one shared. It did not seem likely, but—

Anger made her slam back the trap and burst up into the attic demanding, "Madame, can I be helpin' you some? What is it you be needin' me to do? Or are ye after finished?"

"As if you don't know!" Audrina whirled to face her, pointing a ridged finger. "Look at the innocent sly puss! Your guilt is written all over you. Common thief is what you are. First the locket. And then after my gown!" She wailed. Screwing up her face, she managed to squeeze out a tear.

Cat took a deep breath. "What is it I'm accused of thievin' then—of purloining, Madame?"

"Purloining!" Audrina scoffed. "Listen to that, will you! Fancy word for a common scut. Suppose you are too familiar with all the names for pilfering. In the old days, your hand would be cut off."

Catriona's odd eyes blazed. The hands in question folded in tight fists. Didn't she, now after, come from a line of folk who never overlooked a chance to defend oneself? It became all she could do to keep from socking Lady Audrina on her spiteful arrogant chin. "Sure an' I may be a kitchen maid and all, but I want to ken what you are doing here. This is my room!"

She glared at Madame, whose face flickered aggravation. Put in this position again, Cat faintly hoped for further charity in the face of unequal positions.

In that she was wrong. Madame Solange was weak.

Cat felt a flicker of guilt over the hanky picked up at church services, and it showed on her open face.

"Catriona. It is best you make a clean breast." Madame showed a disappointed face that did not bode well.

Would they find it? The pretty hanky?

Madame shook her finger. "It will go no easier on you if you tell lies. I am certain the good lady here would not wish to lower herself to press charges." She shot a hopeful—or warning—look at Audrina. Cat wasn't sure which.

"Are ye after thinking I took somewhat of this young lady's? Just so I ken what ye are talkin' about?"

Madame Solange wavered, glancing at Audrina.

"Perhaps I could make it right to you—you really did not actually see my kitchen maid—"

Lady Audrina narrowed her eyes into squints, hissing, "I want it back, I said! It is here." Her look was smug and knowing.

She slowly turned, hawk eyes scrutinizing Cat's attic sanctuary. Again. Enjoying every second.

"Aha!" Lady Audrina walked deliberately over to the red Chinese tea chest, smirking. "I spy with my little eye. What is this, pray tell?"

She pointed dramatically at the small chest with the slightly cockeyed drawer. Cat looked puzzled. "But that was me ma's."

"Oh, I don't covet your cheap odds-bin trash!" Audrina scorned.

Audrina had the chest locked in her arms, energetically tugging at the stuck drawer.

"Don't! Ye will be breakin' it." Cat tried to snatch it away. With a sharp cry from Audrina, the box wrenched from their hands, flying across the attic floor, near hitting Madame and shattering against the brick chimney flue. With a face of purple outrage, Audrina stuck her fingers in her mouth, crying, "Oh, you have injured me!" And, rushing over, collided with Catriona for the broken tea chest.

"Oh! See what I found?"

Triumphantly, Audrina, bending at the waist, elbowed Catriona out of the way.

"What?" Cat cried. Madame's eyes too searched the floor.

"And what is this!" Audrina swooped, plucking up the jade brooch fallen from the broken drawer, displaying it in her palm to Madame Solange, then swiveling to shove it under Cat's nose.

Cat swatted it away.

"I ken nothing of this," she cried. "This be not my doing!"

"Ha! Hidden in that cheap piece of junk? Of course not," Audrina sneered. Cat, looking up, stricken, picked up the broken pieces of her ma's treasured red Chinese tea chest, tenderly cradling them. Madame's appalled gaze darted from Cat to the offending brooch.

"Well!" Audrina tapped her foot. "What are you going to do about this outrage? I cannot, nor can my dear mother, stay here with Miss Light Fingers another second, as long as she is under this roof!"

Cat watched Madame's face, terrified of what she would find. For an instant, Madame seemed lost, shoulders drooped in defeat. She studied Catriona for a long sad moment. Cat saw her future written in that expression, as if scribbled in lightning across stormy skies.

"How? Why?" Madame breathed. Anger increased it to a wail as she wrung her hands. Lady Audrina stood with her superior expression, arms crossed, impatiently tapping her toes.

"I cannot and do not want to believe you did this, Catriona…" Madame cried. "All those other times, I believed you. The locket? The dress? You make me a fool and part of your deviousness. I thought better of you."

"You made a slave of me!" Cat cried back. She bit her lip, contrite. "But Madame Solange, please believe me! You have been kind, too. I am grateful for you takin' me in and all. I did not take that… I would never—"

Madame held up a hand ridged as a wall of iron. "Silence! Not one more lying word out of your mouth. Do not insult us. The evidence is clear."

To give credit, Catriona kenned Madame weighed her against the bounteous sums and prestige accrued from the grand gentleman. She mined a small fortune without ever wielding a miner's pick.

Madame took Audrina in with a colder than usual expression. "I shall handle this, milady. You may go. I assure you, we will make it right, and you will find a reward at your table tonight for your forbearance. Please take your brooch and go now."

Audrina sourly studied the two for a moment, then stamped her foot. "See that you do. I want her gone!" And she swept out, clutching the jade brooch so tightly spots of blood dripped on the floor.

Chapter Thirteen
Never Darken My Door

Madame was het up. Her face felt florid. This wasn't good for the baby, and it wasn't good for her. Her temples pounded like hammer blows…all Catriona's fault…her with the eyes.

"I—I have to lie down. My condition," she muttered ominously. With that she tottered out of Cat's attic, at the trap door barking, "Best get your rags and bones together. I do not want to see hide nor hair of you after the sun goes down."

Solange clutched the banister.

How could she? How could that ungrateful Irish motherless brat! She'd tried so hard to put her shame in the past, to put the tinge of the brothel far behind her. *Now this.* A den of thieves, she said.

That had been her first fledgling attempt at business—to be her own woman in a hard man's world. Not her first choice, Lord knew, but one already in the making. The girls had been 'working' the four bedrooms, unbeknownst perhaps to Levi, yet she had her doubts. The four women—Flora, Blossom, Little Mae, and Big Bertha—had no guidance, no rules, no business sense, till she arrived.

She had been a schoolmistress back in Indiana. She kenned discipline of young ladies. She put a stop to freeloaders and those who took advantage, taught the girls genteelness, etiquette, even some reading and writing, and a bit of math in Little Mae's case. Perhaps not Big Bertha, but she had her own attraction and male following.

But now, she had earned hard-won respect. A woman married, soon to be a mother, at her age. Pure and sainted by that title. Securely welded in the relationship. She was going to have Levi's child. How far she'd climbed. All that was behind her now. Levi, her anchor, now she was older, moreover owning half the Longhorn. She did not want the taint again that, knowingly, she harbored undesirables. She turned a blind eye on little Mae. A fixture. She'd been there forever. Discreet.

Her expectant condition had made her increasingly queasy, too. Nervy. Little things bothered her. She burst into floods of tears over burnt toast.

No. Catriona had to go.

Cat had just gaped at her, whilst that snip Audrina gloated.

Was she any better?

She had her suspicions over that sly puss.

"Out of here, tonight." She had repeated wearily, going over the words in her head.

"Tonight? But where will I...?" Catriona's words reverberated.

****

Lady Daphne stirred whiskey-laced tea—oh, how far she had fallen—studying her daughter's frenetic expression.

Glee. Satisfaction. Smuggery.

"You did this," she said, musing, slowly sipping her tea. "Why? The child is nothing."

Her daughter did not deny it. "I have my reasons. And you are right, *Maman*. She is nothing, now."

Lady Daphne, making a moue of sour amusement, followed her daughter's fixated gaze on the fair shining head of Aaron, the innkeeper's son. The lout, loftily crossing the room, had taken on their airs and graces. A bloody mirror, she thought bitterly. *Do we look as ridiculous, as trifling?*

Coming to, she snapped her cup onto the saucer. "The poor girl is of no consequence. She is not a rival. You must make it right. We are, after all, her betters!"

"I will not! She took my jade pin. She took my gown, and the gold locket! I will tell everyone this place harbors pilferers."

When Audrina dug her heels in, a pack of mules could be no more recalcitrant. Lady Daphne exhaled gustily and drained her cup. Something had to happen or they would all go mad.

****

Arabella climbed through the trap with a satisfied gleam. "Step-Ma tossed you out on your ear, you weird-eyed freak. Figgured you wouldn't last. Supposed you had your claws into my brother." She paced a circle. "Thought to myself, I should check your room. See if anything familiar catches my eyes."

"I took nothing from no one." Except your animosity. "Please, Arabella, I need to…" Cat choked back a sob, straightening. "I need to pack my things."

Arabella surrendered her place with the last volley. "That shouldn't take long."

Cat waited until her footfalls died.

All Cat could see in front of her now was her beloved attic, home for the last year.

The cracked mirror.

The child-sized kerosene lamp—Madame had gotten it as a prize from a soapbox—by her cot under the eaves.

The lone window where she traced the Milky Way or watched the moon wane and bloom.

Her clothing neatly hung on pegs, trinkets, her mother's locket, the nice hanky she would never use, and the silver hat pin. She packed them all but the lamp in a potato sack, except the shattered red Chinese tea box, which she wrapped in the end of her shawl as she put it around her shoulders. It did not take long.

Catriona stood at the trap before turning down the wick, wishing she could keep the sweet little lamp. The shadowy room seemed indescribably cozy with the warm rusty brick flue thrusting through the roof. Tugging her shawl close in expectation of the cold to come, she picked up her bundle under one arm with the broken tea chest in the other.

Chapter Fourteen
The Long Hard Road

Catriona found it was almost dusk by the time she slipped down the outside stairs, trying to ignore flakes drifting past, melting on her nose. The late winter day's warmth that had the sun setting like a warm red jewel had turned to dull stone. She said goodbye to nobody, nor did she wish to see them or any judgmental stares. She could have said farewell to the young man, Hugo, feeling unease over the way she had kept him out. Though hoity-toity, he had been ever so kind. She wondered if Aaron would even miss her abrupt absence.

Aaron.

Her heart hurt. She would not see Aaron except by chance, yet he kept flickering in her heart, a guttering candle.

Wandering, aimlessly mulling, Catriona neared the dress goods shop, slowed, and putting her nose to the glass peered hopefully within. Dark as a cave. Not a glimmer of candle for stock-taking on this cold winter night. No doubt upstairs, above shop, the proprietress with a cuppa had feet propped on a pot-bellied woodstove. Already Cat's fingers, folded in the shawl across the tea chest, tingled from cold. The chest soon became heavy, what with her small bundle too. Cat wished she could tuck it somewhere for later, but there was nowhere. Besides, the Vincent House wasn't far ahead, where she really intended to stop. Surely, they might need help. She was surprised she had not thought of it before. The Longhorn was sort of family. For once in quite a long while she now had nothing to do, nothing expected of her. With each step she felt herself fading, until she was thin as the veil of snow mist powdering about her.

Cat licked chapped lips. She would say a hundred Hail Marys for a mug of scalding sweet tea.

She heartened. The Vincent House, its lights turning the shining flakes to gold, was right up ahead. They would need her strong back. Surely, they kenned what a hard worker she was and all. Cat picked up her steps, bundle bouncing on her back, tea chest clutched tight but slipping… Yet it wouldn't be long and she could lay down her burdens.

The thought of the Vincent House's welcoming warmth, the expected fragrance of the baking apple and raisin pies for which they were famous—plus, without the over-laying sour smack of beer, rye whiskey, and tobacco—made her mouth slippery. The Vincent House's enormous fireplace danced before her eyes like a flickering heaven.

Didn't she, now, just ken how to scrub the hardest crusted skillet with sand from the firebox? Dishes, why, she could do dishes faster than a hen lays eggs, and perhaps serve too, already seeing herself in the Vincent House's long starched ruffly aprons, with the enormous bow in back, and a clean cap trapping her wayward curls.

That is not what happened.

She rapped at the back door, trying to look strong and reliable.

"Ah! So, it's you!" She was expected!

The Vincent House restaurant's old cook, blocking the kitchen door, gave Cat the onceover. As she stamped foot to foot, Cat could see the fireplace silhouetting the cook's figure behind her. Wind whistled through the weave of her shawl. Colder. Wished she'd quit gawking and let her in.

"Half-expected you might show up," she accused. "We ain't got work."

"But I'm a good dishwasher…"

"Good dishwasher, or good—?" She made a rude gesture. "Heard all about it. I'll not have your kind here. Never have. Never will."

She folded arms over her chest. Catriona stepped back. "M-My kind? What kind, ma'am? I'm from County—"

"You could be from Timbuctoo fer all I kere. Heard you was in the pond neked as God made you, with two men! Never mind where youze from! It's what youze gettin' up to now! Irish never been more than gypsies! A purty gal usin' her wiles and stealing to boot! Hunh! I ken what you're after. I have two pure, young, impressionable, churchgoing lads who will not be led astray by wanton women, or sticky fingers…"

Cat gawped, speechless at the tirade. She kenned the cook's two boys. Tripping folks on the boardwalk, filching from pockets, and making rude noises with their mouths when a woman passed. Washed-out subjects with pale freckles and buck teeth they were, and she doubted they'd be brave enough to look her in the eye.

Even as Cat protested with that, the cook slammed the door.

"It is all wrong!" she said to the closed door.

Gossip spread like Indian signals, the smokier with

each telling. By the time tales reached the edge of Wylder, she'd be tried for murdering folks in their sleep, most likely. Cat looked both ways. To her right lay the bank and some lawyers' offices. All dead. She turned left, past the desolate outdoor theater, to where a seamstress had her small shop upstairs.

The windows were blank and dark.

Lowrey's dress shop and laundry was just around the corner—still open, windows runneled with steam. Cat hastened. It would be warm working there.

****

"Kicked you out, did she?" Patting her arm, the laundress gave Cat a mug of hot sweet tea. Warming hands around the cup, Cat was near tears as the dressmaker-laundress checked her up and down, as if buying a horse.

"I will do anything. Sweep, clean, cook—look after wee ones." Cat was lying about the wee ones but strived to look her most motherly.

The laundress pinched Cat's arms and thumped her chest, near knocking Catriona off her stool. "My dear. Look at you. A scrawny little thing! Like a sparrow," she chortled, making her stomach heave. Cat had never been called a sparrow. Still, she held a hopeful grin, striving to look robust, though with a red nose, and knees knocking under her shawl and petticoats.

"I need good strong arms, miss. A brawny, broad-backed, big-hipped gal! Why you couldn't wring out a dishrag!" She hooted. "Now, I don't mind you bein' a touch light-fingered, 'cause there ain't nuthin' much to steal here but someone's old scanties. Be off with you after you finish your cuppa. Tell Solange I be visitin' her soon." With that, she ushered Cat to the door as soon as she'd hastily drained her mug.

Catriona opened her mouth to say she didn't work there anymore, and she didn't take anything did not belong to her, but the words were to yet another closed opportunity. Hefting the tea chest, she trudged on, getting more desperate. It was becoming real. She had no home, no place to rest her head. After here, where? It was later and no warmer, the moon a cold silver smile. Must be close to ten. Never been out this late. Blueish light made Wylder a friendless, alien place.

In a weak moment, Catriona wondered if she could tiptoe up the Longhorn's back stairs, but she feared that door would be locked. A final blow she could not face.

Wind funneled as if clean from Chicago, ripped her shawl, and searched under her dress. Cat breathed hard cold puffs as she stood at an empty crossroads. She had no friends. Not really. Little Mae, and she wouldn't ruin her wobbly position at the Longhorn. Hugo had been kind, but he was not her friend. He was highborn. Forlorn hope anyway. No way she could get ahold of him without entering the saloon, and she was quite aware she had not been exactly civil to him either.

Catriona trudged on, aimless, holding her wrap tight, keeping away from the wind as much as possible by skirting store fronts and nipping into alleys.

On impulse, she stopped at a private dwelling with a tiny notice in a window illuminated by a lone lantern. Inside, a baby cried even at that late hour. A child-like woman scarcely taller than Cat, with round glasses and a frizzled pompadour, opened the door a crack.

She smiled gently and shook her head, answering Cat's request with a Scottish brogue.

"Sorry dearie, with your bonny looks, I'd have too

many of the wrong sort hangin' aboot. I have bairns, ye ken," and she gently closed the door, opening it a second later to Cat's raised hopeful eyes and handed out an apple—withered from deep in the straw barrel, yet smelling of heaven.

With foreboding, Catriona stuck it in her bundle for later. She yawned, partially from cold yet, from a rising sense of panic, weary.

'Twas as if tom-tom messages had beaten all across Wylder.

She could withstand anything.

She would figure out what to do.

She was strong, she lectured herself. She checked the train station, hopefully. There wasn't even a stack of platform freight to nestle behind. The next train out wasn't until morning.

Rambling across the steel rails unheeding, Cat was barely conscious she stumbled by the stables until a whiff of hay and manure assailed her nose, and horses gently neighed welcome in their language of snorts and whuffles. Without her even kenning, her feet passed through the small door beside the large double doors. She patted a gray mare, resisting the urge to feed it her apple, and hauled her bundle up a rickety ladder to the loft, wearily forming a nest of straw upon which she laid her shawl. A horse blanket made warm if scratchy comfort. Cat tried not to wet the straw with weeping. Still, she could not wrap her head around the fact she would not see the sun rise from her cozy attic window at dawn, or share a breakfast of eggs and biscuits with Dingy.

Cat nestled deeper in the scratchy hay, trying for comfort that didn't come, hearing the irritating crackle-crunch when she stirred and the chaff tickled her nose, or when she wrapped the blanket more tightly, reminding her she was hungry.

Breakfast at the Longhorn seemed as distant as the moon. She could not eat hay like a horse. Ashamed, she thought of their oat bucket. What was she to do with exactly two dollars in coins and fifty-three coppers tied in the corner of her kerchief, what had seemed a prideful fortune before? Cat nibbled half the apple, wrapping the rest.

"Try again tomorrow after a rest," she mumbled before falling into troubled sleep.

Chapter Fifteen
Stable Hand and Jacks

At the dredge of double doors being wedged open, cold light flooded the loft. Unsure where she was, Catriona blinked awake, almost tumbling off the edge. She peered over. Chaff trickled in silvery glints, settling atop a straw-hatted head below.

For three days, Cat had made herself at home with the stable owner's or the stable hand's unwitting generosity. This morning, the man in question sneezed. Shaking a hayfork, he looked up with a scowl. If he viewed Cat as a young and pretty girl, it didn't show in his dull visage.

"Here! Whut yew a doin' up thar!"

He jabbed the hayfork menacingly at Cat, who was still three feet higher than his hat. The creature below had gap teeth and a snub nose and seemed frightened, with a dash of confusion to season the stew—perhaps because Cat was female, a species she was certain he had little experience with.

There she was wrong. The stable hand, though slow, had a wife and seven stairsteps, all with pug noses and freckles. He was bed-slat-thin below the brawny shoulders at odds with his long, skinny legs.

"Please." Cat placed a finger before her lips. "Don't tell. Can't I stay a while?" She pinched thumb and finger a hint apart. "Won't cause trouble. No one knows I'm here, sure. If you don't snitch. I—I can muck stalls and feed horses?"

It was true. With little sustenance to keep belly from backbone, she ate what she could scrounge fighting off cats and raccoons from scrap bins behind the Vincent House or even the Longhorn—though she would rather cut her hand off. Yet after all it was still enough to manage on—a scrap of gooseberry pie, a chop bone with shreds of meat, half a corn pone dabbed with molasses. Chill nights with naught but a horse blanket, and hay in hair gone greasy and unwashed, Cat was brought low in the world and would do anything to earn her bread.

"Wanna take m' job 'way from me, hah?" He wrinkled his pug nose and pushed out his lower lip.

Cat unfroze, dragging the ladder up. She hadn't the vigor to beg or explain, but let pleading eyes beg for her. It was like pleading to a bale of hay.

A sly grin, or what passed for sly, spread across the stable hand's face. He pointed to rungs fixed to the wall, half hidden by old saddles and other detritus. Cat felt a dunderhead. In the stable's murkiness she'd missed them, watching with apprehension as he lumbered over.

Thumping across the boards, making chaff fly, and plunking beside Cat, the stable hand dug into his overall pocket. Cat scooted back, alarmed, but he cleared a space with a grubby paw and tossed the jacks. Cat giggled, lightheaded, like a fool.

She watched him sadly as he bounced the India rubber ball.

He meant no harm.

Sure enough, he showed her his pet barn mouse, kept in a ragged shirt pocket, its shoe-button eyes peering out at the top. She cooed, stroking its soft gray head, while he beamed. "Nibbles," he said proudly. He scattered the jacks in invitation. Weak from hunger, nearly weeping at the sweetness of it all, Cat could scarce manage tossing the ball.

He cocked his head after scooping up all twelve of the little metal stars. "Why's you up here? Is you gonna stay?"

"No other place to go."

"Oh. I bin that-a-way." He fingered the little furry head in his pocket. "We kin do this ever-day." He unwrapped a sandwich while Cat shamelessly watched his every bite, poised to snatch it from him. Before she could toss him off the loft, he broke the ham-and-cheese wedge in two, mutely offering half.

After she wolfed it down, that simple statement, "We kin do this ever-day," alerted Cat to how puny her efforts had been. How sorry for herself. Playing jacks in a hayloft was not her future, no matter how sweet the gesture. Moreover, the horses ate better than she. Truth, she was weak from attrition, little sleep, never warm enough, and ravenous as a hibernating bear. It was now or never… She grabbed her bundles and the tea box after the hand left.

****

"I heered about you, little girly."

Arms folded across a skinny chest, the stable owner lurked below the hayloft, watching her legs on the top rung. Cat froze in place.

"Folks pondered where you got off to. Right here, abusin' my hospitality, looks to me like. You gotta pay. I heered you likes fun. You likes fun? I kin show you some."

The owner grinned, his yellow picket-fence teeth

showing through a thicket of beard. "Maybe I'll jes' come visit."

She stared aghast as he headed toward the rungs. In a move quicker than a lizard striking a fly, the stable owner was ahold of her arm. Cat lunged aside, hugged her pack and precious box, and scuttled for the ladder. Too late—sinewy arms used for breaking horses clasped her in a vise, dragging her back up. "I said," he hissed wetly in her ear, "where d'you think you're a runnin' off to?"

"N-Nowhere. Just restin' up, mister."

"Hah! I asked, dumb-ass, how long you bin here. Moron's tighter'n an old lady's purse strings. How some ever, he's been actin' mighty strange." He shook her. "You and he up to no good?" He leered yellow teeth between the sandwich of beard and mustache.

"No! 'Course not! Haven't done anything to your old barn. Or him!" Struggling against muscled forearms, Cat instead slipped under them, leaving a strand of hair and her plaid shawl in his grip. He grunted, hunching over as she jabbed her elbow back into a belly as hard as a copper syrup kettle.

"Wanna play, hunh?" he gasped. "Do ya like it rough as sandpaper, girlie?"

He grabbed her ankle as she crawled to the ladder, flipping her as she struck out with her other foot, but dragging her back, with Cat clutching nothing more substantial than straw, aiming for Catriona's mouth. She contorted just enough so a thick mouth redolent of onions and tobacco slid off her cheek. He gripped her chin in another vise of rein-calloused hands, twisting her face, and ground his mouth on hers.

She screamed inside, wanting to be sick, jerking

away for a breath, gaining an inch, and gagging, then bit his lip hard. The stable owner backed, wide-eyed, but in place of holding his mouth he clutched the crown of his head, bellowing, "Owww! Dang!"

Cat, heaving for breath, wiping her mouth, took time to feel fleeting sorrow for the stable hand with the goofy expression. He stood gripping the handle end of a pitchfork as if just dawning what was in store for him.

Cat threw him an agonized look of thank you, wincing, saying sorry with the same expression, as the stable owner staggered, only to land on his rump. She grabbed her bundle, snatched her precious tea chest and her shawl, and half fell past missing rungs, sliding the rest of the way, her palms picking up splinters and wood burns. She raced to the double doors, recalling too late the heavy bar that had been clunked into place. She about-faced, praying the back door used for sneaking in and out wasn't locked too.

"Ain't no place to go!" The man bawled from the loft, the last she heard as she slammed out, save for a loud smack and a guttural cry, hoping that was all the blows the hand suffered in connection with her.

"Never wrestle with pigs!" Cat yelled up from the doorway. "You both get dirty, but the pig likes it."

****

Madame lay in her bed. It was wrong, somehow. Wrong the way she handled it. But Arabella, the sneak, had already spread the word. Perhaps give Cat another chance? They would not be here forever, and Cat had been a hard worker. She didn't believe for a moment Cat really wanted that ugly brooch. Press a few coins— perhaps train fare? It wasn't Christian, throwing children in the street, and that's all the girl from Ireland really was. Madame felt a pang in her flat chest that had more to do with the pickled pig's feet for lunch. Surely, the wretched girl had some relatives? Some friends?

So tired these days, what with Little Levi—a smile flitting across her face, over the thought of the blessed gift of her wee one, so late in life.

With these drowsy, well-meaning notions, Solange drifted into her nap.

****

Straw wove Catriona's hair.

She itched.

Her body was none too fragrant, she decided. She felt like the bottom of a coal sack, all gritty and smudged. If not for the sweet scent of hay, she suspected she'd be worse for wear. It seemed a long way to the pond, shivering with goose-prickles bumping her arms even at the notion, even if it was only five miles from town, even if she did still own the shawl.

She watched, fearful, over her shoulder. The stable owner might even now creep around the corner... She could not tarry.

*****

Tripping, Catriona found herself stumbling up to blue steel tracks dwindling off to unknown territory, once more watching a last mail car clank by. Cat stared west, yearning to jump onto one of those red-and-green passenger cars that would rattle her off to safety, where no one kenned your name.

Instead, she had wandered a mindless path born of hunger between the no-man's land of the firehouse and the sawmill. To her right soared the shadowy hulk of the water tower, where her journey began a lifetime ago when her family's warm, precarious bosom no longer existed.

Its round shape high in the sky on stilt legs bulked dark against the stars, for to her surprise it was night again. Catriona halted underneath its belly, subconsciously seeking out their old tent, seeing nothing but rags whipping in a chill wind, a broken trunk, a dented saucepan.

No time for memories. She raced on, panicked, through the dark, unsure where she headed, but kenning she had scant chances before she gave out. She had used up all her luck wandering stupidly, hoping for sanctuary no matter how slim. Cat caught a faint glimmer like a beacon beyond a stand of cedars. Resting hands on knees, she caught her breath before she went end over teakettle, then headed toward the light.

Chapter Sixteen
Only a Cat in a Gilded Cage

The cold air made tears roll unbidden down her grubby cheeks, and she swiped them fiercely away before they thought her a lily-wristed thing. Cat looked down at Little Mae's dress, wrinkled like grandmam's hands back in Ballygawley. At least her cheeks were pink. And her nose. Catriona kenned where she was heading as certain as gully washers in the fall and winter blizzards.

Pulling the yellow satin, creased and ugly, from her pack, Catriona thought of Ma's wedding dress, yet she would not sully it for what she had in mind. Madame's horrid drab brown was hardly suitable either. Cat was worldly enough to ken that. Little Mae had clumsily cut and stitched the voluminous dress down to her size, more or less. The yellow satin was better than the stained, draggle-hemmed rag she had been wearing, but only just.

Shuddering with cold, Catriona stripped the drab, hay-stuck gown, like a rotting chrysalis, down to knickers and petticoat, quickly shrugging on the satin dress—scarcely warmer—bitterly regretting the plaid shawl left behind somewhere. She scurried on. She only had one candle flickering in her mind—she must find shelter.

****

Golden lights glittered welcome through wobbly

panes, like fire underwater—the gaudy painted balconies and siding gleamed bright yellow and red from the reflected glow.

Before she could think too hard, Cat approached the Wylder Social Club with its wide welcoming porch of swings and rockers, detecting the jolly tinkling piano twenty feet off, as if a cat pranced on the keys, conjuring up BiJingo. Cat looked down at her garb. Perhaps the kitchen might be best for first presentations, even though she was in the yellow silk. Cat washed her face in the horse trough. Using the small broken mirror from her bundle, she plucked hay clinging to her stockings and finger-combed hair—somewhere her precious comb had taken French leave, so she tied the straggly red ribbon behind her ears.

Cat looked at her wrinkled image.

Not too bad.

Bargaining, Catriona hoped she didn't have to do what the other girls did. Whatever that was. After all, they too ate and cooked and needed cleaning and…and bed-changing. Even a country Irish lass didn't ken what exactly happened between a man and a maid, save that, one way or another, you held a baby eight or nine months later unless you were "careful."

Cat faltered at the brilliant red façade embellished with yellow gingerbread and white trim about windows flanked by shutters enameled the shade of Concorde grapes, a wide veranda with "The Wylder Social Club" scribed in fancy gold curlicues above it, the glittering windows framed in swagged violet velvet drapes.

The prettiest building she'd ever clapped eyes on.

Scurrying round back, delaying when she'd meet the formidable Miss Adelaide that Little Mae had told her about, picturing her tall, bosomed like a pouter pigeon, with huge feathers in poofy hair and garbed in scarlet velvet with lots of gold fringe.

Besides, she had doubts over assailing the grand front entrance in her sorry state, despite the grandeur of yellow satin. And she could almost taste food, led by an unmistakable aroma of fried chicken straight to the Wylder Social Club's back door. She would present herself resplendent in yellow, with a red stringy ribbon somewhat corralling scrunchy masses of licorice ringlets.

The dress in question drooped painfully from Cat's pert bosom, draggling the ground in a lopsided, muddy way after another hasty toilette at the horse trough in the lee of the gaudy building, where she scrubbed face and hands, leaving a pale oval above a decidedly darker neck, with hands that appeared as if Cat wore white gloves.

At last ready as she could be, Cat detected laughter and passionate, melodious, sonorous tones of the fabled Italian tenor Caruso soaring from a Victrola's trumpet horn as she waited hopefully in a gown owning only a fading memory of once being a fancy dress, the color of which was nearly undefinable, now exposed to elements, with a mud-spattered hem, after too long crushed into her bundle…

Smoothing the dress a last hopeless time, Cat tucked scuffed boots beneath the mucky hem and boldly knocked on the back kitchen door—in for a penny.

She stepped back as the kitchen door, judging from smells and banging pots and pans, stayed closed. Interior laughter stopped, replaced by murmured voices. To her sorrow, the melodious singing died in a blood-curdling scrawtch.

"Who's there? You be wantin' the front parlor, most likely," an unseen voice ended in giggles.

Catriona shivered and pounded again. "Please let me in," she called without grace. Grumbles now. Caruso resumed.

Abruptly, the door banged open, and she stared into the wizened face of the cook, judging from her splotched apron and brandished wooden spoon. The woman scowled, then darted a suspicious glance behind Cat. "Here now. Whatcher want? We don't do beggars. Go on. Shoo! The Vincent House. They might—"

Cat felt her body waver as if gusted by stiff wind.

The short skinny woman looked her up and down. Cat raised her head and looked the short woman in the eye. "Please," she whispered.

The cook grunted, softer. "Look, missy, whoever you are…" She glanced back, impatient, yelling, "Chuck more kindling in the firebox, and check that oven!" Then she continued with, "Miss Adelaide done already run off a score a gals with that hongry look. You ain't gotta chance of a snowball in Hades."

"Ummm…" Catriona's tongue seemed frozen. What did she want? Everything, and nothing she could explain. Shelter, affection, warmth, food…

"Ma'am, if I could steal a bit of your warmth and a scrap of bread, I might freshen up right sprightly," she breathed. Cat tried to look brave and alluring. "May I…?" she whispered, clearing a throat filled with corn husks. It had been a while since she broke her silence to any but herself. "I…I wish to see the…the madam." Why could she not dredge up her name? "Miss Addie—Annie…Annabelle?"

The cook's face filled with mocking wrinkles.

"Humph! Annabelle! If you please!" She mugged at two gawking women spooning something into their mouths, one wide-eyed and inquisitive, the other frowning.

"Go on, skedaddle now. We don't have truck with you." Cook waved the spoon big as a baseball bat as a weapon.

"I—I wish to speak with her. I must!" Desperation rasped Cat's voice like a hacksaw.

"That right?" Cook laughed. "And what might that be about?" As an aside to the women, she said, "She's got bizniz with the boss!" Then, returning her gaze to Cat, she added, "She don't take no strays, I said. Go on about you. I got supper to red up."

Food! She would not be turned away!

"I am not a stray! I—I worked for Madame Solange—Mrs. Gruenwald." There. It was out. "And I'm so hungry I could eat a goat."

Suddenly, a quick clatter of high heels came near. "I can hear you in the front parlor! What is all that, Bathsheba?" demanded a musical but husky voice behind the cook.

Bathsheba?

Cat winced.

The wizened creature wielding the spoon looked no more the biblical siren than a withered turnip. The turnip jerked her head. "Oh, just this filthy gal a-pesterin' me, when I should be puttin' the taties ta bile. Don't blame me iffen…"

Amusement could be noted in the voice. "Never mind. Stand aside."

"Now see what you done," Cook grumbled. "Oh, don't bother yerself, Miss Addie. Just another tramp, looks like, lookin' for a handout."

Miss Adelaide! Now or never.

Cook raised her stringy arm to shove Cat and close the door, but Cat spied behind her a youthful woman with brilliant gold curls surrounding the face of a doll, clutching a maroon ledger like Madame Solange used. Cat pushed past the cook, not difficult even in her state, for she was still twice cook's size.

"Well! Hello-o? And who is this, gracing our back door?" The musical voice sounded like an angel's to Cat.

"Humph!" Cook snorted, leaning the hefty wooden spoon across her shoulder.

The doll-like woman studied Catriona, mouth twitching as she took in the drooping yellow disaster. Cat saw her glance flick over and dismiss her oily hay-stuck curls and the ring of grime about her neck.

"Hard times?"

Cat nodded, numb. "Yes."

"You the one run out of the Longhorn?"

"Yessum. It's not true."

"I heard a bit of village scuttlebutt. So, she kicked you out. Never did get on friendly terms with Madame. Too many airs and graces. Reckon she didn't want any pretty girls around, if she couldn't use 'em somehow, now she's respectable."

Cook looked back and forth 'tween Cat and Miss Adelaide. Finally, grumbling about "soft in the head" and "needin' to put the taties on," she stumped off.

"Well, better not let the heat out."

Cat heard the "humph" once more, but she scuttled forward before the vision changed her mind and chucked her out, but then her limbs failed, her mind fogged, and she was falling toward a nicely tiled floor. All was dark for a second or an hour.

Cat jerked up, instinctively kenning that to appear on last legs was not the best foot forward, and holding on with tooth-gritting effort, she rasped, "Sorry, ma'am," forcing herself up straight. "Guess I tripped."

Miss Adelaide stepped aside as Cat stumbled in, trailing cold, the scent of horse manure, and mud into the warm clean kitchen, much to Cook's disgust. The woman's muttering grew in intensity in the background. "Lettin' in beggars to muck up my clean floors…"

"Not now, Bathsheba." Miss Addie's voice was the cracking of a whip, but she reached out—her gaze widening slightly when she noted Catriona's two disparate orbs, narrowing her own.

"Are…are you…Miss Adelaide?" Cat whispered.

"None other."

"I didn't think you'd be so—so pretty!" Cat blurted.

"My, my," Adelaide said dryly. "You sure know how to butter your toast."

Cat couldn't help but stare. This confection of a female, big as a minute hand, was store-bought blonde, with dimples and wide blue eyes. Child-sized, she looked like she could be one of the girls, or playing dress up in woman's clothes, except for an experienced icy glint deep in that blue gaze. Miss Adelaide missed nothing. And she was a tad older than first thought, judging by a delicate web about the mouth, which showed through a dusting of expensive face powder laced with crushed pearl.

"Well, come on in, child. How does a warm bath, a mug of strong black tea, and some soda bread with honey sound?" Dimples flashed.

"Like heaven, ma'am, and you bein' an angel and all." Cat tried to strengthen her voice above a whisper.

"Oh, you are Irish. Of course, with that black hair and white skin. Might want to deepen that brogue. Men like that."

Cat nodded, feeling a shiver of excitement, along with fear of the unkenned—but something else too bloomed between her thighs. What would it be like? Her first time laying with a man? Would that it could be Aaron, as she had so feverishly imagined in her attic cot many a night.

Miss Adelaide, her scrutiny once again traveling Cat's frame and finding it wanting, cracked the whip again. "Clean her up. Looks in need of feeding first. Then, I shall see her."

With that she spun on a tiny boot and left for other far more important appointments, her manner said. Speaking over her shoulder, she threw at one of the drudges, "And a good comb out, I should wager. Inspect for lice—fleas too."

The drudge in question, basting a goose, scowled. "Yessum! After she warshes up some! Ain't touchin' her thisaway!"

Cat's face burned under the grime. "No, ma'am. Clean as I could make myself. Had no place to go. Washed off in the horse trough…"

Miss Adelaide whirled her skirts round, widening her eyes in a comical way.

"Really? I've often wondered."

Which made no sense.

Yet Cat would sign a deal with the devil for a bath and a bite to eat. Let the devil take the hindmost, as Ma would say.

The drudge led Cat to a back room with its own pot-bellied stove, humid, scented with lye and soda, strung with laundry, and fitted with large tin tubs. Later, Cat learned elegant tubs with gold claw feet, soft towels, and soap scented with sprigs of lavender were ensconced in special rooms above, but for now it was a yellow slab of laundry lye and rough kitchen towels.

"He'p yarself," the matronly woman muttered, indicating the pump and the large steaming kettle.

Catriona wasn't looking forward to the great flea hunt herself. Chin up, stripping off gray bloomers, and scrap of petticoat, she glared back. "What are you called?"

"Coral. Don't need ta ken your'n. Won't be here that long."

Coral. Cat's mind raced. Pearl, Opal, Ruby, Amethyst, and Coral. "Did you... Were you...?"

"Never you mind!"

When Cat turned, naked and pink in the tub after a fierce hair-yanking and a soul-destroying scrubbing, she spied Miss Adelaide watching from the doorway, nodding at the kitchen help armed with a large comb and menacing scowl leaning against the plank wall.

"Proper clothes. One of the girls might have something. Yes, Pearl's should do." She strode in as if cracking her whip. Cat tried to keep her in sight, but she made twiddly "stand still" signs. "Open your mouth. Show your teeth." Cat stretched her mouth, feeling a fool.

Miss Adelaide studied her. "Devil eyes. Witchy eyes," she murmured. "Might be a bad thing. Could be a draw. We'll see."

Finally, she asked, "You have never...?" And stared in Catriona's eyes from one to the other, making gestures with her fingers, again leaving Cat no doubt as to what she asked.

Catriona without a hint of pridefulness, answered, "No, ma'am. Saving meself for me weddin' night and all."

Miss Adelaide sucked in cheeks trying not to laugh outright. Cat blushed, aware of giggles behind her.

"I'll be savin' meself for someone special, won't I now!" she insisted.

"Apparently not," Miss Adelaide said with the dryness of zwieback, inviting forward two girls Cat later learned were Pearl and Opal. Pearl held a dress across her arms.

"Special." Giving off a wave of lily-of-the-valley fragrance, Miss Adelaide shook yellow curls till they bounced on her forehead, chuckling throatily. "I have a feeling that's not happening, nor why you arrived on my doorstep like a foundling child. Am I right?"

Cat nodded, numb.

Pearl led Catriona, scrubbed to within an inch of her life, to the heartbeat of the establishment—a dizzying blend of a sprawling desk big as the Wylder platform, dwarfing the owner perched in a swivel banker's chair, and file cabinets not out of place in a New York lawyer's office, mixed with rose chintz overstuffed chairs, pink velvet drapes weighted with gold tassels and fringe, feathery fronds in epergnes, gilt-framed oils of unclothed females, two fluffy white cats in a miniature canopied bed before a fireplace with rose-imprinted tiles and featuring a gilded mantlepiece—lastly, a gray steel safe large as a baby elephant, with a spin wheel big as Cat's head, plus a humidor by Miss Adelaide's elbow.

****

Cat waited before that desk in the clean gown—pale

pink, adorned with a large coffee stain on the bosom and a torn ruffled hem she'd stitched up, intending to embroider a rose over the blotch.

Her hair, after a wicked war with the comb and thereby ripped free of devilish snarls, rested now in a fat braid. She swallowed hard, while Adelaide tapped the pink shells of her fingernails on her desk.

No matter how helpful Cat made herself, causing more than one dropped pan of biscuits, she'd found no place in the kitchen. Moreover, there seemed a surplus of women showing lines of age around mouths and eyes, "in retirement," grumpily toiling under the withered taskmistress—whom Cat had already crossed swords with—and begrudging any younger interloper.

At Miss Adelaide's bidding, Cat winked cheekily and awkwardly sashayed in a circle, swaying hips and looking coquettish over one shoulder in a desperate attempt of appearing "knowing."

Not fooled, Miss Adelaide raised a perfect golden brow. "Try again."

Cat looked at her toes, one foot over the other, bowing her head.

"As I suspected. You have never…?" Miss Adelaide made a gesture.

"Didn't I after be saying that?"

"My, what a treasure!" She mocked in a not-quite-believing manner. "I have to be assured. Most gals when they arrive, have already 'sampled the wares' and have a taste for it. You, my dear, are clumsy as a calf on crutches, true. Nevertheless, there is a certain, as the French say, *je ne sais quoi*. Hidden fevers. Obvious charms."

Cat looked back, mulish, in confusion.

Miss Adelaide sighed. "A pearl of great price!" She gestured impatiently for Cat to perch, then scrutinized a large calendar printed prettily with flowers. "Your debut will be spectacular…" She flicked a fond glance at the large safe. "And very profitable…"

Cat frowned. Puzzling it out. "Profitable, ma'am?"

"Mmmm, yes," she murmured distantly, already marking her books. "Quite a treat for one lucky gent. We must get readied for your…" She slammed the ledger shut, showing dimples belying her businesslike demeanor. "For your unveiling. We must not peel too much innocence away, yet we shall lend you certain skills to enhance your untried state."

At Cat's confused look, she added, "We shall make you seem even more naive and virginal than you are." Tapping the desk, she continued. "I wonder if perhaps we should…" She paused, cocking her head. "Advertise? Mmm, no. On second thought, we'll let it out as a delicious secret for only a privileged few. That should get the smoke signals all over the territory, and they will come flocking."

Cat swallowed hard. Imagining a herd of people descending on her in a great cloud of dust.

Miss Adelaide leaned back, lit a black cheroot, and watched Cat through a fog of smoke, offering Cat the silver case, and blew a long gusty plume as if mulling her fate.

"No, ma'am." Cat didn't want to say the habit made one's teeth brown.

"Good." Miss Adelaide took another puff. "Clients don't like girls smelling of tobacco—spirits mayhap, or cloves, but not tobacco, neither chaw nor smoke."

"And the men?"

Miss Adelaide laughed. "Young and old, fat, or thin, it matters little, as long as they wash up and have the—" She rolled thumb and fingers to indicate cash. "At least we pretend," she avowed, squinting though the cloud. "How old are you?"

"I'm—" Cat hesitated. "Thirteen?"

"You don't rightly ken?"

"Not rightly, ma'am. I think maybe fourteen. Could be fifteen? I kinda missed a year, sure."

"And your birthday?"

"Next month, I'm a-thinking. Ma and Pa never made much fuss." Cat lifted a one-shoulder shrug. "Back home, busy in the fields and all, then here fending off the cold, bandits, and rough trails, but when they recalled, it was always next month, if this be November. Think Ma said I was almost a Christmas baby." Cat shrugged, reddening.

Miss Adelaide studied Cat with a look that struggled with sympathy…and lost.

"If you wish to stay under my protection and…instruction, you must be willing to perform certain acts, and expect a humiliating experience for some, but—" she smiled, revealing small pearly teeth, "a pleasurable experience for most. Some gentlemen appreciate sassy gals, others a lighthearted lass full of jokes and teasing. You must read their wishes. We do not cater to the rough trade. In time, if you accrue regular clients, you will ken their desires."

She smiled, ruefully shrugging a pink ruffled shoulder. "Most just want a good poke. Yet even range riders off the trails, or trappers or miners are obliged to smell sweet as summer roses. None of that ridden-hard-and-put-away-wet stink."

She stared through Catriona.

"Dishwashers grow on trees in Wylder. Comely girls do not, or I should not bother. If any of my girls—Pearl, Opal, Ruby, or Amethyst—need help, you will aid them, at least for the present." Miss Adelaide poured a tumbler of spirits, offering Cat none. "I have standards. Few do. But here, a young girl must be at least fifteen before she begins…work."

Cat looked steadily at Miss Adelaide, throwing a sharpish glance, not revealing the tempest within.

Miss Adelaide smacked the desk. "That's settled then. We shall see how it works, until you are of—as society so quaintly puts it, 'the age of consent.' "

Which gave Cat the feeling Miss Adelaide had dark shadows somewhere in her own youth.

"So!" Miss Addy stubbed out her cheroot. "Till that happy day, let us say you are in training, grooming. Sand off rough edges, teach you the arts. In the meantime, you will not be idle. Work the kitchens, doing all the old bat says. She's my mother, by the by, so treat her with all the respect you can dredge up." She twinkled a smile at Catriona's discomfort.

"Nothing too strenuous, however, to wrinkle the cream of your skin or roughen your hands. We must keep you all fresh and dewy."

Chapter Seventeen
Sows' Ears and Silk Purses

The girls, on Sunday morn after church, giggling, gnawing oatmeal cookies and fruitcake, sloshing tea liberally laced with spirits, dressed Catriona like a large doll with abandon, delighting in dragging out fripperies—flouncy short petticoats, corselettes which showed off the bosom or left it bare, a pair of bloomers that didn't seem to own a bottom. Deep-throated gowns of lemon yellow, sea green, robin's-egg blue, and scarlet velvet.

They whirled Cat around, ripping off one outfit after another and as quickly slipping on new combinations and having a jolly good time. Cat chuckled, high on fruitcake and unaccustomed attention, gazing at her reflection. "I'm not seeing meself, sure!" She giggled. For the time she could forget what all this was for, though she didn't allow her mind to wander into that unknown territory often anyway.

Pearl had tossed over her head a lavender-blue rustle-y taffeta confection, strangely enough, making her odd eyes nearly match, the heart-shaped neckline dipping between her bosom. Her waist appeared tinier than ever cinched between flaring skirts.

Opal, good with hair, did wondrous things to Cat's snarled wayward tresses, pinning and twirling, practiced with chignons, and braids wrapped round the head or looped over her ears, or let the back hang free to her waist.

Finally, Pearl, Opal, Ruby, and Amethyst crowded to the pier glass, giving great gusts of satisfaction.

Cat had never felt so beautiful, or imagined she could be.

****

"Slowly, slowly! The garter! Then, a glove…never too much! By the time you are disrobed, the polecats will be easy to tame, tether, and ride to the finish," they chuckled while Catriona wondered if she'd have the sand to put such practices to use. Pearl, Ruby, Amethyst, and Opal delighted in illustrating a bewildering array of advice.

"Look at them from under your lashes."

"Wet your lips, then your nips," Amethyst suggested in earnest.

"Now, slip one strap, shrug as if by accident—the other now."

"Show a breast, not too much, like your shimmy is loose. Hold it up as if you are very shy."

Not too difficult, Cat thought, feeling a right eejit. Cat's shimmy slipped to her indented waist, sliding on down narrow hips. She made a grab for it.

"Aah, there," Miss Adelaide crowed, unannounced and quietly watching from the doorway.

"A natural. Clumsiness adds verisimilitude." Whatever that meant. Cat vowed to look up "verisimilitude" in the parlor's forgotten corner of books featuring *The Lustful Turk* and *Night in a Moorish Harem*, both by a Mr. Anonymous, for the gentlemen's pleasures whilst waiting.

Cat had spied a lexicon there and overheard Miss

Adelaide late as she said, "What lovely little rosebuds…now slither slowly from those petticoats… don as many as you can. A wriggle here, a twist there, gazing over your shoulder… No! No!" She clapped hands. "Not with eyes wide open as if they were a plate of flapjacks and you melted butter and blackstrap. Tease them—you have naught beneath your petticoats."

Cat learned how to undulate belly muscles and whisper certain things in a man's ear. She practiced on one of the girls, giggling throughout, to Adelaide's stern amusement. Biting her lip to keep from grinning, she finally flicked the imaginary whip, tiny fists on hips. "Won't need to know all that till later, yet while I give room and board, you take my tutelage seriously."

Cat looked chastened, yet the instructions mortified. Treacly and stupid to call a man her "forever lover" and "making her hot all over."

Even so, Pearl eyed her critically. "Aye. She'll do. When's her day-byou?"

"Soon," Miss Adelaide muttered cryptically, giving a slight shake of the head at Pearl.

****

There were more serious discussions, it seemed…

"…and before, you know, you—do it—be sure to tuck this in."

Opal held up a sea sponge, knotted and tied to a long black silk thread in one hand, and a small jar of apple vinegar in the other, whilst the girls nodded solemnly, as if they offered Cat the wisdom of the ages.

Which they had.

Cat, clutching the tiny jar of vinegar, looked at Pearl blankly. Pearl sighed. Ruby snickered and whispered in her ear, then knelt and looked at Catriona full in the face.

188

"Are you certain-sure y'all understand? Don't want no babies before-time."

Cat nodded, clutching the jar tighter, feeling her insides twist and snarl. She was on a runaway train hurtling down crooked tracks into the vast unknown.

Chapter Eighteen
The Virgin's Undoing

"We will have a private auction."

Miss Adelaide's' blue eyes were steel bullets. "I assume you have been truthful and are, as yet, untouched. I will check! So don't lie."

Four months had passed. Cat was either fourteen or fifteen. Miss Adelaide leaned toward the latter. The imaginary whip smacked the desk. Cat jumped.

"Have you slipped out, lain, screwed, tarradiddled, or fornicated with any boy since you arrived? I need to know now!"

Cat felt heat rising. "No! Ma'd skin me. Father Patrick said, 'Stay pure till wed with bans read and priest sayin' words and all." She looked at her feet—though, truth, some did not wait till the words.

"All that folderol, eh?" Miss Adelaide managed a twitch of the lip, then cracked the imaginary whip again, raising a golden brow and watching her closely. "And never been taken advantage of?"

"Taken?" Cat flushed. "No!"

"This event is important. I do not wish to be made a fool of. I must be certain." She did not look the least bit apologetic.

Cat looked up with such flashing strange eyes, Miss Adelaide leaned back in the massive swivel banker's chair that made her seem even more doll-like, possibly assessing if she had the tiger by the tail.

"Those eyes." She tapped her nails on the desk. "Might be off-putting—or an exotic attraction. We had a one-legged gal here not long…"

She let the thought trail.

Cat straightened, striving to appear grown-up, though her innards were aquiver, her mind a beehive of questions. "When do you expect this of me—this event?"

Miss Adelaide cocked her head, fingering one dangly pearl earring. "Don't get many virgins here." She gave an unladylike snort.

"Whoever bids the most—gets the prize." She pointed her fan. "You."

Cat's face remained smooth as a porcelain plate, yet her thoughts shattered.

****

They had held Cat's birthday party in the kitchen. Miss Adelaide ordered beer for all. She raised her stein. "For Catriona!" They gave Cat the fifteen whacks on her bottom, and one to grow on.

Hiding her pride, the kitchen drudge grimly brought over a lemon sheet cake for Cat to slice, after hot pasties, the sight of which brought a lump to Cat's throat, but she gamely thrust melancholy away. There was even hand-churned vanilla ice cream.

Opal, Pearl, Amethyst, and Ruby indulged in lemon cake and pasties. Miss Adelaide said something about her figure. Cat was too happy to do anything but nibble. At last, something was happening—this frightening milestone, gateway to an unknown world, but far better than what she had been accustomed. No more kitchens. No more cold. Or being alone. Having a warm bed, sleeping late, enough clothes to cover one's body, and more than she'd ever need, and never, never being hungry.

Could anything be better?

****

Came the night before the grand auction: The bidding would be not on horses, or livestock, but on her. Catriona.

Against Miss Adelaide's wishes, Cat concealed herself behind one of the heavy pink velvet drapes in a forgotten alcove near the kitchens where she could nip back in, if exposed.

She had never been allowed in when the girls entertained in the parlor. Adelaide had given strict instructions, cracking her whip again, that should not happen, to keep her "fresh," whatever that meant. Cat half wanted to "get it over with"—not the term she would have used for losing her virginity, but she quashed those thoughts.

This was what it was. Perhaps here, she'd save a small grubstake and start anew. Farther west. Fabled San Francisco came to mind.

All these thoughts raced through Cat's mind as the clock struck three times in the grand salon and men arrived in a trickle at first, from the train, shaking snow from coats, stomping as if they owned the place, already looking girls over. A few with expectant smiles seemed to be searching for specific girls.

Perhaps she would soon be a special someone.

Shortly after, the parlor milled with clients of all types and ages.

She would not let Miss Adelaide down. She'd strive to recall everything the girls and Miss Adelaide had instructed her upon. Instructed was one thing, but to watch experts in the art of flirtation and seduction was quite another. Opal had already disappeared upstairs with a portly gent in a bowler hat, and Pearl was sitting on another, ruffling his hair and biting his ear.

Cat gasped and shrank from the drapes, wishing she could disappear.

Aaron!

Cat peered out again.

Please, not Aaron. Maybe it's some other—

It was him. His tall frame, and his hair like gold silk spilling down his neck, among other newcomers streaming in, was unmistakable. As he called out to someone, his recently acquired British accent grated on Cat's ear. "Oh, I say, old chap, fancy seeing you again."

"Again! What is he doing here?" Cat moaned.

What do you think? Cat's devilish imp suggested.

"I thought he was savin' himself," Cat whispered in despair.

Ha! Even her angel laughed.

Cat felt ill. What if he were here tomorrow! Her grand unveiling! Her debut! Not into society like Lady Audrina, or even Arabella, but into his league of so-called "soiled doves." This became real. Her heart felt like lead, and her stomach twisted into pretzels. Stricken, Catriona saw Amethyst of the violet eyes and wicked grin leading Arron upstairs by his cravat.

****

Catriona stood in front of the pier glass, gazing unseeingly at her nude reflection. She might have butterflies and bees in her tummy, but the rest of her was numb. Her head seemed not to be working. Try as she might, she could not dredge up the anticipation of the coming event, or even what it was about, or what the girls had taught her, and especially what to do after.

Aware Miss Adelaide rustled up behind her, Cat's lips spread a wooden smile, beaming, though it felt like cracked plaster. Adelaide frowned back without noticing, concentrating on two shockingly short dresses, holding one after the other before Cat's image.

"Here," she snapped tossing her the garments.

Could Miss Adelaide be as unnerved as me? Cat wondered.

"Put those on." She handed Cat sheer white stockings, gauzy pantaloons, and pink ruffly garters. Gone was the fun of dressing up.

Miss Adelaide slipped the chosen dress, a frothy confection, over Cat's head. White lawn, childish short puffed sleeves, boasting a wide pink satin sash with an enormous bow in back and a flouncy skirt that only came to Cat's knees.

Motioning Cat to thrust her foot forward, Miss Adelaide fit on black patent slippers, fastening the strap with mother-of-pearl buttons about her ankle. Next— pins in her mouth, she parted Catriona's hair, secured each side above her temples with crisp pink bows matching the sash, and let the rest hang to her waist.

Cat gazed at herself...her other self. She looked about twelve. If that.

Her cheeks pinked without aid of rouge. She swallowed hard. She tried to yank the skirt down past her knees.

Miss Adelaide slapped her hands.

"None of that, now! You know what to do."

"Yes," Cat lied.

Chapter Nineteen
Highest Bidder

Catriona peeked over the staircase. She wasn't to be seen until her "unveiling," but she couldn't help it. She still had time. She had been readied early. Other preparations bustled below in a panic of activity.

Maybe no one would arrive. It was all a lark at her expense.

Yet she could not avoid the hustle-bustle, the hectic baking of savories, pork pasties, mince tarts, Saratoga chips, relishes, Parker House rolls, and cheeses laid out on starched tablecloths lining one wall, or the casks of spirits and other supplies trundled in. Cat gulped, feeling her palms spring with moisture. The event grew like Topsy to frightening proportions.

As Cat peered down, the server arrived, a short man, hair parted in the middle, a walrus mustache, long apron reaching his ankles, plus a snappy red bowtie. A fiddle player entered via the kitchen, striding to his place on a small platform after a short confab with the piano player.

The over-warm room reeked of masses of drooping hothouse lilies and roses, Miss Adelaide's pride. Deep alcoves dotted the circular lounge where, presumably, more intimate exchanges were held, as heavy pink velvet drapes could be drawn at whim.

Some alcoves circling the sumptuous front parlor showcased nymph statues performing unclothed poses—

all except the largest, in the center. This was where Cat would be concealed until the Grand Event.

Cat wondered why the bother, with half-clothed girls lounging unperturbed, even relishing the freedom from corsets topping froths of sheer petticoats, and unfettered bosoms or scantily clad bottoms—it seemed never both at once. Cat intuited that would seem crude in Miss Adelaide's mind.

Yet now, not a sighting of the other girls could be found. This was her night…until, presumably, later.

Cat spied a Victrola beside stacks of thick dark disks proclaiming titles like *Romany Violins*, *Bolero*, and *Caruso*. A roaring fireplace reflected off crystal, gold rococo, and silver cutlery laid out next to candlewicks. Cut-glass decanters on the bar glittered flame, along with a plethora of spirits sparkling like stained glass. A black bartender in starched white, with a maroon fez atop his bald head, filled a large punch bowl ringed by silver cups.

All this was frosting on the cake, Catriona thought, admiring the rest of the vast parlor. Circular pink velvet settees, pillow-heaped brocade lounges, sumptuous yellow-and-green-striped silk recamiers, and of course, elaborate oil paintings of languorous *zaftig* nudes in extravagant gold frames all glowed with erotic life.

Surveying all of this from her lofty perch, Cat swallowed hard. *All this for me? Because of me?*

Tonight was her night.

Cat felt a fluttering like trapped birds in her chest.

Her tummy buzzed with bees. She felt sick.

A pattering of footsteps. A swish of skirt. Her arm grasped.

"There you are!" Cat, was subsequently yanked

harshly back into the dimness of the hall, well away from the gallery.

Miss Adelaide's infuriated face was directly before hers.

"I have sought you everywhere!"

Cat kenned then Miss Adelaide's fear that she had done a runner, that this whole grand affair would bring ruination and mortification, if that were true. It would leave Miss Adelaide the butt of Wylder's witticisms for years to come—had Catriona vanished.

Miss Adelaide's ma looked up sourly from slicing a huge ham down below.

"Yes, ma'am. I'm sorry, I am that," Cat stuttered.

"Stay in the kitchen for now. Right before I place you," she ordered.

Miss Adelaide tugged her down the back way to the kitchens, warning her not to get dirty. Cat had assumed she would be led downstairs to great fanfare. "Keep that dress clean!" She admonished again, bustling off. Miss Adelaide herself wore a magnificent gold dress glittering with spangles, stiff with tulle ruffles about the deep neckline, and flowing with a long fashionable train.

****

Aaron strode into the Longhorn.

Time for a quick tipple, not that there would not be a surfeit of libation where he was heading, but it might be smart to prime the pump and not seem eager, like a country bumpkin who just fell off the hay wagon.

Big night, not that he was nervous. He had some saved up, but he wasn't a sucker…a day-old biscuit could be just as hot as one right out of the oven if warmed up. He pondered idly which virgin in town was the lucky gal. *Probably had to ship one in from out of town.* He snickered, kenning smugly he had something to do with the lack of suitable young virgins in all Wylder.

Smirking, he spied that long drink of water Hugo, per usual, long nose bent over the ledgers of "Mad Mortimer of the Mines"—Aaron's moniker given Lord Greville. *Busy as little bees, ain't you, son?* Hugo was transcribing notes or some rot, and on such a fine anticipated night.

"Dolt," Aaron muttered, gulping his rye.

Shooting his cuffs, on impulse and with mischief on his mind, Aaron sauntered over. "I say, old chap," he sneered. "Burning midnights oils, or slowly going blind?"

Hugo looked up and blinked, and blinked again, nudging his spectacles. "Mmm. Well, rather." He checked Aaron out. Aaron seemed more dandified, even for him. His hair reeked of bay rum.

"Yes. Well…" Hugo coughed, waiting for him to leave.

"I say. Care for some fun?" Aaron perched on the edge of the table, nudging the precious ledger aside and nearly upsetting the inkpot.

"Fun?" Hugo repeated as if it were an alien concept, his hands busy fussily setting things to rights.

"Yeah. Ever heard of it?"

"Of course," Hugo said stiffly. "I believe you showed me some fun several weeks ago."

"Ever been to a cat house?"

"A cat house?"

"Crib? House of ill repute?" Aaron laughed in his face. "Bet you never been with a girl. Am I right?"

Hugo laid down his Mont Blanc pen. "Of course. Naturally, I've been to a cat house," he lied. "They are called brothels or bordellos where I come from."

"Prove it. Now?" Aaron picked up the Mont Blanc, stabbing the paper with the nib and making small ink splotches until Hugo rescued it.

Hugo frowned. He sat back and studied the ledgers and plat maps spread out before him. His eyes swam. Almost done. Tedious stuff. He couldn't let this lout get the better of him. "Now."

"At this very moment, my friend! This is a special night." Aaron smirked, touching his nose as if he had a secret. "Might want to bring your wallet."

Chapter Twenty
Love for Sale

The largest alcove, suffocatingly shuttered in the ubiquitous pink drapes and grandly flanked by two gilded columns, now concealed Catriona until the auction.

Shaded lamps on either side afforded a watercolor of light washing Cat's face and baby-doll dress of virginal sheer white muslin, showing her shape and hint of color beneath and a modest swell of bosom.

She held a childish nosegay in slippery hands. The hem, no matter how she tugged, stayed stubbornly above her knees. Enormous pink bows quivered like butterflies, long white stockings and slippers with straps, and her reddened lips and pinked cheeks completed the portrait of innocence, with Catriona's hair dressed in long, youthful, sausage curls cascading over white shoulders.

Uneasy in her little-girl get-up, with her legs disturbingly bare, Cat felt like a *leathcheann*…an eejit, upon hearing the growing hubbub, clink of glasses, disembodied laughter, joshing, and raucous jokes beyond the drapes, detecting more noisy arrivals from the swish of the front doors, stamping feet, polite offer of removing coats by Miss Adelaide's elderly retainer, until it sounded as if a herd of Belgian Congo elephants stampeded the Wylder Social Club.

The scent of cedar fires, the lingering jasmine and

lily-of-the-valley fragrances, plus male bodies crammed into tweed and leathers and smoking cheroots, plus a new odor, of Sweet Caporal cigarettes—slim white tubes of tobacco now becoming popular among young lions—all invaded her closed space, making her want to sneeze. Conjuring hordes of boys and men just beyond, Catriona felt like a red-tailed fox at an Englishman's hunt—slavering hounds baying, ready to chase her down, ripping at her clothes.

She clenched fists with the undeniable impulse to ease from the drapes, hugging the wall to the kitchen, and run—run as fast as she could.

Sweat trickled between shoulder blades. Goose bumps prickled her arms. The room was humid. She suffocated behind the thick pink drapes. She couldn't breathe but sucked in rapid gulps of air till she felt dizzy. Increasingly, Cat had to quell the urge to dash screaming through the unseen mob out there. She put her hand on the drapes to rip them apart…

****

Cat started. Her eyes opened wide.

It began.

Too late to run.

Trembling, Catriona heard Miss Adelaide's enchanting purr of husky laughter, used only when males were present, apparently in a small speech to the accompaniment of huzzahs, whistles, cheers, and hoots of approval. The piano's fanfare pounded away…

"Gentlemen! Gentlemen!" Miss Adelaide chuckled throatily. "Rein in your impatience. Prepare to be delighted and content. I assure you! We all know why we are here, gentlemen. Have your purses ready, prepare your hearts to rejoice, and set your minds open to a rare possibility and opportunity. Raise your hand, nod, or even wave a silk Chinese fan to place your bid.!" Miss Adelaide jested to laughter but impatient laughter, attested by one lone voice.

"Well! Let's get this rodeo started, Miss Addie!"

"The bidding will begin shortly. Until then, avail yourself of our libations and our bounteous buffet for your other appetites." Her husky chuckle came again, promising everything, followed by expectant nervous laughter and an increase of cutlery clatter.

The room quieted.

"Gentlemen all, and a few rogues, without further ado," Miss Adelaide announced, "I present for your pleasure, as your reward, a young miss straight from Ireland. An unspoiled Irish lass fresh from Londonderry County for your bidding…"

Cat then realized few, if any, had ever witnessed her back in the kitchens here or at the Longhorn. She was an unknown to most, and even then, they'd scarce recognize her out of the drab brown dress and the cap that had concealed her conspicuous hair.

****

Aaron urged Hugo along.

He smiled wickedly at the flame-haired youth. "Not far now. Gotta surprise for you."

"Surprise? How infantile. It is not my birthday." Hugo commented loftily in cultured tones.

Those tones tripped so lightly off this fool's tongue, Aaron thought, and he himself strived so hard to emulate them… God, he hated him!

"Oh, but it could be!" Aaron smirked, taking his crop to his horse, and cantering on, leaving Hugo to his own solitary devices. He was not going to miss this, just to show the fool up. He grinned as he heard Hugo's mount canter up beside him.

****

At a tug of gold silk cords, the pink velvet drapes swished open.

Catriona stood stiffly on the stool Miss Adelaide had bade her to pose upon in full view. She gave a sharp intake, along with the mob avidly eyeing her. Cat was instructed to look down, shyly, slightly scared, then look up and tremulously smile. Instead, she crushed the nosegay, holding her breath until faint.

With a thousand eyes belonging to men of all sizes and ages, the mob ten figures deep pressed forward as one, followed by silence as before a storm.

Was she not pleasing?

Then at that moment an excited murmur swirled about the room like a prairie dust devil.

Eyes opened. Or narrowly squinted. Faces brightened and bloomed.

They were pleased.

Eager. Enthralled. Calculating.

Most well-dressed, the bon and ton of Wylder—the banker, the mill owner. One intrepid trapper noted only for his eccentricity, filthy rich yet choosing to wear rough mountain garb. In the back, Cat saw several youths pretending indifference.

She hoped it wasn't one of them.

Oddly, Catriona did not wish for a youth. Too close in age. Nor did she wish for inexperienced fumblers in this, her first time, but a gentleman who kenned his way around women. "Masterful" was the word Cat searched for, in her romantic heart born of reading *Jane Eyre* and *Pride and Prejudice*.

203

One cowhand stood out with a face of gentle longing. Cat's heart went out to him.

"Well, when does the bidding start, Miss Addie! Can't shoehorn another one in?"

"Don't we get a sample?" one jested.

Cat eyed the crowd from below sooty lashes resting primly on pinked cheeks. She was not easy prey. She would show whoever won her. Even if Miss Adelaide kicked her out into the streets. Thankfully, Aaron's golden head was not bobbing among the crowd. The blood was too rich for him tonight. She breathed relief, making her bound bosom heave in a way that caught men's throats.

Why not leave then, with honor intact? A small voice spoke in her head, but it was too late…men of all sizes, conditions, and ages pressed into an interlocking mass, the doorways were covered, and stragglers kept arriving, vying for space. She backed into the alcove till her spine scraped the molding, effectively trapped, high and teetering on the small footstool. It made her seem she was trembling. Another ploy? Cat saw a few eyeing her as if she were a new horse to be broken, pressing harder against the rounded wall as the mob grew ever more raucous and demanding. She looked anxiously at Miss Adelaide, who stood behind a small podium holding a tiny gavel affixed with a pink bow, aware of the pounding cadence of *Bolero* just beginning…

"Here's my money, Miss Addie!"

"Everybody in Wylder's here and fer twenty miles around!"

Guffaws of encouragement greeted this.

Miss Adelaide, looking like a fluffy yellow canary in her tulle and glitter, rapped on the small lectern, and suddenly this was real.

"Gentlemen!"

Miss Adelaide's voice cracked the whip, this time sheathed in velvet. Her words poured out in a rich strong burr, like aged whiskey. "Gentlemen, this is not a cattle stampede, but an auction. Please retain your places."

She waved a tiny hand for Catriona to slowly revolve. "This young lady is most refined, gently brought up, and quite innocent. Her father, a pastor, sadly expired in her tender years back east, hence her orphaned state…and brought up by the good sisters of…" Cat couldn't make out what order of "good sisters" had raised her.

"I'd like to be her daddy!" One jokester hawked while Cat turned, gasping when Miss Adelaide's short crop, usually used on her small-sized mare, lifted her skirt slightly.

Catriona completed her slow awkward turn in the small space allotted.

"Catriona just celebrated her fourteenth birthday." Miss Adelaide's dimples deepened. "We think." She winked. "Pure. Untouched. A day many young girls look to be wed and become mothers. But not this shy young lass—yet with a wayward streak, I fear, gentlemen, just waiting to be tamed under the right—tutelage. Now you've had a good gander, who among you randy stallions shall start the bidding? Let us say fifty dollars, bidders for a newly-minted young lady, fresh and innocent as a baby chick."

Catriona gasped. That was a bit rich!

There was a murmur and some frowns. "In gold, silver, or blood money?" One of the stern men in back, bursting in tweed, sweat rivaling red jowls in the heated room, demanded.

"American Eagles, gentlemen, and no Confederate!" Miss Adelaide chivied and pointed a fan at the man with a southern flag on his hat.

Cat's breath caught in her throat as if a fish hook pierced it, not hearing the rest of the repartee.

Her eyes widened before she caught herself. "Oh, no!"

Miss Adelaide darted a venomous look at her.

Chapter Twenty-One
Dark Night of the Soul

Aaron.

Aaron here, half hidden against a stand holding an enormous epergne stuck with fronds. Her downfall from grace was complete. He was here not as one seeking her hand but her very soul. Yes, Catriona wanted Aaron, had yearned for his touch, his merest glance, at nights in the attic, had shamelessly dreamt of him even after that time, and here he was.

Perhaps. Perhaps? He had a plan…he was shocked, though. Outside of a widening of the eye and a nonplussed look, he made no gesture that he recognized Cat.

Her heart lifted. Yes! Here to rescue her! That's why he pretended.

The room faded, along with avid faces, to only Aaron eyeing her from across the room. His expression told her nothing. Not love, pity, or desire. He seemed an observer.

Bid for me! Aaron!

Pleading eyes sent the message. His declaration of love. He would "buy" her, whisk her from Miss Adelaide, and plight her his troth—she forgot, for the moment in heady dreams, the specter of his stepmother who had banished her.

She fretted. Crushed petals drifted to the floor. To

the room, she must look terrified, not kenning quite what to do, no matter her instructions. Catching Miss Adelaide's frowning question mark, Cat slipped back on her wobbly shy smile as "the girls" had instructed her, while looking worriedly at the bidders...coming out of her mental musings to hear...

"Fifty dollars!"

Cat searched for the bidder. She flashed an anguished look at Aaron, but he gazed nonchalantly over the throng as if he too was intrigued by the bidder, sensing the first sting of animosity. He must hurry before it got too high. Fifty dollars was an unimaginable sum.

But even now Aaron looked on with a bored superior air and stifled a yawn. Cat watched him turn to speak to someone and was startled when Miss Adelaide rapped the lectern like a hammer pounding nails.

"A fine start, gentlemen, but just the beginning...shall we say, sixty?"

"Sixty-five!"

"Gentlemen all! Let us not nickel-and-dime!"

"Seventy-five!"

"I hear seventy-five. Come, come. An untouched flower? A mere seventy-five? Let us get serious!" Miss Adelaide smiled roguishly at them, reproving. "Are you men, or little boys shooting marbles, perhaps, or betting on mumblety-peg?"

The trapper edged out. The rest stayed.

Cat felt a scream welling up, like a rattling steam kettle's whistle, as hands rose, some with jerky hesitant motions, a few waving energetically. Heads nodded, each bidder eyeing the other with fever pitch, to win the prize, heating the room as they egged each other on far beyond their means, perhaps.

Her ears closed down, registering only odd buzzes and rumbles, and the room swung back and forth. Her face flushed and arms chilled as bidding turned to a frenzy, rising higher. Yet one tiny part of Cat's mind gloated, the one where the devil imp resided, as serious bidders pressed closer, jostling discreetly at first, then elbowing sharply, leaving discretion at home with the wife. These were feverish bidders, horses racing for the finish, neck and neck, though a flurry of bidding was in five or even one-dollar increments.

One man, hooting and hollering for attention, waved bills. Several cityfied characters, who had come in by train, carelessly flicked cigar ashes, yet their eyes betrayed them in glittering rapaciousness as they raised eyebrows and lifted fingers.

One serious bidder sat, lordly, in an armchair at the fringe. He merely waved his cigar a fraction, below a lizard smile and half-slitted eye, beyond the smoke's gray pall.

Cat gasped. The last bid was three hundred and twenty-six dollars—the six was met by groans and laughter.

"And fifty cents!" The cowboy. He was laughed to the sidelines.

But in the end, it was from an undistinguished fellow lost in the crowd.

"Four hundred!" He bellered the declaration. The humid, overly masculine parlor was stunned to irritated silence.

Cat sensed currents of rage and frustration as the mass parted, staring, murderously irate because their blood was in such a state, at the man with his belly and bull-like shoulders resembling a salesman of cattle feed plowing sideways through their midst, in a grubby stramming-tight tweed suit, baggy at the knees. His face was blooming red above a too-tight celluloid collar, his large-mustached mouth clamped on a soggy unlit cigar.

He leered up at her, or grimaced around it with teeth brown with tobacco, or worse.

Cat swayed. *No! no!*

She swiveled, reaching out. "Miss Adelaide. No!" she whispered hoarsely.

Miss Adelaide was by her side then, clamping her arm in her tiny hand like a sharp-boned vise. "No, you don't, my girl!" she hissed, smiling past small white teeth, turning to face the mob in a teasing, lighthearted manner.

"Are there any other hale fellows out there? Any more range riders ready for a wild untamed virgin? We have this sweet rose to be plucked. Might be a few thorns, but nothing you stalwart men cannot handle. Bidders? Surely, my fine gentlemen, such a rare treat should not go fallow so early on. This gentleman sees a prize. Do I hear four hundred—six?" She jested.

Cat kenned she knew that sum was a tease, and the mob out there, the sea of faces, would take it so.

It seemed to douse the bidding. Already the bidder, reeking of a devil's brew of tobacco, onions, and whiskey, was diving for her with a proprietary air and red-rimmed eyes that spoke no good.

"No-no-no…" she moaned. *Please, Adelaide.*

Once again Catriona backed into the alcove till her spine scraped ornate molding. She eyed the slit 'tween the wall and the drape. The kitchen wasn't very far off…

"Here! One thousand!"

The voice was commanding, but its owner was

secure enough not to raise it above the crowd's rumble. Even so every ear picked it up.

The tweedy man twirled, furiously searching. To Cat, he looked as if he'd discovered a snake in his boot when the rare prize was almost in his grasp. A free room for the night came with the girlie. He knew what all he'd like to do with the twelve hours promised, by God. He'd show her a few things she'd never thought of, all righty, and some he'd never had the chance to try. He owned her! He could do whatever he—

Her bidder's sparse greasy hair sprayed out from below his derby hat as he whirled to spot the craven interloper, while Catriona frantically searched the crowd for the new bidder too—was it the man with the lizard smile? Even he was indescribably better than this one, if it had to come to pass.

The frenzy, the rising tide of excitement, had seized her. For a second, she forgot what the end was, why she was here.

Disgruntled bidders drifted to the sidelines to watch the entertainment, but not enough for her to see who was the new bidder. She heard only grumbles of conjecture, but that voice was familiar. Cat's thoughts winged back to the Longhorn, yes…but where was Aaron? Why, wasn't it his bid? But…one thousand dollars? Even Catriona realized this was not possible, unless he put old Levi's saloon on the block.

"Where'd he come from?"

"Ya ain't in it at the start, you ain't bona fi-dee."

She heard the confusion. Cat kenned no one would up the sky-high bid. It was all for show.

"This here's a plant to up the ante, by gum!"

"Biddin's done bin over!" the greasy man shouted.

"Gentlemen, gentlemen," purred Miss Adelaide, but her reproaches held a panicky burr. "Now, let us hear this mysterious bidder. What say you, sir? Where are you hiding?" She flirted, shielding her eyes.

When there was no immediate answer, she sashayed, lost in the crowd, save for yellow plumes waving overhead, so Cat kept track as Miss Adelaide swirled in their midst, tapping men on the shoulder with her fan. "Come now."

Vexation tinted her voice—this was close to becoming a farce. Did someone trick her with the outrageous bid, only to remain silent now? Cat could hear her thoughts as plain as if they came over the Morse telegraph.

"Come, let us get a gander at the big spender."

****

"I say."

Cultured tones fluted from the back of the room. "I should correct myself."

This announcement was followed by waves of snickers and guffaws.

"Too late, ya done bid!"

A few looked speculatively at Cat again, liking what they saw.

Perhaps there was still a chance, if the outrageous bid was disqualified.

The lizard man fidgeted in his chair, sardonic, or disgusted. Either way, he eyed her hotly under his wide-brimmed hat.

A shock of bright red hair rode above the sea of men, like a red-sailed schooner, as Hugo thrust through the mob—which parted reluctantly—removing his gray bowler to become unmistakable.

Cat gaped. Hugo! Hugo was her high bidder!

Hugo doggedly continued until he stood before Miss Adelaide, now back at her lectern.

"I am unsure quite how one thousand American dollars translates. I bid in English pounds; you see." Hugo turned to query the mob. "That is right? I assume we could possibly exchange notes at an exchequer, or mayhap a bank?"

Murmurs rose to excited babble. Pounds was more than American dollars. Would Miss Adelaide accept *furrin* dough? From a stranger in these parts? *Don't seem right.*

Cat drank in Hugo's gray suit, wool so fine it shone like charcoal satin, his long legs encased in knee-high glossy black riding boots, the pale maroon brocaded waistcoat and crisp white ruffled shirt with a stock, rather old-fashioned but stylish, and his flaming hair—an interesting counterpoint. He was by far the most elegant man in the room, including the swell Cat had christened "lizard man."

The greasy salesman blustered and made a grab at Cat, missing her as she shrank.

"Come on, girlie-girl. Yer mine!"

He whirled on Miss Adelaide, spraying, "Can't flim-flam me!"

With his other hand, he dug in his pocket and dragged out a wad of filthy, crinkled, limp bills tied in dirty string. Cat had no notion if it signified life savings, a bank robbery, or a sudden death in the family. Moreover, she scarcely cared.

Without grace or ceremony, the man swayed and drunkenly threw the wad at Miss Adelaide. It bounced off her bosom. Her cheeks pinked. Her expression cracked the whip.

"There! Paid for, by gum," he bawled, "and this off-eyed gal better be worth it!"

He managed to reach into the alcove and grab Catriona's wrist, half-dragging her out; the nosegay lay crushed underfoot. Cat cringed at the hard dry calloused palms, dirt under the nails, scruffy beard, acrid scent of tobacco and unwashed clothes.

"The bidding had hardly begun, my good man, when I arrived. If you were a gentleman…?" Hugo cocked a scorching red brow at Miss Adelaide. Miss Adelaide bit her lip.

"Good man! I ain't yer good man! You lily-white furriner."

"You would not find me a naysayer, sir," Hugo rejoined smoothly.

The bidder spat at Hugo's glossy boots, missed, and hawked for another glob of ammunition, but he was dry of spit. Not letting go of Catriona, he swung a hard fist in a straight shot to Hugo's jaw, not an amateur's wild haymaker but a practiced street brawler's punch.

Cat spied Miss Adelaide calculating, making eyes at the "enforcer"—a tall grizzled black jack-of-all-trades garbed in an ill-fitting tuxedo, even now thrusting through with a well-polished ax handle. She waved him to stay. This was turning into an embarrassing farce, her expression spoke—should she give over to this new bidder out of nowhere, and disgruntle her best clients? Or…?

Even so, it was getting ugly, far from the dignified ceremony of bringing a young girl into adulthood and the highlight of a successful bid, but not for this disgusting scum of manhood. Perhaps she could still rescue the situation. No one seemed overly fond of the winning bidder, at any rate.

Discreetly kicking the wad of bills with her toe, Miss Adelaide deliberately gave her back to the swaying pugilist fists doubled, glaring at Hugo, who seemed unaffected beyond a reddened jaw. The man blearily offended, building up another head of outrage, tried to swing around Miss Adelaide. By this time, he noted the tall black man with the ax handle and subsided, and waited, fuming, for justice, by fist or reward. Either way, he promised Hugo bloody revenge.

Miss Adelaide, digging deep for inspiration, grinned roguishly at Hugo, tapping him with her fan.

"Gentlemen! Do we let our prize go to a foreigner? With all of our red-blooded Wyoming males? Surely, we could have more successful bidders."

She sashayed among them, swinging hips, tapping them on the cheeks with her fan and madly flirting.

"Red-blooded we may be, but we don't wanna bleed to death though our wallets."

A man with the rough leather vest of a miner barked out angrily, "I can fetch a gal for fifty cents, cash money."

The enforcer subsided, resting the bat.

The men looked sheepish at that comment, all but the enraged bidder, and lizard man, taking amused interest, fingered his elegant wallet but nevertheless returned it at the same time "greasy man," as Cat thought of him, swung a weighty cutglass decanter, wielded by an arm thick as a log, at Hugo's head towering above him.

Inebriated as he was, it would have broken Hugo's jaw.

Hugo simply raised one arm, blocking the blow—
"Fool me once, sir..." and threw a swift hard punch to
the belly with his other fist. His opponent inadvisably
doubled over, butting Hugo in the chest while clawing
up at his face.

Hugo slammed the back of his neck with a swift
heel-hand chop. The greasy man exploded a gust of air.
Staggering, he bulled forward single-minded, eyes red,
arms ending in meaty flailing fists, all technique flown
the coop.

Hugo seemed to have limbs forged in a blacksmith's
shop for all his willowiness. The gob-smacked room
heard the creak of bone and shoulder tendons, as the too-
effete man, in their estimation, sidestepped, snatched,
and twisted his opponent's arm as he sailed on past,
bending it far up his spine.

Hugo made a motion so swift the attacker flew over
his shoulder with his arm twisted oddly sideways before
the mob kenned what was happening. The room heard
the crack like a firecracker exploding—drawing *ohhhhs*.
This was turning into quite a show. None would leave
now, even if threat of the gallows hung over them. This
beanpole, pale, flame-haired, four-eyed, mushy-
mouthed toff was not only taking on but overpowering a
brute of a man, a feed salesman, used to brawls and
bareknuckle fights and pugilistic events for money, it
was told, and the toff was winning!

The greasy man howled as his knees thudded to the
floor, until Hugo whiplashed him back, accompanied by
another howl and another bone-crack somewhere in the
shoulder region. The man instantly grabbed toward his
side, spitting, drooling from his nose, with a face ruby as
a beet. He reached in and withdrew a bulldog pistol,

wavering it unsteadily.

Hugo gripped his wrist, forcing the gun hand up, where it fired at the ceiling—fortunately missing the chandelier—and gave a snake-swift uppercut to the man's jaw.

Cat too marveled that such a fragile-looking instrument as Hugo could wield such force. Hugo's hands were too long, pale, and aristocratic for such manly efforts; more as if he played fine instruments like a violin or pianoforte than indulged in fisticuffs. Then, flushing, she recalled his sculpted form, hewn apparently of stone, at the swimming pond.

Hugo booted the greasy man's rear. Slumping, struggling for breath, her erstwhile bidder tunked his forehead on the floor, unfortunately bare of carpet in that spot, resounding like a hard winter melon hit with a bat.

Stubbornly tenacious, he grabbed Hugo's ankle with his good fist. Hugo jerked it back, giving him, as any common street brawler, a sharp kick in the head.

Miss Adelaide groaned inwardly, seeing the brawl was a runaway freight. Moreover, the crowd seemed spellbound by the pugilistic display. This was spoiling her grand gesture, her event of the year. She couldn't recall the last time she'd had a genuine virgin here at the Social Club! She pondered briefly if pugilism could be a side attraction out back where bloomers usually fluttered on the clotheslines.

The man rolled heavily over, showing an agonized face. He heaved onto all fours as Hugo danced, butting Hugo's knees like a billy goat, attempting to surround his legs with one arm and topple him, as the mob backed. Hugo grasped him round the midriff, swung him up, and squeezed until the bidder's face turned into a purple swollen plum and his eyes like two boiled eggs.

He struggled, kicking back, swinging a clubby fist and spewing invective, while the crowd now cheered Hugo on, urging him to finish the man.

Chapter Twenty-Two
The Wrong Bid

Though with grudging respect, a certain abhorrence, a bigotry of class emerged, though few felt likely to intervene. Here was this youth in his foppish gray satiny outfit, casually, like effin' magic, with a minute flip of the wrist here, a shrug of a shoulder there, or one long pale hand with a telling chop, making Christmas mincemeat out of the poor fella who really was the rightful winner, all said and done, or so they nodded to each other.

Were the rich and hoity-toity to lord it over them in this way too? The one area where they felt supreme?

As if judging the throng, Hugo stepped aside, staring down at his attacker.

"Truce, sir?" He held out a hand. "Also, an apology is in order, I believe."

"Truce be damned! You can believe the sun shines outta yer arse. I will see you in hell, you frail quean, fricking she-male, before I apologize fer what's rightfully mine." The crowd muttered agreement.

He swung on Catriona. "Harlot! All your doin'! Leadin' a man on, and you!" He snarled at Adelaide, sticking his dirty finger in her face. "This madame of the house! A cheap doxie with unholy tricks to rob a man's pockets and self-respect."

Snapping his shoulder back in place, he spat at her.

Miss Adelaide's cheeks turned stony, her mouth pressed. The invisible riding crop crackled and snapped. She looked about her, first picking up a vase, studied it briefly, put it back and selected another and cracked him over the head. Shards clattered on the floor.

He howled and clutched his noggin, declaring loudly, "Fetchin' the sheriff, I will."

"I'm right here." A man stepped forward, trying not to grin behind his mustache at Miss Adelaide. Miss Adelaide decided her path and said, "Take your money and scat." She snapped her fan. "I don't cater to your sort." She kicked his wad of bills to him.

"And ya do the likes of him," he sneered—and lunged with a wild haymaker aimed at her belly for another go-round.

He didn't learn.

Adelaide waved off the sheriff, raised a derringer from somewhere in her waspwaisted skirts, and held it steady on. The man knocked it away and, straight-arming sideways, without looking, managed with one hand on Catriona's neck to drag her choking, sputtering, clawing at his grip, off to the stairs, howling, "Come on! I earned you, by jingo!"

Picking up the derringer, Hugo swiveled, thunked the greasy man on the head, and the greasy man dropped like a sack of rocks. The sheriff stood down.

"You sir, have not learned your lesson, it appears," Hugo commented mildly in his perfect tones, as the man lay moaning and clutching his head. Several of the mob looked ready to intervene. Undeterred, greasy man crawled to Hugo, spitting out teeth, howling cuss words and dire threats.

Hugo hefted him up by collar and waistband and,

with the intense interest and awe of the entire stunned audience, threw him out with such force he landed in the midst of the street in a pile of horse patty.

Miss Adelaide eyed him appraisingly.

The bidding was over, and the greasy man's cash, which he'd taken from his innermost pocket, had most mysteriously evaporated into other men's pockets after he dropped it. The crowd cleared out, save for a few who, ceding the show was over, had more interesting business upstairs. Pearl and Opal were eyeing Hugo with more than a professional gleam. Cat felt a twinge—okay, more than a twinge—of little green leprechaun-ache, she conceded.

Not looking at Catriona, Hugo withdrew an elegant leather wallet.

"One thousand, I believe," he proclaimed coolly and peeled off the correct amount to Miss Adelaide, who looked a tad dazed. "It is in pounds. I do apologize. I do not have the amount in U.S. dollars."

Rallying, with a pained look as if she ate a pickle, Miss Adelaide waved it aside. "What do I do with that? Might as well be wallpaper. The bank won't take it."

Hugo looked nonplussed for a flicker of the eye. "A bank in a larger city—say, Cheyenne, madam?"

She looked resentful and put out. The eyes on multicolored bills featuring Queen Victoria's puffy face gazed sullenly back as Miss Adelaide murmured, "That face would stop a clock."

Hugo's alabaster flesh pinked. "Many have made mention of that. How gauche of me. I mean about the exchange. Might you accept a letter of—how do you say, IOU? And I will have proper funds wired forthwith."

Adelaide was increasingly aware she was fast losing

authority and *dignitas* among the remaining audience.

An onlooker, another trapper by the look of him and his scent of hides, snorted. "Ya figure ya ken all about us? Cheyenne's got more sense too than ta take paper ain't worth more'n wooden nickels over here."

"I fear that is all I have to offer, madam, but the offer was made with true intent." Hugo eyed Miss Adelaide with more coldness than Catriona would have imagined he owned.

"These—gentlemen are my witnesses, and the lovely young ladies." He swept a gracious hand toward Pearl and Ruby. Amethyst and Opal must be entertaining, Catriona supposed, checking the stairs leading up.

Hugo's mouth parted in a charming smile, the corners of his lips curving into his thin cheeks, revealing perfect white teeth. He gave Adelaide a courtly bow. "Then you must accept this. It is worth…much more than a paltry one thousand, I believe, with my sincere apologies over unfortunate distractions."

Hugo tugged a hefty gold ring with a carnelian bas relief of a Roman emperor ringed with diamonds from his right ring finger. Catriona gasped. No one had ever made such a gesture over her.

Miss Adelaide kept her face poker-smooth as she held her hand out, then flipped the hefty ring, catching it as if weighing, lifted a shoulder as if to say, "Guess that'll do," and was secretly delighted, as Cat noted by her smug smile that said, *This gent from London doesn't ken its true worth.*

Miss Adelaide kenned to the ounce.

"The bidding is over, gentlemen. I thank you all for your enthusiasm. And please avail yourself of our other many amenities."

There were faint grumbles, ignored with a fixed smile. Turning, she swept her hand toward the curving staircase. "You may please yourself, sir. Take your prize."

Cat caught movement on the stairs.

Aaron made an arrogant descent, trailed by a bedraggled, sullen-faced Amethyst, who cast Aaron a poisonous glare before flopping down in a deep red armchair clutching a pillow to her breast, as if it were a fortress.

"Did I miss something?" He raised a brow at Cat in passing, while her gaze followed his gloriously Adonis-like figure—wide shoulders, narrow waist, long muscular legs in tight trews. His hair was straggling and limp, shirt half misbuttoned, trews drooping as if not fastened.

He wasn't worth her spit, she told herself as he sauntered to the small marble-topped bar, leaned on his elbows, and watched the scene. So why did it feel as if she was hurt by a hundred cuts? Or had swallowed glass?

She belatedly recalled Hugo.

Stiffening her spine, she breathed deeply and revolved, waiting for Hugo to make a move. She wasn't frightened. Somewhere in between... No, she wasn't.

Miss Adelaide's' eyes weighed heavy as stones upon them. She clapped hands when Hugo made no move.

"Come, gentlemen, shall we escort our lucky bidder and his blushing prize?"

The unlucky bidders and kibitzers crowded round, cheering them on. Opal and Pearl fanned and flirted coquettishly at Hugo and blew kisses.

She had hoped her first time was to be with her beautiful Aaron in the bridal bed. She had imagined it so many times. What a foolish muddling colleen she was. He with eyes like holes in the sky letting sunlight in, lighting her day, and hair pale as yellow silk, thick and wavy, the long, square-jawed face with deep chin cleft—she groaned inwardly at her forlorn fancy. This was here. This was now. She was with Hugo. Make the best of it. Tomorrow was another day. Time to put childish fantasies aside, Aaron included.

From now on…

She eyed Hugo with a face like doom.

Chapter Twenty-Three
Winner Takes All

Instead, Hugo bowed to Miss Adelaide. "I will take my leave now, madam. My business here is concluded." He spoke loftily and gracefully to both Catriona and the madam, performed an ungraceful bow like the Hugo of old, smashing his elbow in the eye of another chap, shorter than he, who had the misfortune of hovering behind.

Pushing Cat aside, Miss Adelaide rounded on him, bright yellow hair bouncing loose, drawing up to her full five feet, two inches, to Hugo's gangling height. With her chin aligned with his third shirt button, she addressed him with blood in her eye, despite her short stature.

"So! My sort ain't good enough for you higher than mighties," she hissed, mindful of her audience. "My girls are pearls of great price. You've better, I s'pose, in those London slums you toffs likes to waller in."

Her background was showing, her speech broadening. Being Irish, Cat could not place the Appalachian twang.

"You bid fair and square on this one," Miss Adelaide whispered urgently. "She's caused enough trouble. Sticks to her like the tar baby." She checked over her shoulder at avid speculation further tarnishing her grand event. Why had she not shooed the mob out and locked the frickin' doors? This debacle would burn across Wylder faster than prairie fires in August.

"Not getting this ring back. Might as well spit on it and shake hands."

Hugo assured her he wasn't planning to take it back. A flush colored his high cheekbones as he held back anger, not chagrin.

Go or stay? Hugo gave no indication.

Miss Adelaide spun on Catriona in a voice designed not to carry. "You seem to stir problems like a pig does mud. I can't have that. I shan't let you upset my apple cart. Either go with him—he won ya—leave without, or go on upstairs."

Cat flashed agonized appeals. "But 'tisn't my doin'."

Hugo gazed at Cat, smiling with a faint expression that could mean anything. Nevertheless, Cat flinched. He read her every emotion like flip cards, or carousel lamps making moving pictures.

Hugo bent close to Cat as if Miss Adelaide were a mute china doll. "This is the third time I've rescued you."

"You do wind up in some odd places for my benefit," Cat hissed back, forcing a smile, discomfited by Miss Adelaide's demeanor and Hugo's hateful reminder. Miss Adelaide's gaze would frost the equator. The jerk of her head to the stairs said, "Don't dilly-dally. Do not embarrass me."

With a cleft flashing in one cheek, Hugo placed a hand on Cat's back. "We shan't tarry then, madam. We don't wish to disappoint well-wishers." He threw a cheeky grin at the onlookers, gave a regal wave, victorious, to the crowd, which was mollified now there was a winner in the gent who gave them such a fine bare-fisted match.

Prodded, Cat trod the steps as if treading to the guillotine. Hugo gripped her waist, leaning his long frame, whispering, "Courage! Smile! Laugh as if I told you a wicked joke. You are not going to a Tyburn hanging."

His long face took on a sardonic grin, lighting the luminous gray eyes that flashed like cold rain for an instant behind his glasses.

Cat stiffened. With that, Hugo lifted her effortlessly, threw her over his shoulder, and bounded up the winding stairs to rousing cheers and bawdy comments from the rapidly inebriated crowd.

Miss Adelaide watched from the bottom, stony-faced.

****

Down the long gallery overlooking the parlor below, a door stood ajar, emitting soft rosy light. The designated room opened to a wide, gilded, heavily cupid-embossed bed, inviting rose velvet coverlets pulled back, lacy pillows heaped and plumped, the lamp—painted with violets—with wick turned low.

Over the bed hung an oil of a rubicund reclining harem girl.

Hugo released Cat, gazing into her odd eyes. Closing them, Cat waited, supposing he would proceed now to kiss her and rake in his winnings.

"You are free," he murmured.

She stared at her feet, hands clasped behind her, not wanting him to see her confused face. "You—you bought me fair and square."

"I believe the days of slavery are over, madam. Did not your Mr. Lincoln just suffer a massive undertaking in that department?"

Cat looked up, spying Hugo's back.

"But wait!" she blurted. "Wait!" Her mouth unfroze, the lump in her throat unstoppered. "Where are you going?" Then she caught herself. Was she not a girl of Ireland? Did she not have the dignity of a flea on a dog?

"I wish to thank you, sir." But her eyes slid sideways. Aware of the scene below, she shamelessly tugged his fine silverish coattails. "But what should I do? You—bought me. They will be thinkin' ill of me and all!"

"Nay. But any gentleman could not but see what would come to pass. I sensed you did not—wish it."

"You have more stars in heaven than I can ever count, sir…but—" In truth envisioning her "small treasure," the last she owned, to be taken by force by the brutish bidder who looked like he bathed in a horse trough once a year, Catriona was beyond grateful.

He checked the lush interior, with hubbub of gaiety and noise below, puzzlement drawing his burnished brows together. "You came here to Miss Adelaide's. You do not wish to stay?"

Cat wanted to say, am I that unlovely? Do you not wish what you bid for? What is wrong with me, that even such as you does not find me with favor, she yearned to speak with the bitterness of a wild persimmon on the tongue.

He gravely mulled her anguish. "Then you must leave this place."

Hugo's ivory face, with its furze of red mustache and fiery hair flipped over thick lenses, gave away nothing but vague distaste, as if he smelt a bad aroma from far off. Catriona hoped it was not her but a scent of cheap cologne, the cloying jasmine one of the girls insisted on dousing herself with, hanging heavy in fetid air the room could not conceal.

Catriona glared over his obtuseness. Nervy, she snapped, sharper than intended, "So easy to state what you will or will not do, if you are a toff!" Or close to one. "I cannot go back to the Longhorn! I cannot go anywhere. No one will have me." A suppressed sob strangled her voice. "Madame Solange! She kens where I've been, doesn't she now! If she would not accept me before, she would rather take in a—a stray cat than a Catriona. She's more pride than a lord mayor of London's wife."

"You have no real bed to lay your head, then. Only here."

She shook her head. "No. No one will suffer me. And even Miss—" She left the thought unsaid.

"I will."

She looked up, confused. "I will—what?" Catriona placed her hand on his chest, giving him a shove far from gentle.

"I will have you. Come with me."

"From one pan to the other? Both in boiling water. I would be your—your—bit on the side?" Hugo was no different, she thought bitterly. No better. A grasping male taking advantage of her miserable state, like others that had tried to undo her knickers, or grab where they shouldn't. Cat sniveled, inelegantly wiping her nose on the back of her hand like a gutter hoyden.

He offered a fine linen handkerchief.

She ignored the monogram in which she noisily blew her nose. Hugo demurred accepting it back.

"No, little one. I only want to be with you, upon your invitation, and…I cannot see that fortunate event occurring." He gave a short bow, his long elegant hand on hand on chest.

Cat sneered.

His smooth demeanor changed like storm clouds squalling from nowhere across leaden skies—gray eyes darkening, slashing lightning glints.

"Don't stay!" Hugo threw out a hand, pacing in frustration. "Return with me! My uncle is still at the Longhorn. He's—" He sighed deeply, throwing her a lopsided smile. "Negotiating for a hole in the ground—or several. It will take eons. A meteor could crash to the earth and stars wither to walnuts before he makes up his mind. I do believe he enjoys the hunt, solitude, and renunciation of the usual stuffy London society. He's taking French Leave—playing 'hooky' I think your term is."

A rueful smile chased the storm clouds.

"I…" Hugo hesitated, pale face turned aside, gazing off. "I can protect you."

"I don't need protection. You see you have gained nothing! I would never…"

Catriona could not go on. She should be grateful. What flaw was in her? Why blame him for her pickle? Catriona boiled over like a kettle of burnt sugar, bittersweet and quick to turn brittle and crack, spinning from Hugo so he could not see her fear, truth be told, of not seeing Hugo's melancholy face.

It was the culmination of pain, loneliness, and the abandonment by parents in a strange and hostile land where all seemed to despise her for her foreign country ways, when half of Wylder seemed to be from somewhere else. Kindness was her undoing. She did not ken how to act.

Oh, why was he vexing her so? Staring with what?—pity!—through those thick lenses. She hated him, with his cultured tones. "You remind me, sir, of the British landlords that made Pa and Ma think low of themselves," she hurled.

Hugo was a burr under the saddle, which she could not stop long enough to remove but could not abide, either. What was he rabbiting on about now? Why not go gracefully and leave her with a flyspeck of dignity?

"Catriona…?"

"What! Why are you still here? If you suppose I'm beholden when all you want is…" Catriona threw herself dramatically on the bed, making it bounce, staring grimly at the ceiling and making an ungainly snow angel on the pink velvet coverlet, appearing every inch a delectable but grim Irish martyr. "Go ahead. Ye've paid for it."

Hugo fought for control. Anger flashed, but then humor knitted his face in suppressed laughter till all forbearance unraveled into a long loud hoot. "HAHAHAAAAHAHAhoho…" Choking for air, he sputtered to a stop, wiping his eyes.

"Forgive me, miss…" Chuckles still erupted from that straight proper mouth as he vainly strived to press it to silence.

Cat sprang up like a wind-up toy, making the comfy bed bounce once more, her feet thudding on the floor as she flounced off, defiant and miserable at the same time. Not really, she told herself, after a small imp nudged her, carping that she was not exactly gracious no matter the motive this ungainly fellow might have.

She stared aghast at Hugo. *He's gone all doolally.*

He bounded over and tugged the weighty brass bed post, shoving it side to side, so the whole bed shivered and rattled, then lifted the weighty post and thrice let it drop, making floor-shaking thuds each time. Scarcely breathing hard, he dropped it once more for good measure and swiveled to her, his wide attractive mouth grinning.

"Now with all that heaving and bouncing on the bed, and me laughing until I'm breathless as a spavined nag, and the floor given a good thumping, no doubt we have put on the appropriate and titillating show for all beneath us, including your rapacious Miss Adelaide. Don't you agree?"

Cat gazed, dumfounded, at the rumpled bed, snapping her mouth shut, blushing from toes to cheeks. "Oh! Oh! Then the tale will spread."

Hugo eyed her sardonically and with less patience. "I think that is the proper assumption."

"But all of Wylder will... Aaron will..." Cat sobered at Hugo's expression as if a fire curtain had dropped at a theater— Blank. Ominous.

"Ah, Catriona, my little Irish ragamuffin," he said smoothly, still with the cold blank fire-curtain expression. "You will be the death of me."

"But what will they think?" She sulked.

"The usual!" he snapped. "You may stay here now that your virtue has been supplanted. I'm certain Miss Adelaide could be seduced...or... We could wed."

She whirled on him. "What are you on about now? Haven't you done enough not to be after teasin' me, an' all?"

Chapter Twenty-Four
Sea Change

"I will take you back to the Longhorn. Lord Greville is deep into contract considerations. Mulling over"—a faint twitch of the mouth—"which mine, or rather how many. He gets this way—obsessed. His lordship will be here, as said, for"—he sighed—"a while." Which sounded as if doomsday would come and go before the duke made his decision.

"What has that to do with me?" She crossed her arms and tapped her toe, conscious of her long bare legs. Apparently, Hugo was too.

"I said, then we will wed…"

Catriona stared with all the comprehension of a wood stump, as if Hugo asked her to fly to the moon on gossamer wings. He sighed again.

"Wife. You could return as my wife."

His face told Catriona nothing. Calm. Matter of fact. Eyes behind the lenses unreadable, already roaming the room as if searching for something she'd need to collect, flickering a smile as if in reassurance.

Catriona gaped as if he spoke Hindustani. "We will—wed?" Or did he say, "We will bed"?

"We will wed. Hang it! Be married. How do you say—'hitch our wagons together.' Simple. I take it you are without wherewithal, acquaintances, or relatives." He said it as a given. "So why not? I could do worse.

You're not a lady, true, but it takes more than fine clothes. All you have to do is look at my companions. If I dress you up, and we tame your, ah, hair, you could pass anywhere," he muttered off-handedly as Catriona eyed a hefty candlestick.

His white porcelain face held a slight blush almost matching his hair.

"Oh, if ye sand rough edges off, and take me out of me pig sty, and make me be wearin' me shoes an' all, I just might pass muster!"

But her ire was performance only.

Cat's mind galloped ahead in a wayward race—if he was willing to wed, why could he not simply lend her a few coins to get on the train, to go far away to another place—another chance? She'd be damned forever if she would ask. A true gentleman would offer…

As if her thoughts were writ in purple ink across her forehead, he spoke with his usual stiffness. "I put that awkwardly, as always. When we are away from this establishment, you may stay or go, as you please. Yet I will assure myself you are safe. It is not fitting for a young miss to venture alone."

That was his class speaking. Catriona fumed.

"But why?" She looked at Hugo with helpless appeal. "I've been so *mí-thaitneamhach*." At his expression, she whispered, "Ungrateful."

Catriona studied her shoes.

Hugo's face held no more expression than a cast iron skillet. "True. Why? No particular reason."

"That is not an answer."

"It is the best I can do, nevertheless…" He looked away. Cat saw he meant to say more. Biting his full lower lip, Hugo stopped himself, shying like a horse

234

would shy from going over a cliff.

Cat felt her tummy claw as if she had swallowed nettles. All was going so fast. She could not wrap her head around it. "I do not believe in divorce, sir. If this is a rich man's game, it is cruel."

He sighed to his great booted feet. "I believe in the Orient there is a saying something like, "If one saves a life, they are beholden to keep on saving it until doomsday… At the moment, doomsday seems a welcome option." Hugo appeared as if he had saved a bobcat in a sack, regretting Catriona's claws. He cocked his head, and red hair fell in a fiery waterfall over one eye as he slowly thought.

"We could say we were."

Cat scorned. "There be no secrets here. No proper priests and all. Anyone would know we were deceitful, and they'd laugh." She sulked unreasonably.

"Why so obstinate?" His voice was as if he asked her what her favorite color was. "Because I am so ugly? Awkward? Never fear, I am well aware of my reputation, as I am reminded repeatedly and tediously. I won't touch you, if that is your concern. You will be kept pure." A faint note of derision mixed with, she'd like to think, regret coloring his tone.

Cat watched, oddly hurt and contrary. "But I don't know you."

He grinned suddenly. "Oh, I think you know me better than most young ladies."

Cat flushed, kenning he referred to the pond when yes, indeed, she got to know every inch of Hugo! Here, this tall drink of water offered her a rope made of pure gold and strong as she wished…and she scorned him.

Cat tried to weave whole cloth from the tangled

skeins. Flight. Madam Solange. Poverty. What would Ma and Pa think? Was Aaron hopelessly lost, with fate slapping her face? *Wake up!* Cat's imp prodded. *Still maundering on about that lout?*

While the mind is logical, the heart cannot be. What did it matter, in the end? She'd be elevated. Made safe above the flood waters of hunger and homelessness.

Cat wavered, faint. The excitement of the bidding had topped off a long day that seemed a lifetime ago, during which she had not eaten a bite since the gulped breakfast of coffee and dry toast eaten whilst they dressed her.

Hugo reached out one long hand, catching her arm.

She pretended she tripped, snatching it away, faltering.

Chapter Twenty-Five
For My Sins

She shook her head. The day crashed down as if its hours were stones pressing her below earth. She blinked awake. She was in Hugo's arms, knees bent over one arm, her neck the other, as he cradled her next to his chest. She felt his heart thumping.

Or was it hers?

"Let me down," Cat whispered. Yet his arms, no matter the chilliness of his ice-gray suit, were warm and strong. Instead, he tossed her over his shoulder with her bottom in the air and long black ringlets bouncing to his waist.

"What do you think you are doing?" Her voice was the wail of a cat as she strived to tug her dress down. He muttered something dire under his breath, tightening his grip. "I cannot, in good faith, leave you on the street, miss."

"But where are we going?" she wailed.

By this time, they had broached the gallery in full view of the throng below. Hugo marched down the stairs to applause. He could have been in an empty room for all he noted others, including Miss Adelaide's calculated gaze.

"The midden heap!" he snapped when they got to the veranda. "I don't know yet," he muttered more softly. "Now I am stuck with you. Damn!" He eyed the empty hitching post, with irony. "This puts a cap on a perfect evening! The scoundrel has absconded with my *horse.*" With a bitter laugh underlined with absurdity, he sighed and started out.

"Didn't exactly think this out, did you? Don't walk so fast!" Cat stuttered mid-bounce. He released his arms and dropped her unceremoniously to the road.

"Obviously." Hugo strode ahead.

"Wed," Cat said simply.

His long legs out-paced her. "Wed, I said, for my sins."

"Or mine!"

"I heard you."

They were almost back at the Longhorn. Cat's breath seized. Was he now leavin' her, sure?

Hugo lapsed into silence, grim, formidable, gazing first at the Longhorn, where his judgmental kin were, then at her, and marched on without a word.

Cat raced, skipping and hopping to keep up with his long-legged stride.

"Well! You bid for me," Cat growled, truculent, breathlessly challenging. "Is your gallant, noble, kind-hearted, charitable offer yet on the table?" She would think about it tomorrow. Besides, if the pastor wed them, would it be a proper wedding, if a priest had not done the vows and if the banns were not read for six weeks an' all? If Hugo were truly noble and his motives pure, she would at least be fed, warm, sheltered, and untouched, wouldn't she? Was he still wanting to?

"Come, come. Not a moment to waste."

She ran to keep up, until he saw she couldn't, and he unceremoniously slung her over his shoulder again, until they reached the main thoroughfare. There, Hugo slowed as they neared the saloon, and he put her down again. His face reflected the moon—pure, white, expressionless.

"Wait," he commanded, bounding up the steps. He returned in minutes with a frothy gown Cat recognized as totally unsuited to the chill, trailed by an extremely irate Lady Audrina with hailstones of demands and queries raining down from the veranda. Cat heard Lady Daphne's protests out the side window.

****

Cat and Hugo stood before the pastor and his sleep-stunned good wife, fetched from their comfy slumbers into the wintriness of the night. His feet hastily jammed into boots, their tongues flapping, his nightshirt tucked into pants under loosed suspenders, the pastor wondered if it was the usual emergency, involving a self-righteous gun-toting father and a repentant yet jubilant daughter.

To his bewilderment, it was the jumped-up whelp spied at the Harvest Festival and Solange's kitchen scut—a girl the rector found himself wishing he could forget in the dead of night when the devil conjured her up. She was gowned as if for a fancy-dress ball, and her wilderness of hair, out of place in the unfinished church, appeared downright wicked in this place of worship.

Drawing his nightshirt over his chilled shaking hand, the rector held the Good Book open, intoning, "Wilt thou have this woman to be thy wedded wife, to live together after God's ordinance in the Holy Estate of matrimony? Wilt thou love her…"

Catriona stood stiff, barely hearing the words, glancing dazedly from Hugo to the minister to the wife, and down at Audrina's gaudy spangly dress, thinking absurdly that at last she had Audrina's gown—but she had given it to her. Upon awaking this morning—was it

239

only today?—she would never have read in the tea leaves or dreamed she'd be now standing before a pastor and repeating wedding vows.

She became aware of Hugo's impatient answers, "Yes, yes!" and aware the pastor's wife, their only witness, shivered under a quilt made into a cape.

Cat whispered, "I do," at appropriate times.

"…for richer, for poorer, in sickness and in health, to love and to cherish, till death us do part, I do pledge…"

She swayed at a nudge from Hugo and raised brows from the pastor perceiving late the words, "I now pronounce you man and wife."

The pastor looked askance at the two. To his mind, it seemed the groom scowled, and the bride stood in a trance.

"You may now kiss the bride," he said as a question, urging with his hands.

His wife smiled tremulously with her head cocked, puzzled.

Hugo looked coldly upon Catriona, then turned, bowing to the pastor and his lady. "I think we have done quite enough." He flipped a coin, shining gold rather than silver, at the good man. The wife gasped and made a curtsey. "I thank you, sir! God's blessings!"

"Or the devils," muttered Hugo, dragging Catriona away.

****

"Why would you do this for me? You obviously despise me." Catriona wailed from her doorway. It had been an exceedingly long day.

"Why not?"

They were in the Vincent House and Hostelry, as

"there was no place at the inn" for the newlyweds at Hugo's old lodgings, bunked in as he was with the duke. They had endured the owner's stares and flusters until Hugo shoved a scrap of paper at him, the one which the good rector had bestowed after he and Cat signed a register. It had been accompanied by the minister's words, "with hopes for continued wedded bliss," which died on his lips as Hugo snatched it from him.

To the owner's further bewilderment, Hugo signed for two rooms. Hugo shrugged, in answer, as if he had nothing better to do.

****

Catriona found her natural combativeness returned.

Hugo, stripped to the waist, stood at the floor-length window, his sleek form and alabaster skin limned in a haze of blue moonlight. Leaning his forearm on the frame, he gazed out at Wylder's quiet thoroughfares.

She contrarily found her attentions traveling his sinewy frame before making her presence known, dwelling on Hugo's taut muscular buttocks encased in his usual tight gray trews and broad muscled shoulders, before studying the ceiling, blushing, and confused.

She had never seen him unclothed save at the pond, months ago now. Without his fine linen, silk, and cotton shirts, she once again thought Hugo remarkably sculpted and muscular, like a cold marble David come to life, with throbbing veins and pulses in his neck and arms. The only color about him was a feathering of bronze emblazoning his forearms and chest, and a shock of hair undone from its ribbon, flowing like scorching waves down his neck.

Hearing her, he looked over his shoulder, searching her face. He was not wearing his glasses, she saw. His eyes seemed liquid mercury with the moon glinting off them.

Cat inhaled deeply. He dropped his arm and leaned against the wall with no encouragement she could detect on the finest scale, suddenly aware each whisper of cotton against her flesh felt like flaming fingers, for the proprietress had lent her a nightgown. Studying Hugo's fine clothing, she had lent Cat her best, so now she stood in a simple but elegant white cotton shift, not sheer, yet showing hints of pink skin where it brushed her flesh, kissing her hips, outlining her breast with suggestions of rosy nipples.

Watching her bare toes, Cat folded her hands virtuously in front. She kept her eyes to the floor a long moment. She studied the walls. She looked over his head, then nailed him, square in the face, with one green and one blue eye gazing deep into Hugo's unflinching silvery ones, a faint question lurking within his that Cat did not ken how to answer.

"I'll be takin' you, then, as proper husband an' all, if you want. I will. Or you'll be takin' me. 'Tis only fair an' all. I'll be a good and proper wife. I ken ye did me a great boon."

"I want no favors back. I want nothing from you that you do not wish to give, Catriona. I expect nothing. I did what I felt right at the time, as I said."

"A Christian duty, is it then?" She couldn't fight a faint curl of lip.

He spread his hands in a placating gesture. "Hardly." A mischievous smile curled. "Even Jesus had his Mary of Magdalen."

"Don't you be blasphemin'!" she demanded, proper as a preacher's wife. "And now?"

He shrugged, checking the window once more. "I had nothing to lose. I do not have young heiresses—or old ones, for that matter—flinging themselves at my head, tossing sweet perfumed notes with locks of hair under my door," Hugo muttered with unaccustomed bitterness. "Besides, I'm in Wylder, and you, my princess, appear to be 'the fairest damsel in the land.' " He cast a faint smile, removing the sting.

Is he already after regretting it?

"Don't be a fool!" Cat said, pleased. "What of Lady Audrina? Or—or Arabella!"

"If one cares for ice queens or false springs," Hugo commented enigmatically, studying her a long uncomfortable time. Did he find her wanting? Fetching? Off-putting? Her ways too crude?

"For now, let us both keep our heads."

Cat nodded coolly, as if her mind was not spinning like a child's whirligig. Wasn't it every week she was garbed like a child strumpet? Bid on and found wanting? Wed and alone with a half-naked man who rejected her out of hand?

She nodded, brooding.

The look lent her a dark wild gypsy façade as she peered at him hotly from the corner of her eyes.

Couldn't help noting how tall Hugo was, could she now? The wretch topped the frame of the window. How sleek and broad his shoulders, how muscled his arms, noting his hide, in place of appearing milksop-weak, made him chill hard marble. She longed, to her disquiet, to run her palms along that silky cold smoothness.

The gold-shaded kerosene lamp gave a flickering glow to the perfect white canvas of his skin. Silken hairs gilded russet until he seemed formed of gold, his mane in the growing dusk now the color of ox blood.

Catriona glided to him.

Her feet had a mind of their own, while her heart beat a—*no-no-no!* Her mind wailed, *Stay away…don't demean yourself. He doesn't want you. This was an unrealistic favor—a charity.*

Without conscious volition, indeed an urgent need forming somewhere in her primitive body, Cat laid a hand on his arm, feeling an answering tremor within. Was he detesting her? She withdrew. He made a small noise, a gruff clearing of his throat—she saw a pulse pounding.

He moved away—

"No, look at me! Am I charity? Am I a stray dog you take in?"

She saw the bleakness, the despair. Already regretting his generous impulse. The wedding was a sham.

He spoke harshly. "This was not mercy. No compassion. Catriona?" He ground his teeth. "Don't stand so close."

"We are wed. It is right we are alone."

He turned on her with a fury.

"Fool that I am! I thought I was being righteous. Righteous!" He flung at her. "Oh, yes, so unselfish, me!" He gripped her arms, boring into her eyes. "I have wanted you! My bones ached for you. Blood roars through my veins whenever you are near me until I hear nothing but the singing in my ears. My heart beats turbulent rhythms like a child beating a drum. Surely you are aware!"

His voice still anguished, softened. "I have—admired you since first I saw this lovely flower of a face, with your wild gypsy hair, peering from the kitchen in that hideous rag of a dress. You were all, I was not. Your tempestuousness could never be caged, least of all by the likes of me. You have a right to despise me."

Cat studied his mouth. His words faded to mist.

His eyes, large, slightly slanted—showing his Cornish roots, perhaps—glowed from his pale face in the moonlight. Catriona needed to trace his lips and found her hand hovering. Hugo caught it, turned it over, and passionately kissed the palm. Quivering from the sensation, Catriona felt his tongue on her tender skin. Her body trembled inside. Her knees knocked. She snatched her hand away.

"Forgive me—" he said stiffly—"for my liberties—"

"Hugo…" The word was a silken sigh. Cat placed her palm on his cheek. "No, wait! Wait," she breathed more softly, more urgently.

Without thought, a longing conquered her body, drawing her to him as if she had tiny magnets stitched to her skin. Standing on tiptoe, Catriona cupped his face between her hands and brought it down to hers. His lips were soft and sweet. If Hugo was a novice, he was a natural lover, knowing all the right moves to bring her to a passionate state. The kiss bloomed tender and growing. His mouth betrayed experience in the art of kissing. Soft at first, playful, then deep and deeper still as he crushed her slender waist to his lean hard length, exploring her body through the sheer gown. When Cat came up to breathe, she grasped his hair and dragged his face to hers once more. Hugo bent his head to her height, cupping her bottom and the back of her head, kissing her hard and thoroughly, as if it should last a lifetime of remembrances. His lips were mobile and talented, hungry and demanding, then harsh, unrelenting in pressure and longing until Cat at last thrust her head back, laughing, gasping.

"Now, is that what you want?" he demanded.

"'Oh…yes…" she breathed. "It was like—like…"

"Magic? No, little one. Return to your room before I shame both of us by rude attentions."

"I— I have no room. I am a woman married!" Catriona felt stubborn.

He gazed with hooded eyes. "True enough. The gossipmongers are working overtime. I will kip on the floor like my ancient relative's stable hand." He threw his half-sided smile. "You wanted none of this."

"No! No!" Cat stamped her foot. How stupid could this man be? She hopped up in a very unladylike manner to wrap her arms about his neck and legs about his waist , to cling to Hugo.

He let her down gently.

Cat frowned up, wearing a warring look. He shook his head in defeat and pulled her to him. Her head thumped his chest, her belly pressed his manhood.

So icy Hugo was not formed from stone, but very like it.

She giggled softly.

Cat pressed her lips to his as if she were starving, kissing, whispering nonsense and kissing again.

With a deep groan starting from the floorboards, Hugo finally lifted her and carried her firmly to bed. They scarce made it out of their clothes.

****

Their lovemaking was two thunderclouds crashing together with lightning strikes illuminating secret parts and faces, and sparks flashing from half-closed eyes as they devoured each other with kisses and caressed each alien territory of flesh, exhaustively, long into the night, to begin anew as each reached for the other, blending and re-blending, until both lay exhausted, momentarily satiated, gazing at each other with wonder, humor, and affection. How could she ever have thought Hugo ugly? He was beautiful. A work of art. Aaron was crude—a badly-cast copy, rough with slag.

"But where shall we live?" Cat, lying with her head on Hugo's shoulder, murmured idly. His arms were strong and sheltering. She was safe. She was loved. She was already home.

She smiled, letting her mind play games.

He gazed fondly down at her curly mop of hair and yawned. "Most likely Sandringham Cloisters."

"His lordship's home? He won't mind?" Catriona thought tenderly of a wee thatched cottage somewhere in a parklike setting with a garden and a dog, or perhaps even the great house itself, sharing meals with jolly, good-hearted servants and helping the cook… She gazed up at his contented face, one arm crooked behind his head.

"Or are ye a help mate, a valet or somewhat?"

"Oh," Hugo said, off-hand, "something like that."

Chapter Twenty-Six
Revelation

Audrina stormed onto the Longhorn's broad veranda, blazing at Hugo, and performed an abrupt curtsey that could be rude, it was so insolent. "Your grace!" She sneered from an obnoxiously low position, hands stretching skirts wide.

Cat looked questioningly at Hugo and noted his aggrieved expression, a pucker marring the bridge of her perfect nose with the two cinnamon sprinkles. His pale aristocratic face turned a faint rose shade. She had commanded herself not to dwell on the eventual meeting.

"Not now, Audrina. Let us enjoy our day. I merely wish to inform his lordship."

"Oh, inform, will you? Tell him the next in line has done a runner!" She smirked at her own slang. "With a scrub tart!" She affected a cockney accent. "An alley Cat, *guv'ner!*"

"Enough, Audrina," Hugo said mildly, glancing with adoring eyes at his bride—a glance that warmed Cat all over. "You will not insult my wife, even if you do not approve."

Audrina made another wide, low, sweeping, affected curtsey. "Yes. I hear and obey, your most noble lordship!" She snapped her fan and, with one turn of the heel, flounced inside.

A few seconds later, a raw shriek, sounding very like

248

a fishwife hawking her wares, erupted from upstairs. One could suppose it would be the Right Honorable Lady Daphne, if one did not ken better.

Cat's large blue and green eyes grew wider. Her thick glossy lashes blinked. A furrow formed between her brows. Her rosebud mouth formed a perfect pink O before she asked, "What is happening?"

"Oh yes. I suppose I forgot to tell you. But this is not the time or place." He shot an irritated glance after Audrina's retreat. "Now, I must see the duke and gain his blessing. He will be pleased."

Cat came down with a thud. She had been hoping they could put that off—that she and Hugo could just…vanish.

****

"If you had not, I would have!" The old duke winked, taking Catriona's slim white hands in his two gnarled ones. "Our family needs fresh lineage, God knows. Jolly good show, Hugo!"

****

"What did he mean, Hugo—my love?" Cat spoke shyly, still unused to the fairytale she was in.

"Awful bother. Sometimes, why, my uncle likes to, as you say, play hooky."

Cat frowned in confusion.

"I am the next duke. The next Duke of Sandringham. My mother married milord's' younger brother. He was lost in India. Died of malaria…I never knew him." Hugo made a forlorn gesture. "When mother returned, I think she died of heartbreak. I was lost in the shuffle, passed from relative to relative—one a rather dotty auntie—and in time, no one recalled quite who I was." He spread his hands in an "It just happened" way. "That is my bloody fate. The fifteenth duke of the House of Sandringham, and a few thousand hectares of jolly old England, and Lord know what else."

Cat nodded, dumbstruck.

"Kissing babies and attending flower shows, pinning on prizes at the pig fairs, battalions of servants to be subservient to, practicing husbandry on thousands of hectares, being a noble landlord…sitting in, God forbid, Parliament… "

Hugo smiled down at her. "But not for a long while, I hope. We must take good care of his lordship. You," he touched her nose, "will be—" he smiled lovingly, showing beautiful white teeth with puckish humor—"a duchess. I hope you don't mind."

Cat didn't.

She puckered her brow then. "It is all rather frightening. Is there just you?"

"There are no others. No heirs beyond me." He cast an eye at her. "We shall have to make amends, and do something about that."

"How many little heirs do you wish to have running around?" Cat dimpled, unbuttoning his shirt.

Hugo reached down and swept her into his arms. "Let us have nature take care of that."

His smile was wide, sensual, and warm. He kissed her to seal the bargain and undid the corset of the next Duchess of Wylder, Wyoming…

Epilogue

Lady Daphne, puffing on a long black cheroot, leaned over the taff rail and idly watched the moon play on muddy waters spraying from the riverboat's enormous wheel. The night was humid, even for Mississippi, but her dress was finest lawn, though she denied the expense of it, brought from Paris. This boat suited her, even after the splendor of Monte Carlo glamour and Biarritz casinos. She tossed the slim cigar into the tan water of the flowing river and turned back to the gaming tables, refreshed, smiling warmly and in secret code to her partner, the handsome cardsharp from Wylder, Wyoming.

He grinned knowingly at her, touched his forehead, and shuffled cards in a dazzling and intricate display.

****

Pouting Lady Audrina snuggled up to Aaron. Already she was feeling the first stabs of regret after their mad elopement. If Hugo could, so could she! However, Aaron had cooled when he discovered she was a threadbare heiress. In turn, he was surprisingly mean regarding their money, which she found to be little indeed.

****

Arabella literally rode off into the sunset behind her rugged, good-looking range rider. She found she relished campfires and long cold nights under the freedom of a thousand stars, and strong black coffee in the morning.

But mostly the nights.

****

Madame Solange, Mrs. Levi Gruenwald, gazed down with crushing love, and held her strapping child close. A girl. Levi already spoilt her.

****

The fourteenth duke of Sandringham, His Most Noble Lord Mortimer Greville, eagerly thrust his face into the frigid, frost-sparkled wind, silver hair whipping past his eyes as he squinted for the long-awaited Alaskan shoreline.

Sky, sea, and snow blended seamlessly, yet he kenned Juneau and the Alaskan gold fields lay not half a league ahead, according to the sailing captain. "Ah, the Alaskan gold mines await!"

A word from the author…

For my sins, I scribble novels and scripts in Myrtle Beach, on ships at sea, the car, my palm, or anywhere there is a phone, laptop, matchbook, or paper napkin.

Visit me at my websites:

ship11233.wixsite.com'sarys-diamonds-twrp

ship11233.wixsite.com/sarys-gold

Thank you for purchasing
this publication of The Wild Rose Press, Inc.

For questions or more information
contact us at
info@thewildrosepress.com.

The Wild Rose Press, Inc.